George

The Story of a D-Day Dodger

Based on true events

By Mike Lemmon

The Author recognises and gives his thanks for the kind permissions given in the production of this book, especially those of Matthew Parker and his tremendous work; Monte Cassino – The Story of the Hardest-Fought Battle of World War Two.

In loving memory of Michaela Elizabeth Lemmon

1971-1997

Dedications

This book is dedicated firstly to my dad (George), who this story is – partly but not entirely – about. Although sections are fictional, the military encounters are not. I was teetering on the brink of giving up, due to the gaps in my father's military history, when a friend told me to continue to write the story. "Get it down first and worry about the correctness later," were his encouraging words.

My father was an obstinate and awkward character, quite often a frustrating person, to whom I have been likened on occasion. Perhaps this is why I have continued with the writing; it may make you appreciate the sacrifice of the men who took up arms and fought in the Italian campaigns, did their duty and died while doing it. All I ask is that they are given as much recognition as those that fought bravely on D-Day in Normandy.

I would also like to dedicate this book to Ben Kerrridge, whom I interviewed while writing and who served in 5th Tank Regiment. Unfortunately tanks proved quite ineffective at Cassino due to the terrain. Ben was a lovely man, who gave me his time to tell me how it was in Cassino and his previous encounters. His frankness and good humour was his saviour. When I asked him how he managed to stay alive when so many died around him, he simply replied, "A four letter word." He then spelt it out for me, "L- U- C -K."

Ben died at the age of 94 in June 2016; I thank him and his family for allowing me to talk with him. Like so many men in the war, my father never spoke of his experiences and so it was a privilege to speak to Ben. I am just sorry that I was unable to make a second visit before Ben died; I enjoyed his company; his good humour and the twinkle in his eyes reflected his enjoyment of life.

Prologue

A tragic and deeply moving account of George, a Royal Fusilier in the 1st Battalion City of London Regiment.

As a young man, George is deployed to India 1936-39: from the East End of London to the exotic East. His experiences and encounters are far removed from the grime of London, where he is seen shuffling to school in his big brother's cast-off shoes. He is thrown into the horrendous tragedy of war, in the deserts of North Africa, Egypt, Syria, and Iraq 1939-44 and then to Monte Cassino 1944-45, where comrades he has known from the age of eighteen are dismembered before his eyes in gut-wrenching bombardments.

He finds love and tranquillity in the green hills of Italy, where he is shown love and caring where there has only been blood and destruction, and ordinary Italians open their doors to him and show willingness to share their bread. Their concern and affection opens his eyes to another potential life.

George's story began some considerable time ago. His attitudes, his approach and what he would become were formed in a past that sculpted his nature and outlook. His childhood days and the loss of his mother moulded his feelings. He was happy to be an individual, didn't care to be the most popular or to lead or be led, so the decision later in life to join the army was an odd choice, one might say perverse. It could be argued that the lack of work and opportunities in the 1930s was a reason, but this was not the only deciding factor. His older brother joining the military may have swayed him, but George was the sort of character to do just the opposite. Like all of us, he was complex and very individual. His story would take him across the world; for him this was an eye opener, as it was for many of the men who travelled for the first time in their lives. Their insular existence in a few square London miles formed their characters and their attitudes. Many found it difficult to adapt; others like George met everything head on and felt that it was a challenge, firstly to show no weakness or emotion and, secondly, to rise above it all.

George was one of millions of men that came from all over the United Kingdom and Empire to fight in a war in which they had no choice and which, in many cases, they did not understand; the same applied to the Allies from all over the world. This story is not set down to justify actions; it concerns what happened and is still happening, with service personnel being sent across the world and then left to their own devices when they return. Some of the battles were the bloodiest ever recorded and yet are not remembered in the same way that D-Day and other conflicts are today. This story is to highlight the plight of these men, known as the D-Day Dodgers, who were so called because they were thought to be having a great time in Italy, when in fact the opposite was true, and to share their sorrows and losses and their anger at the establishment that gives them very little recognition, despite several of them having won the Victoria Cross. It is also for the men who are still trying to gain recognition for the work that they did for the UK in the Second World War, not forgetting the sacrifices made by the Gurkhas, Indian regiments, Canadians, New Zealanders, Americans and of course the massive sacrifice made by the Polish regiments, plus many others.

The stories in this book are not set down to glorify war but to show the atrocities, while also revealing the courage of the human spirit.

Those of you who read this story should perhaps also read *Monte Cassino: The Hardest Fought Battle of World War 2* by Matthew Parker, who has been generous enough to allow me to quote from his book. I have read Matthew's book a number of times, the most poignant occasion being in Monte Cassino, as I lay in my bed in a B&B in comfort, looking up the hillside where men had lost their lives in appalling conditions. I do not distinguish between enemy and ally when I say "men", I mean all men, as enemy and ally alike had family and friends who would miss them or would suffer with them on their return to a 'normal' life.

Matthew has been recognised by another well-known historian, James Holland, who wrote in the *Daily Telegraph*:

> Superb…I suspect that few people today realise that British and American soldiers fought in a battle that compares to Stalingrad for human suffering. *Monte Cassino* is a fitting tribute: an important and beautifully written book, told with real understanding and pathos for those who withstood the Western Allies' bloodiest encounter with the German Army.

James Holland's book, *Italy's Sorrow*, is also an excellent account of the battles in Italy and Cassino.

A further recommendation from James Holland is Peter Caddick-Adams' *Monte Cassino: Ten Armies in Hell.*

Comments on the conflict at Monte Cassino:

"The seemingly unending succession of mountain ranges, ravines and rivers of the Italian terrain demanded the soldierly qualities of fighting valour and endurance in a measure unsurpassed in any other theatre of war," wrote the British General, Harold Alexander, in his memoirs.

The German commander, Lieutenant-General Fridolin von Senger und Etterlin, wrote: "We found that divisions arriving from other theatres of war were not immediately equal to the double burden of icy mountain terrain and massed bombardment."

Lady Astor and the 'D-Day Dodgers'
From the beginning, soldiers serving in the Armed Forces made up their own parodies to the tune of *Lili Marlene*. Perhaps the best-known of these parodies was created by British troops serving in Italy in 1944. This came about after the British politician, Lady Nancy Astor, was reputed to have claimed many of the British troops serving in Italy had deliberately avoided taking part in the Normandy Landings on D-Day. From BBC *WW2 People's War*.

The Ballad of the D-Day Dodgers (one version)
[Anonymous – sung to the tune of 'Lili Marlene']

We're the D-Day Dodgers out in Italy –
Always on the vino, always on the spree.
8th Army scroungers and their tanks
We live in Rome – among the Yanks.
We are the D-Day Dodgers, way out in Italy.

We landed at Salerno, a holiday with pay,
Jerry brought the band down to cheer us on our way
We all sung the songs and the beer was free.
We kissed all the girls in Napoli.
For we are the D-Day Dodgers, way out in Italy.

The Volturno and Cassino were taken in our stride
We didn't have to fight there; we just went for the ride.
Anzio and Sangro were all forlorn;
We did not do a thing from dusk to dawn,
For we are the D-Day Dodgers, way out in Italy.

On our way to Florence we had a lovely time.
We ran a bus to Rimini through the Gothic line,
All the winter sports amid the snow,
Then we went bathing in the Po.
For we are the D-Day Dodgers, way out in Italy.

Once we had a blue light that we were going home
Back to dear old Blighty never more to roam.
Then somebody said in France you'll fight.
We said never mind, we'll just sit tight,
The windy D-Day Dodgers in sunny Italy.

Now Lady Astor, get a load of this.
Don't stand on your platform and talk a lot of piss

You're the nation's sweetheart, the nation's pride,
But your lovely mouth is far too wide.
For we are the D-Day Dodgers in sunny Italy.

If you look around the mountains, through the mud and rain
You'll find battered crosses, some which bear no name.
Heartbreak, toil and suffering gone
The boys beneath just slumber on.
For they were the D-Day Dodgers way out in Italy.

So listen all you people, over land and foam
Even though we're parted, our hearts are close to home.
When we return we hope you'll say
'You did your little bit, though far away
All of the D-Day Dodgers out in Italy'.

Court Martial - 1945

Chapter 1

Field Court Martial

George is under close arrest, he is being held at the Allied armies' HQ in Villa Rossi, just north of Cassino. He is standing between two burly 'Red Caps', staring at the large doors to his destiny, just inches from his nose. The house is a crumbling wreck, although outwardly majestic, even after numerous close battles. No one is speaking, although there is a bustle of activity behind them; he is unable to take even a casual glance at the frantic activities surrounding him. He is not afraid or anxious about the outcome of his court martial. Originally he had feared that he might be shot, but over the past five years, he had been shot at, mortared and shelled many times; he hadn't been killed, yet.

He is hearing the steady heavy breathing of the men guarding him. They needn't have bothered; he had given himself up willingly. No big hunt, no searching for this East London lad over mountain and hilltop required. A lad, he thought, I am now a veteran; he was fast approaching his 30th birthday. The furore behind him had quietened a degree, but he could still hear vehicles mobilising outside.

Time was passing to the beat of a large clock, from somewhere behind him. He began to stare pointlessly at the doors. Seen better days, he reflected; the paint was peeling and the bare wood showed in places. He could see several layers of paint, some blues and creams and even some gold, perhaps it was gold leaf. Very posh, he nearly blurted out but contained the comment, as he felt the gaze of the larger of the two guards fall upon him. The guard's breath changed momentum as he moved closer to George, who could feel the warmth of it on his neck and smell the sweet sickly aroma of tobacco and something else. George inwardly questioned: what have you been eating? The doors came back into focus and he thought he heard someone approaching from the other side. The guards pulled themselves to attention in readiness then relaxed as the footfall moved away.

George was thinking about the past months, the warmth of the sunshine and the good nature of the people he had shared it with. The time had passed without a thought of the previous period spent up to his neck in muck or of the comrades that had fallen beside him. Now the various and many routines of army personnel: lower ranks saluting, stamping feet and 'yes sirs' burst into his consciousness. The accustomed smells of polish, Blanco and NAAFI food wafting on the air from the distant mess halls also added to the sense of familiarity gained from his past years in training and in the camps where he had been stationed.

George hung on to the thought that it might not be so bad. He was alive after all; he could have a whole new life in front of him. Back to staring at the door again; nothing else to see, except for a small creature, some sort of bug running up one of the panels. This bug should be court martialled, along with him, obviously for insubordination; this made him smile at the thought of it. George had done a bit of that too. Few officers impressed him; he had seen first-hand some of them cowering in their dugouts while sending others into the fray. Not all were like that, but many were ill-equipped to deal with the issue of war and death; but then, weren't most men?

These doors, he thought, would be nice on our little terrace in Hoxton. Then he couldn't help himself, there was a sort of suppressed escape of air to stifle the laugh.

"What's the matter with you, you snivelling little bastard?" the larger guard exploded. "If I had my way, I would take you outside and shoot you through the fucking head and done with it!"

George was not at all fazed by this outburst; he just kept facing forward with a stoic look on his face, wondering whether this tub of lard had ever seen any action. George's temper would usually have flared; he would have floored the guard with a few hard and fast well-placed blows. Maybe the past months had tempered his behaviour. He let the matter pass, controlling his temper with an inward sigh.

No sounds passed any of their lips for the next ten minutes, until the doors were flung open unexpectedly and George was facing the court martial board. It consisted of three officers, all seated behind a long trestle table bearing mounds of paperwork: Lieutenant Appleby, a rather gangly individual, with a neatly trimmed moustache, his legs reaching the top of the table, Captain Titchmarsh, who was short and stocky, with reddish hair, reddened cheeks, and a dour expression permanently engraved into his features, and Major Frensham, whose impressive handlebar moustache covered most of his face. It seemed he spoke without moving his mouth, which gave rise to a much affected clipped form of speech. They all looked rather stern, and the major, who sat in the centre, gestured to the ensemble to come forward. One of the MPs barked his orders and they moved forward as one. George wasn't actually listening at all to the military police sergeant, who stated whom he was delivering to the court martial. Both MPs then stamped their feet and withdrew a pace behind the accused.

George stood alone facing the officers. The judge advocate, who sat to one side and whom George could only see through his peripheral vision, stood to read the charges relating to George's desertion, his voice slightly nasal and whining as it navigated its way through the list of charges. The judge advocate, who sat to one side, stood to read the charges relating to George's desertion. He was a rather thin, wiry man, who fidgeted as he laboriously read through the charge sheet, standing first on one foot and then on the other.

George drifted into a world of his own; mentally, he was not really in the room, and he felt relaxed at attention, if that is possible. He knew that this was all a performance, as he had already pleaded guilty to the charge of being absent without leave (AWOL), but this was the army and they had to do their little dance around the maypole, before finding him guilty as charged. The only uncertainty is: what would be the sentence? Would he be sent home or remain in Italy? He would rather stay here and if possible return to where he had been for the past months. Shortly, this could all be taken out of his hands; it dawned on him that he is not the one in control.

The major was speaking, but George's mind was elsewhere, until he was snapped back into the room by one of the MPs barking at him.

"Answer the officer!"

George came out of his daydream and responded with a quick, "Guilty Sir." The major spoke,

"In light of your admission of guilt, and under army regulations, we have a number of avenues that we may take. In the past it was within a court martial's remit to impose the death penalty; this rule has now been rescinded. You did not leave your post in the heat of battle but rather after the battle had been won; this is a puzzle to us all. You have been absent without leave for some considerable period of time. I believe from reports that you were a good and dependable soldier prior to this." The major fumbled through some papers, conferred with the captain and the lieutenant on either side of him and then returned to his summation. "Erh some seven months I believe, which is quite some time to be missing. The court martial would like to know where you have been and what you have been doing for all this time. Do you have anything to say in mitigation?"

George shuffled his feet and was about to reply, when one of the MPs breathed a note of warning, “Stand still when the major addresses you.” The major, who seemed to be more than curious about George’s disappearance, was not the least bit put out by the fact that George had done a soft shoe shuffle.

“That’s perfectly alright, Sergeant Major, let the prisoner stand easy.”

“Yes Sir,” bellowed the sergeant major, stamping his feet as he did so.

“Quietly, Sergeant Major, we are not on the parade ground now.”

“Prisoner stand easy,” said the sergeant major, as quietly as his training allowed.

“It was like this Sir,” began George. “As my record shows, I have been a regular soldier since I was 18 years old; I have spent my time in India, North Africa and then Italy. I have seen many terrible things in the past years and some would say I have done some terrible things. The worst part of all was my mate Bertie being killed next to me; one minute he was there and the next gone. He was a good sort, Sir, and it was such a waste. Now don’t ask me why Bertie being killed did it for me, but it was a sort of turning point.”

The major didn’t seem to like the way this was going, so interrupted George, “Yes, yes, I understand that certain traumatic events can affect a person, but this is not what the court martial has asked you. Where have you been and what have you been doing? That is the question we have put to you.”

“Sorry Sir,” George replied, “I was just trying to give you background and my reasons for going AWOL in the first place. You see Sir, I don't remember much after the surrender at the abbey, and therefore the first few days after are a little foggy. I wandered for what I assumed was a day, but it could have been much longer. I managed to get up into the mountains on the far side of the valley from Cassino. I can remember it being very peaceful and green in the mountains, far away from the sounds of the battlefield and I fell asleep for a long time. Whether this was the same day or another day I am not clear; it was getting dark when I awoke, I was thirsty, disorientated and rather bemused about my situation. I couldn't recall how I had managed to get so far from the battlefield without being noticed or challenged by anyone. I didn't have much of my uniform left so I must have discarded it, but why and where I did this, I just don't know. The timescale of my journey, that was lost to me. I was weeping rather a lot. I must have travelled for some days; I was exhausted, cold and hungry."

George paused awhile to gather his thoughts and then, to the court martial's surprise, asked permission to ask a question. Although the major said that it wasn't his place to ask questions, they would allow it in the interest of clarity.

"Will the family that aided me be punished in any way for helping me?" George asked. "They are good people and shouldn't be punished."

"The court martial has no interest in these people. The fact that they aided and abetted a deserter is not this court's concern; we are only interested in your actions, Private, that is all.

However, this does not mean that the court exonerates them either," was the major's reply.

"Thank you Sir," George replied, then continued with his account of what he recalled about his sojourn in the hillsides, outlining the work he did in return for food and accommodation.

The major stopped the proceedings, as the officers felt that they had heard sufficient to make their judgement. The board agreed to take a break; they would reconvene after lunch with their verdict. George was marched out of the courtroom and told to sit on some benches in a locked room, where he saw a faded outline of a fresco on the wall opposite him; this place had seen a lot better days, George assumed. He sat alone, while his guards went off for a break. No lunch for me, he thought. Enjoying the quiet, his thoughts turned towards home, his parents and brothers, as he travelled back in time.

Chapter 2

Childhood

George is nine years old; he is running home from school, pushing aside the washing strung between the buildings in the street; it hangs limply on this windless day. He's sliding in his oversized shoes on the wet cobbled areas where the market had been earlier. Usually George would walk through this part of town to see if there was any free stuff from the stall holders. Occasionally he is lucky enough to find discarded fruit or vegetables, which, after a bit of a wash, are good enough to eat.

However, today is different; his dad had promised him a gift, not that George is expecting much, as he is one of five brothers. The eldest, Harry, is like a beanstalk and nearly six feet tall; he wouldn't be going to war in the future, he had an underlying defect with his vision. His brother Jack, also known as 'Jack the lad', whom he looked up to most, was a bit of a mechanic. Tom was the serious one and destined for higher status, while Albert, whom they all looked out for, was George's youngest brother. Albert had a winning smile, and losing his hair early in life did nothing to deter the girls from being drawn to him, preferring him to the other brothers.

George was incredibly bored with the repetitiveness of school; he couldn't wait to get out and travel. Tom was planning to join the army and George thought that this might prove an excellent way to escape the drudgery of the East End and fulfil his own ambition to travel. George liked to read; he picked up discarded magazines in the market and managed to read some of the books on travel, in the so-called school library. This mainly consisted of a few creaking shelves, on which stood much-worn tomes, which had seen better days. They lay in despondent array but, amongst these, were some books with sketches and travel stories. He also devoured books about explorers and adventurers. In his fantasies he pictured himself standing on high rocky outcrops, above a jungle somewhere, as he looked across a vista of circling vultures, which were preying on the carcass of a dead animal.

The other boys at school picked on George, not because he looked or acted odd; he wore his brother's cast-off shoes that were obviously too large for him. This made him trip up quite often and if he didn't, some of the boys would help him on his way. This was a dangerous game to play with George, as he had a quick temper and would lash out at the nearest tormentor with his fists, with inevitable results; he floored his opponent, the outcome being that he received the strap or cane on several occasions for fighting. He never blamed anyone for this or 'squealed' on the other party; it wasn't the East End way. George was not averse to 'knocking the block off' kids much larger than himself; his mother despaired when he returned home bloodied and grubby.

"It's these shoes," he would complain. "They call me Coco the Clown."

"Well George, you will just have to put up with it until we can get you something better," his mother, Ivy, replied. "Money doesn't grow on trees you know, and if it does, take me to it and I'll be right there with my largest basket."

"Oh Mum, I'm sorry. I know we have to be careful, but if we can find some shoes that fit it would be better." George was satisfied he had made his case.

George reviewed these discussions with his mum on many occasions in later life; he would feel bad about what he had said and for the unnecessary grief and feelings of inadequacy he may have given her. Had he in fact hastened her death, by adding to the constant worry and struggle? The workload for his mother was great, with a mass of washing – all to be done by hand – and stretching their meagre income to cover the cost of their food and lodgings. Ivy was strong and determined, but the dampness of the house, combined with the fact that, without anyone knowing, she fed herself less, constantly drained her life strength.

Slum clearance: that was the cry from local authorities in the 1930s East End of London; they announced a major scheme to clear the East End of the deplorable housing that blighted their streets. They proclaimed the houses were shoddily built and the roof timbers were rotten and collapsing and no amount of re-tiling would save them. The buildings were damp and infested, generally having no toilet, bathroom or running water. Most of these properties had shared facilities, including a standpipe tap, from where a number of neighbouring households fetched and carried their water requirements back to their kitchens, in buckets and bowls. Little did they know that, in a few years, Germany would assist in the demolition of many of these houses.

George and his family lived in one such small terraced property on the Hoxton/ Shoreditch borders; it was fiendishly cleaned by his mother, who, in common with many of the residents in his street, suffered from bronchial problems, due to the damp and poor living conditions. Ivy was becoming frail but always put on a brave face and was frequently heard to say,

"Things aren't so bad, others are worse off!"

Some of the residents had smaller properties and were crammed into one room, where a whole family ate, slept and lived. The men were out all day searching for work; most were employed at the docks, on a casual first come, first served basis. They had to queue each morning, to see who would be fortunate enough to be working that day. The employers had the pick of the men; you had to be strong and in the know: where to go and whose palms to grease to get the prime jobs. The work was backbreaking and dangerous, but as the men were all too willing to do it, they could be easily replaced. Should anyone dare to complain, the employer's attitude was,

"If you don't like it, then clear off somewhere else, there are plenty waiting for your job."

George's father, Arthur, was one of the men that had to 'bow and scrape' to get the work required to keep the large household fed, with clothing on their backs and a roof over their heads. Each day he would stagger back from some backbreaking task and slump in the chair by the stove, exhausted. The work at the docks and the power station was feeding his family, but it was also killing him. All the brothers were destined for a similar life, unless somehow they could break the mould.

On this particular day, George was right not to build his hopes too much, regarding the gift. When he reached home breathless and red faced, he burst into the scullery of their little terraced house, and there it was on the table. At first he looked with excitement and anticipation at the item lying on its side. On closer inspection he noticed its wheels akimbo and a dented body. His mum called from upstairs.

"George, is that you? Have you seen the engine your dad has brought home for you? He said that you will be able to fix it up ok."

George's shoulders drooped, he had wished for something more than a-fix-it-up type of present, but he was a pragmatist and so he pulled up a chair to the heavily scrubbed table and, using the kitchen knives, began to dismantle the little clockwork engine.

When his mum came downstairs, she saw George intently at work on the clockwork train and said, "Oh George, not with my good knives. You know I'm trying to keep them for best."

"Sorry mum," said George. With a wicked twinkle in his eyes, he added, "Are the King and

Queen coming for tea then mum, that we need our very best cutlery?"

"You cheeky little beggar," said Ivy. "Just wait until I get hold of you, you monkey you." After a quick chase around the kitchen table, with George's mum flicking at him with a tea towel, he made a break for the stairs. Just as he thought he was clear, Mum made a spurt and caught him on the back of his bare legs, with a positive and satisfying 'twang'!

"Ow!" George shouted in mock pain.

"Serves you right, you little beggar. Get back down here and sort this lot out before your father gets home."

The engine was still on the table when his father returned home. Looking at George, he said, "You'll be able to fix that up, won't you Son?"

"Yes it will be fine once I've cleaned up all the parts and put it back together, Dad; there isn't much broken."

With a feeling of pride and a light smile on his lips, George's dad then puckered up and began to whistle tunelessly, while he moved to scrub up in the scullery sink. Water splashed on to Arthur's head as he shook it under the water pouring from the bucket that Ivy held over him to rinse off.

"George," his mum called. "Go and get some more water, I need it for the potatoes." Rising from the table and collecting the bucket, with a superior sounding voice, George said, "I believe the word is 'please', Mum."

"Why, you've got the cheek of the devil, you have. You just get out there and get that bucket filled or there will be no tea for you tonight!"

"That's what you always say to us, Mum," George said as he leapt out the door, with his mother's shoe following in quick order. His father laughed at the pair of them, grateful for the moment of levity, after such a gut-wrenching day.

The stew on the stove was bubbling away, the rich meaty smell permeated the house, the potatoes were cooked and the rest of the household seemed to arrive by magic at the table for their tea. They were all hungry boys, growing at a fast rate, although George was lagging behind his brothers and sometimes they referred to him as 'shrimp'. This caused a lot of fighting and tumbling around their small house, and it was always Ivy that had to pull the bundle of limbs apart. "You boys will be the death of me," she would often say.

Chapter 3

Mum

George was still a schoolboy aged 9, when as often he arrived home pink faced from running. He knew that something was wrong as soon as he returned home. Neighbours were gathered around the tenement, smoking and chatting, in a sombre mood. It was like that in the East End, everyone knew each other's business: births, deaths and marriages were always at the top of the agenda for discussion and dissection. George had no time for the crowds outside; he pushed his way through to the kitchen and saw his dad sitting at the table, with a glass of something in his hand. A neighbour had brought his father a drop of the 'good stuff', just what was needed in times of trouble. Women from the tenements were fussing by the stove and making pots of tea. How many women does it take to make tea, thought George.

"What's up, where's mum?" was George's question. The ensemble looked towards him and one of the women said, "Poor mite; look at his poor little face."

"Never mind all that," George exploded. "Where is mum?" His father looked at George, his face grey, tears welling in his eyes, which he hurriedly wiped with the back of his hand.

"Your mum is gone, Son. I'm sorry."

"Where has she gone, Dad, where?"

"She collapsed this morning and a neighbour found her gasping for breath. She was taken to the

Royal London, where she died at two o'clock this afternoon."

"I don't believe you; you're telling me lies. Where is she?"

"Like I said, Georgie, she's gone, she's dead, and I can't make it any clearer."

"What did she die of then?" was George's angry retort.

At this point a neighbour stepped in and said that she would take care of George, taking him gently by the arm to lead him away to her house, but George would have none of it. Snatching his arm from her hand, he ran out of the house. He ran until his lungs felt as if they would burst and his legs could carry him no longer. He made his way to the canal, where he played sometimes; sitting on the wall, he dangled his feet over the edge of the canal. Sobbing until he could cry no longer, he then rubbed his eyes dry; he didn't want to be seen like this by anyone. He realised that his dad and his brothers would need him, they all needed each other.

The next few days, leading up to the funeral, were the worst days of George's life. Friends and neighbours kept calling in to see if everything was alright, "in the circumstances", and asking the family to let them know if there was anything they could do. What does that mean, thought George. Yes, there is something you can do; you can bring my mum back, that's what!

After all the preparations were completed for the funeral, the assembled crowds gathered around the little tenement once again. The coffin stood in the middle of the kitchen on a trestle, with the hearse purring away outside the front door. Four men in black lifted the coffin as if it were empty, loading it with all due reverence into the back of the hearse. The family would remember the day as being grey and miserable; it wasn't, mostly the sun shone, with just the occasional cloud, but for them it would always be remembered as grey.

There were no others cars; for one, they couldn't afford it and secondly, the cemetery was a short walk away. The family and mourners then followed on foot the short distance to the cemetery. The mourners held bunches of flowers, and a few shed tears. George looked around him with dry eyes; he had no more tears, his feelings had been drained. All he felt now was a hard lump in his chest, as if he had eaten something in a rush and it didn't agree with him. He just wanted, needed, this to be over and for these people to go away and leave the family in peace. As young as he was, he also knew that they meant well, but that did not stop his irritation at their fawning words, head rubbing and patting. What was this head rubbing business anyway? He wasn't some small animal that needed petting and stroking.

He was angry at everyone, but he also felt guilty, as he had learned that his mother had been unwell for some while but had hid it from them all. His brothers walked in solemn silence in the procession alongside him and he glanced over to his father, who seemed to have shrunk and become wizened and bent over, like a really old man. George was able to hold it together at the graveside, but he had a terrible urge to throw himself into the grave with his mother, as the coffin was lowered. Although George could not express his annoyance at the priest or the words spoken at his mother's funeral, if he could have done, he would have said that it was cursory, meaningless drivel, spoken while pontificating over his mother's life and serving up hypocritical platitudes. But he did not know such words. George was aware the priest hadn't known her; he hadn't even spoken with her. What did he care? He was getting paid to do a job, so he should just get on with it, take his money and leave them to grieve, and stop all this shit about God and a new life somewhere in the clouds.

The funeral was over at long last; he thought that he would now be able to escape these people, but, unfortunately for George, neighbours had prepared food and drink for the wake. They returned after the internment to the small house and enjoyed the refreshments until late into the night. George looked scathingly across at his father, who was much the worse for drink and his brothers were drunk too, all except Tom, who had a very serious frown and an extremely angry expression. No one else seemed to notice Tom catching George's eye; he nodded to him and the door, and they slipped away to their favourite spot by the canal, where they sat and talked into the night.

Tom would be joining the army soon, so they spoke about that. George said that he would like to join up too. Tom smiled at him and said, "When you are old enough Georgie. Just a few more years and perhaps we can be in the same regiment; how would you like that?" George did like it. He smiled at his big brother, the first smile in many days.

George left school before he was 14 and began the search for work like his brothers. He moved from one job to another as work became available. He was thin and relatively small, so few employers risked him carrying out heavy labour, but he was always ready to surprise them with his strength, by picking up the largest man he could, lifting him with ease into the air. However, party tricks were not enough to keep him permanently employed. One day he might be working in the vegetable market, another at Billingsgate fish market or Smithfield meat market. He simply moved where they would take him on and give him work. His father was unwell, so it was down to all the brothers to bring in what they could, but George just longed to join his brother in the army. When Tom joined the army, there was one less to feed but also one less to bring in an income. He missed his brother greatly and never felt more alone. He could not wait for the day that he was 18 to join up and become a fusilier.

Chapter 4

Joining up 1934

The recruiting sergeant looked up from his desk and said, “What can I do for you young man?”

“I want to be a fusilier,” piped up George.

“Well do you now? We don’t just take anyone in the Royal London Fusiliers, now do we?” Despite his warm welcome to the Fusiliers’ recruiting department, George signed the relevant documents and waited to hear from the army about the next stage of his military service. If successful, he was to be sent for a full medical, to complete further forms and be interviewed by an officer who would deem him either fit to enter or otherwise. George had grown a little but not a great deal, and his mere 5’ 7” and slight frame worried him, as he thought it might disqualify him from army service. However, after a short wait, a lieutenant colonel approved him fit for army duty, having completed the required ‘Attestation’ and sent him for his medical examination at Great Scotland Yard Recruiting Office. This completed, George returned to the Royal Fusiliers two days later and, in the presence of the approving officer, Major M.C. Moulshell, he became a Fusilier on 29th March 1934. Barely two months after his 18th birthday, the ‘shrimp’ was in.

His training was based at Aldershot, Catterick and in the Brecon Beacons, the latter being the toughest and wettest. This training would stand him in good stead for the endurance that he would require in future theatres of war.

The part he did not like was the classroom exams that followed. Having left school prior to his 14th birthday, he had missed a good deal, and part of the time had been spent grieving for his mother. The school had not been at all sympathetic; the attitude was very much, 'get over it.'

George's time in the Tower of London HQ passed mostly without incident, apart from a tiny case of being absent without leave (AWOL), although he maintained at the time that it wasn't his fault. He had a further posting as a guard at Buckingham Palace; this, he thought, was a great experience, and the tourists passing by the gates of the great house encouraged the guards to march up and down. The soldiers had been ordered not to comply, but the tourists could take photographs of the Fusiliers changing the guard. George felt that he looked the 'bee's knees' in his uniform. During the past months he had put on some weight, even a little height, he had also broadened considerably with the training and exercises, which consisted of a large amount of drill, bulling his boots, running up hills and down again, sometimes with full kit (over 60 kilos) pulling you backwards. The gym ropes were hard at first, but as time passed his strength grew and, due to the combination of his light frame and now more powerful arms, he shinned up and down like a monkey after a new food source. He thought that this type of soldiering wasn't bad at all, but things were about to change.

Chapter 5

Embarkation 1936

The First Battalion Fusiliers were mustered at Liverpool Docks after travelling from London; they were to gather their kit and follow the colour of the tickets they had been given. These matched the designated walkways to board the ship that would eventually take them to Bombay. The purpose of the coloured tickets was to ensure equal loading of the craft and to deploy the men safely and swiftly. Some of the men with George began removing their tickets and in the jostling throng switched them with others: not for any particular rational reason, just for a laugh.

The men with the swapped tickets were piling up the gangways, where a sergeant spotted a blue ticket amongst the yellow. George saw what was going on and turned to the fusilier behind him.

"There's going to be some trouble here in a bit. Did you see the men messing with the tickets?"

The fusilier replied, "Yes I did; I'm saying nothing, that sergeant down there's not to be messed with."

Looking about him, George saw the massive effort that had gone into today's embarkation. The faces of the men were of a mixed nature; some were talkative, others were passive, but all were probably wondering what they were in for. The mass of men in khaki could be seen stretching out through the dockyard. George wondered if they were all to board a single ship or whether there were others in front or behind. The sound of men settling in and the smell of damp clothing, the heat from the men around him, gave off an odd odour, like damp washing that had not been properly dried, and the exchanges of men discussing everything to nothing joined together into a deep rumble. The only clear sounds were those of the strategically placed sergeants shouting instructions to the men who were not moving fast enough for their liking.

Suddenly there was a sound that pierced George's awareness. He looked at the fusilier behind him, who just raised an eyebrow, as they heard a yell from the nearest sergeant.

"Where do you think you are going lad, are you colour-blind or something?"

"I don't know, Sergeant," the unknowing culprit replied lamely.

This seemed to send the sergeant into a fury; he halted the embarkation at his gangway and sent the ticket holder back to the blues. The lad had tried to tell the sergeant that he was sure he was in the right line, but it just didn't wash. This gave the gang of reprobates a good laugh and cause for much merriment in the reiteration of the yarn over the next few days. Unfortunately, the sergeant was passing one day and heard the repeating of the tale; he was so furious that he immediately put the offender on a charge. No matter how much the soldier tried to explain that he was just repeating the story, the sergeant just increased the punishment for his perceived lies. This gave the men even more to talk about and more reason to retell the story once again, of course being extremely careful to look about them prior to retelling the tale.

Apart from this little diversion, the rest of the journey went smoothly, and the days on board were to be a trial of endurance and tedium for all. Although the sea journey was uneventful in most ways, they were still expected to carry out exercises and drills. The sergeant major wasn't having any sloppy pink-faced weak-kneed recruits in his army, so he marched them until they dropped; many did, from sea sickness, from the massive cocktail of drugs they pumped into them and from the sheer hard work the sergeant major insisted they engage in. They were reassured that the drugs that were being administered were for their benefit, even if the immediate aftereffects left them feeling sick and disorientated. The drugs would protect them from all nature of ills, including malaria, black water fever, yellow fever and dysentery. To be fair, there were games, and George participated in some; skittles and rope hoops over cones were enjoyable, but those of a more sporting and competitive nature appealed to him more as a way to rid himself of his frustration, in particular boxing. Although of slight build and a southpaw, he loved his ability to dance around the larger men; it reminded him very much of his school days, except this time the army was encouraging him to fight.

Chapter 6

Bombay to Jhansi

The Bombay dockside was teeming with workers, lifting, carrying and running around to what was considered no particular purpose by the men disembarking. The smell of fish pervaded the air and, although painted in bright colours, the buildings looked dilapidated and tired. The lower walls were rough red, with an uneven texture, they conjured up a feeling of some ancient ritual with blood-spattered walls. It turned out to be something more mundane: local men would chew betel nuts after a meal to aid digestion and spit the discarded husks against the wall, leaving the red colouring.

Looking about him George could not only feel the heat, but he could taste the uncommon smells. He felt the trickles of perspiration running down his back, soaking the already dampened shirt. Taking in the crowds surrounding the disembarked soldiers, he could barely discern any ground between them; such was the jostling and pushing of the people. One of the fusiliers came alongside George, thinking that he must be looking at something in particular.

"What you looking at George?" he enquired,

"Nothing in particular, mate," he replied. "I just can't take it in, that's all, it's just so…different from back home. There are just people, cattle, and noise all around us."

"Well George, all I can say is, welcome to bloody, smelly India!" said the fusilier.

Trucks were lined up along the docks to take the men to the railway station for their onward journey across India. Sellers of all sorts of goods crowded the dockside, hoping for a sale to the British Army. Too dazed after their sea journey, the men endeavoured to push their way through to the trucks. Bellowing commands, the sergeant major shoved the natives out of the way without a thought to where they might land; some fell into the dockside's greasy water, floating with diesel oil and other indescribable objects.

Named after Queen Victoria, the train station was a magnificent building, known as Victoria Terminus. It towered above a shanty town, which contrasted with the splendour of the city. Its detail and colour were impressive: bright red brick, domed turrets and towers with spires; cathedral-like in its appearance, it dominated the surrounding area. The terminus served the whole of the country's mainline long distance trains, as well as the local links around Bombay. The local trains were incredibly busy and the commute into Bombay for work seemed to run all day, with men, women and children hanging on for dear life if seats were not available – and they usually weren't. Not a scrap of floor space was vacant, and somehow vendors plied their trade through the trains as they rattled their way through the outskirts and into the city.

The men, now exhausted by heat, carrying their equipment and the constant buzz of voices and activity around them, were relieved to at last board the train that would take them away from the stifling heat of the city, they hoped.

The train seemed to be travelling along an endless line cut into the side of a hill, catching branches of lush green foliage as it wound its way along the apparently precarious track. The endless clickety clack sounded somehow different from the British trains, George thought; maybe the closeness of the jungle muffled the noise. The mesmeric murmuring's of the train's movement and the motion of the swaying carriages was enough to send you off to sleep, if it were not for the bloke next to you poking his elbows in your rib cage and the one opposite with the symphony orchestra of sounds emanating from his mouth – and sometimes from elsewhere. George felt uncomfortably warm as the train rumbled through the hills overlooking Bombay; he had a very stiff neck and his oppos were sleeping in disarray, arms and legs in places they shouldn't have been, kit strewn through the carriage like abandoned refuse. The jungle seemed as impermeable as the thoroughfare through his carriage. George stared intently into the greener world until he thought he saw movement behind every leaf; he was hoping to catch a glimpse of the wildlife: tigers or even elephants.

George and one of his fellow fusiliers were staring at the wonder and depth of the greenery.

The fusilier turned to George and said, "Cor, this is just like Kew Gardens, where my old man used to take me."

Laughing, George replied, "I've heard of Kew Gardens, but I've never been there. What's it like?"

"Blooming marvellous," he chuckled at his own pun. "I liked the tropical house best, but that's before I knew I was going to see the real bloody thing. I don't fancy strolling around out there without my rifle."

George was thoughtful and said, "When I get back to England, I think I might visit Kew Gardens and have a look for myself."

"You do that mate; there's some beautiful stuff there. My old man knew a lot of the names of plants and things, but I just liked being with him. Dead now, he is, heart attack. Still he liked his beer and his Sunday lunches and his pork sausages for breakfast. You might say he went out with a banger!"

Both men laughed at the sick joke, gently bumped each other on the arm and returned to their positions within the melee of the carriage.

They were headed for Jhansi. It didn't look that far on the map, but it was translating itself into a formidable journey. Although travelling through the jungle was hot and sticky, with flies everywhere, at least they were on dry ground, or mostly, as the jungle dripped moisture from the overhanging foliage, which ran in tiny rivulets down the inside of the carriages.

George's thoughts were of home. Although she had been dead for some years now, he missed his mother and wanted to be able to tell her that he would be all right and that this was an adventure he wished to undertake. It had come as a surprise to George that he was being packed off to India, but he had been told by many that he would love it and that it was far from anything he had encountered in England, especially in the East End of London. He was going to the East from the East, he joked with his mates back home. At least he would have three square meals a day, plus other rations, and training too. He hadn't yet learnt the intricacies of smoking and didn't see the point of it, so his cigarettes were good currency for chocolate and other niceties.
George had already been in trouble; he had been AWOL from barracks and it was particularly annoying because he hadn't meant to be but had got into a drinking contest while on a short leave home from The Tower of London, where he was stationed. He had passed out, trying to be the best at drinking down the most pints until someone gave up. The killer was the whisky. He had won the competition, for which the prize was a bottle of whisky; they badgered him until he opened it, and, although he shared it around, he found that even a small quantity of whisky mixed with all that beer would prove fatal. The publican found him the next morning fast asleep on top of some crates in the backyard – not the most comfortable of spots – where even the light rain that had started in the early hours hadn't wakened him. George ran all the way back to barracks, in the hope of sneaking in,

but it was too late and he was put on a charge, losing a day's pay.

The night's celebration had been a prelude to his imminent departure for India – he had been given leave to say goodbye to his nearest and dearest. Soon after the drinking competition incident, he was on a troop ship to India without seeing his family or close friends before he left. Now he was sitting in a train chugging across the Indian subcontinent, relishing the thought of a nice pint of beer in his local. He thought of Dicky Herbert in the pub competition, throwing up all over Mrs Bradshaw's bulldog. She was furious, but Dicky was unrepentant and said, "Well you shouldn't come in here if you can't have a laugh." She gathered her belongings and went off in a huff, shouting back to anyone who cared to listen.

"Wait until my husband hears how I have been treated; he will knock your heads together, he will." Dicky ploughed on unperturbed and shouted back at Mrs Bradshaw.

"Is that after he has finished knocking up Mrs Millington from number 28?"

"Steady up boys," said Alf, the publican. "We can't have you upsetting Mrs Bradshaw like that." But Alf was struggling, hardly able to contain himself, and with that the whole pub erupted in laughter.

George sighed at the thought of home and squirmed into a more comfortable position, well, as best he could between these sweating, snorting beasts. How he longed for a good soak in a nice bath, with that pint just within reach, perhaps served to him by an Indian lass – an image resembling some of the pictures that the older men had brought back with them from their time in India. The exotic and bright colours of the East captivated his senses and had him dreaming of wonderful adventures and pleasures. With that, someone let off a terrible stink; everyone in the vicinity groaned with displeasure – the perpetrator would not be found as many of the men were fast asleep or pretending to be. The moment was shattered; he was back in the train with its rickety clacking along the interminable track.

They were pulling into Jhansi; they could see the town ahead of them, as the train made its slow twists and turns in between the makeshift-looking houses. The heat intensified as they approached the outlying districts, the town and its surroundings acting like a basin absorbing the sun for even more heat. The soldiers couldn't believe the intensity of the heat, which was building as the train slowed even more, increasing with each passing minute the train was exposed to the direct sunlight. As they slowly pulled alongside the platform, they became aware it was a jostling mass; how they were to get onto the platform seemed impossible to work out. There were tea *wallahs* and fruit sellers, together with a goat being pulled by an elderly man; in fact, the sights and sounds were so numerous they were hard to take in. Colours and smells also pervaded their senses; the strong smell of the oriental spices was a delight and a distraction, bringing a myriad of comments from the men, from "what's that pong?" to "what have you trod in now?"

The men were soon shaken out of their sightseeing by a sergeant major, who bellowed and cajoled them into some sort of order on the train, while an array of pristine Indian soldiers from the 4th Indian Regiment moved the assembled crowd away from the train. This they did without much thought for their wellbeing, pushing those that, to their minds, were too slow off the mark. The 4th Indian was a proud regiment; their turnout was impressive and, to the natives crowded on the platform, intimidating.

The soldiers on the train were struggling with their kit; trying to load it onto their sweat-soaked backs was the last thing they wanted to do and it was also proving an impossible task in the confined space of the carriage. As the sergeant yelled at them to disembark before trying to put on their kit bags, the men fell over each other and their kit in their attempts to get off the train as quickly as possible. The heat was rising in the stationary carriages, the humidity and smells within them were now more than unbearable. Having got the men in some sort of order, the sergeant barked at them again to line up with the 4th Indian, who would guide them through the now disgruntled throng. The appearance of 'new blood' was a great sight for the assembled crowd, but being unable to get to them to sell their wares was a major frustration. They continued to jostle the 4th Indian, who were not in the mood to take any nonsense, and a few rifle butts were seen to thrust their way into the crowd, cracking a few heads, but, apart from a few murmurs, there was no further dissent.

The Fusiliers were to be billeted at 4th Indian HQ, bringing the regiments into closer contact and boding well for future relationships. The 4th Indian, the Punjabi Rifles and many other Indian regiments, such as the Gurkhas, were to be an integral part of future conflicts and an asset in the battles across the globe.

Chapter 7

Colour and Spices

Life in Jhansi was idyllic for an east London lad; George loved to wander through the markets when off duty. They were much brighter, nosier and even more full of life than the markets in the East End of London. The grey, drab streets seemed a million miles away to George and, in this reality, they might as well have been. Live chickens, geese and ducks in cages were carried off by eager consumers, whom he assumed had large families waiting back at home needing to be fed. Piles of colourful spices, the smells of which reached George's nose, were olfactory pleasures beyond imagining. The colours were breath-taking, with large cloths, rugs and pots reflecting the sun's heat and adding to the vibrancy of the sweltering days. The crowds, busying themselves with their daily tasks, pulling carts, pushing past with large baskets of freshly picked produce – the like of which George had never been exposed to – overdosed his senses.

He found a place to sit in the shade of a building; it was not so much a café in the true sense, more a hole in the wall. The assumed proprietor rushed to George's side, bowing and nodding his head as he asked this new arrival,

"What is your pleasure?" The proprietor asked.

George requested tea; it was the only drink that he had been told was safe in this new world of experiences, and he didn't really know what else might be on offer. The rickety chair on which he was seated seemed most unsafe; he was unable to move too much for fear of it collapsing. A young woman appeared, her head covered in a gold and red cloth, seemingly part of the long dress that touched the ground as she moved towards him, carrying the tea in a large polished metal pot; it had an unnecessarily long spout, which she tilted towards a tiny clay pot at arm's length. This show of dexterity displayed a skill that had been acquired after much practice – the tea was drawn to the pot as if by magic; then the show was over and the tea was standing on a small equally rickety-looking table. The table had no cloth; it seemed to be made of some matted fibres, with legs of bamboo or something very much like it. As he thanked her for the tea, the young woman was withdrawing from George, walking backwards, bowing as she went. George felt very awkward at the way in which the locals seemed to revere the troops. He felt their smiling, bowing and scraping was all too undignified. The young woman had almost reached the hole in the wall before George noticed how very pretty she was. The whites of her eyes glowed from under her headdress, yet the centres were as dark as night; her nose was pierced and bore a silver stud, and bangles of gold and silver adorned her arms. Her dark black hair shone with a blue hue in the bright sun and framed her face under her headdress; her forehead bore a painted red spot (a *bindi*), signifying her married status and faithfulness. She was a stunner; her complexion was the colour of strong coffee, her gloriously white teeth shining through her succulent red lips when she spoke. Wow! George thought: no girls like you in the East End.

The sun was moving on its circuit; gradually George was becoming very hot, as it first reached his legs and then crept up his body as the day moved on. Time to go, he thought, as he got up and went to the hole in the wall to pay. Coming from the brightness of the sunny street, he peered into the darkness of what must be the kitchen. Fires burned in the corners; the young lady, together with another older woman, was making round flat breads and baking them on the sides of the clay ovens over the fires. The room was smoky and possibly even hotter than the street outside. He moved in towards the staff at the back of the room, only to be intercepted by the proprietor, who began the ritual of bowing and walking backwards as George moved forward.

"I just wish to pay," George said.

"Yes Sahib, certainly Sahib, no need for you to come; we come to you."

"That's ok," said George, proffering a handful of rupees in paper money and coins.

"Too much, Sahib, far too much." The proprietor riffled through the money that George was holding out until he found the correct coinage, bowing and walking backwards once again. George thanked him and turned to go as the proprietor thanked him, asking him to return and bring his friends. He also began to explain that they provided an array of food that would delight him and his friends.

"Please return Sahib, please return," were the proprietor's parting words.

George, who had enjoyed his day in and around Jhansi, was even more pleased once he returned to base and had a wash and freshened up for his evening meal. He had heard that a number of his platoon had visited a tea plantation further north; that would be his next port of call once he had leave, the time and transport. The men returning from the tea plantation had reported that it was cooler in the hills; the types and flavours of tea that they were served seemed endless. George thought that it sounded too good to be missed: cooler climes and endless tea, what could be better? He would wait and see if he could get himself on one of the many transports heading towards the Punjab.

It was on such a trip that he met a soldier who had been on a later transport; this man was to become George's closest and best friend. Bertie Bakewell was a likeable and amiable young man, who did not follow the pattern of many of his compatriots, who drank, were loud, swore a lot and were used to chasing young women at every opportunity. Not that Bertie was a saint; he was known to swear when the situation called for it, and he liked women in his own way. He had a cheeky grin and was not averse to a bit of kidding his fellows along with tall stories. It was while travelling to the hills that George met him in the midst of one such story. George was quickly onto Bertie's tongue-in-cheek account and listened quietly as the lorry bumped and ground its way up the ever-circling hillside road. Bertie was telling the tale of a corporal he met, who had recently returned from a tour in the northern territories and was noted to be a fairly shy man. He was persuaded by his fellows to go out for a few pints one night. The tale centred on the said corporal who, having fallen into a drainage ditch, drunk, was sleeping off his boozing from the night before. He awoke becoming aware of a pain in the lower trouser area. Bertie continued:

"The corporal, believing that he needed to pee, undid his trousers to find that he had the most enormous dick; he was pleased and horrified at the same moment. Pleased because of the size of his old man, horrified because he could not pee and his engorged dick was turning a nasty shade of deep purple. At this moment a patrol came across him sitting in the ditch weeping with the pain. They helped him out of the ditch and immediately transferred him to the medics. They were amazed at the corporal's story and at the massive size of his dick. Doctors were summoned and on closer inspection, they diagnosed that a leech had slithered its way into his penis while he slept and had created the bulging with the corporal's blood."

Catching George's eye, Bertie realised at that moment that here was a fellow who perhaps could not be fooled so easily. He winked at George, who was smiling as Bertie proceeded with his cock and bull story, while the men sat intently listening to Bertie as he wove his yarn, their mouths wide open with amazement as they waited for the next instalment. Bertie left them hanging with anticipation of the conclusion, when the lorry pulled into the tea plantation.

"The story to be concluded on the return journey," said Bertie with a twinkle in his eye and another wink in George's direction.

There was a chorus of groans from the men, who, like children, were being told they couldn't have what they wanted just now. As they formed into ranks, George leant towards Bertie and said,

"Quite a story."

Both men grinned, whispered their names to each other, and briefly shook hands, before they were called to attention.

Chapter 8

Friends and Others

As a soldier, George soon began to realise that the locals either loved the troops in their country or were of the opinion that they should leave the indigenous people to their own government. Tribal infiltrations of the barracks were of prime concern to its security, with firearms being the main goal for the tribesmen that had managed to work their way into the secure areas. Chai *wallahs*, cleaners and tradesmen were all under suspicion, since materials began disappearing. In India, to lose your rifle was a particular disgrace; much was made about the procedures to secure them, as every weapon stolen could be used by tribesmen against the soldiers. Each company barrack room had a rifle rack in its centre, to which weapons were padlocked when not in use. At night, two orderlies slept on either side of the rack, rooms were visited by the orderly officer and the weapons were counted. By day, one orderly was always on duty in each room to safeguard weapons and equipment not in use while the men were training. After shooting on the rifle ranges, every round and empty case had to be accounted for, and the men's pouches were inspected by an officer.

At this time weapons were even carried on church parades, a precaution dating back to the mutiny at Meerut during a morning service back on a Sunday in 1857. Old suspicions died hard.

The primary role of the soldiers in India was one of internal security when not deployed on engagements across the country. Much training time was allocated to this, and demonstrations were given to show how the military should take over from the Indian Police on the authority of the local magistrate when rioting got out of hand. This seldom happened, but when it did the presence of well turned out and highly disciplined British troops was salutary. The separation of troops from rioters was a fundamental feature of internal security training, and internal security drills for crowd dispersal were clearly laid down in the 1930s. They were based on a banner, inscribed in both English and the local language, calling on the crowd to disperse, and a bugler to draw attention to it. After that came the opening of carefully controlled fire by skilled marksmen at specified agitators, followed by a pause to assess the effect and provide the opportunity for the mob to break up and move.

George was left to ponder the fate of these poor wretches. He was not the sort of person who felt the British had the right to subjugate the locals. In fact, he felt he had more in common with the local man in the street than with the British Government and the high-handed manner of the officers around him. After all, he was the common man, who had toiled in any manner he could to make a living in markets and the docks of the East End of London. Not so different from these poor beggars, he thought.

These thoughts about the common man came back to him with a vengeance when news of a massive earthquake in the far northern region of India was relayed to them. They might have to mobilise troops and transport them to help the Queens Own Regiment, who were fighting a terrific battle of recovery of the dead and injured. Jhansi was the hub of transport for the whole of India, its railway station built in the 1800s was extremely robust, distinctive, and of great importance to the British. Resembling a fortification rather than a railway station, it had been built to stand for a hundred years or more. Besides, the transport hub was of vital significance, allowing them to move men and equipment at speed across the whole of India.

An official Government communique issued on the day of the earthquake from Simla stated:

> "On 31st May 1935 at 3.40 am in the early morning the city of Quetta and the countryside for 100 miles to the south-west including the town of Khelat were devastated by a severe earthquake which lasted three minutes. There was another severe shock on 2nd June.
>
> 1. The whole city of Quetta is destroyed and being sealed under military guard from 2nd June with medical advice. It is estimated that 20,000 corpses remain buried under the debris. There is no hope of rescuing any more persons alive. The corpses extracted and buried number several thousand. There are about 10,000 Indian survivors including 4,000 injured.

2. All houses in the civil area are razed to the ground except Government House, which is partially standing but in ruins. The church and club are both in ruins, also the Murree Brewery.
3. One quarter of the cantonment area is destroyed, the remaining three quarters slightly damaged, but inhabitable. Most of the damage was done in the RAF area where the barracks were destroyed, and only six out of the twenty-seven machines are serviceable.
4. The railway area is destroyed.
5. Hanna Road and the Staff College are undamaged.
6. Surrounding villages are destroyed, with, it is feared, very heavy casualties. The number is not yet ascertainable. Military parties are being sent out to investigate and render help.
7. Outlying districts, as already reported from Khelat and Mastung.
End."

The men were mustered earlier than usual the next morning after hearing of the quake. The sergeant and two officers were looking to the men for a trip north with vital supplies for the recovery of bodies from the aftermath of the earthquake. The captain spoke first, telling the men of the utter devastation, the need to provide aid to their fellow comrades, who were also badly hit by the earthquake, and to the locals, whose houses were not so sturdy and fell at the first tremors. The quake hit the population while many were asleep, meaning they were caught out by the suddenness and the ferocity of the event. The airfield, aircraft, married quarters and outlying buildings were also destroyed. All in all, the captain said that it was a right bloody mess; men and materials were urgently needed to restore the base and aid the locals. The sergeant thanked the captain, spoke very quickly, said he didn't want any messing about, he wanted men to go with the support materials to help with the rescue and recovery, restoring services as required. On this basis he wanted skilled, strong men who would be an asset to the operation. Men who thought they could be of service should take one step forward, stating what they could bring to aid the situation. They would be volunteering to be away from base for however long it would take to reinstate order.

George was one of the first to step forward, stating that he could fix anything mechanical, was trained as a lorry driver and a motorcycle rider and, if it came to it, was strong enough with the lifting and carrying, as he had done a great deal of this at home.

"Good man," said the captain, "I will leave the rest to you, Sergeant. You seem to have a good bunch of men wishing to assist; sort out those that you feel will be of most use." With a, "Well done men," the captain and lieutenant moved back towards the HQ office.

The 20 men selected to be of most use were marched to the side of the vehicles being loaded with everything from picks, shovels, crowbars and cases of explosives. There was a myriad of identifiable crates, marked medical, others were not readily identifiable, but they were told there were shrouds, blankets, tarpaulins and sundry items. Also being loaded were cases of tinned produce, from corned beef to peaches. All the produce would be taken to the railway station at Jhansi and loaded onto the train taking the men and supplies as far north as the railway would permit. It was estimated that at least a one-hundred-mile radius from the epicentre had been affected by the earthquake. The reports coming from Quetta did not state whether the railway was still effective. Should they discover, as they travelled further north, that the railway had been destroyed; the contingency plan was to muster as many vehicles as possible to take the goods and men to Quetta, dispersing them into the provinces as required. They would be joining up with the Queens Own and the Punjab Rifles, who were already on site. During the next few days, every squadron in India sent aircraft up to Quetta, laden with doctors, nurses and medical supplies. They returned carrying injured women and children.

*Tremendous losses were incurred in the city of Quetta in the days following the event. On the streets, people lay dead, others buried beneath the debris, some still alive. On the eventual arrival of George's contingent, they joined the other British regiments, who were scattered around the town to rescue victims, which was becoming an impossible task. Men were putting their lives at risk to help others; they were to be awarded gallantry medals for the part they played in the search and rescue operations, not that this entered their heads; the issue was the speed and efficiency of the recovery. The weather did not prove to be of much help, and the scorching summer heat made matters worse. Bodies of European and Anglo-Indians were recovered and buried in a British cemetery, where soldiers had dug trenches. Padres performed the burial service in haste, as soldiers would cover the graves quickly. Others were removed in the same way and taken to a nearby *shamshāngāht* (crematorium or cremation platform), for their remains to be cremated.

*While the soldiers excavated through the debris for a sign of life, the Government sent the Quetta administration instructions to build a tent city to house the homeless survivors and to provide shelter for their rescuers. Fresh supplies of medicated pads were brought forth for the soldiers to wear over their mouths in fear of a spread of disease while they dug for the dead bodies buried underneath the rubble of the town.

In a quiet moment of taking refreshment, the rescuers sat looking around them at the work still needing to be done. A military chaplain sat with the men, his clothes indistinguishable from those of the rest of the rescuers. Some of the men looked at the chaplain and asked him the inevitable.

"Why? Why has God allowed this to happen?"

The chaplain seemed lost for words and exhausted by his efforts in the search for life. The men continued to pester the chaplain, until George couldn't stand it any longer.

"Leave the man alone, will you?" he spoke out. "He has been digging, just like us, can't you see he's tired and in shock like the rest of us?"

The chaplain replied, “Thank you my son, but it is alright. These men have seen some terrible things of late and it’s only natural to look for someone to blame. I could go on about free will and that God cannot intervene in every situation, disasters will happen, whether they are natural or man-made. I too question God and what he is doing in his infinite mercy and wisdom, but we rarely have all the answers; sometimes, it seems, none.”

Trying to discover more, George spoke to the chaplain.

“I believe that there is a God, or something like a God. I have felt it and seen it sometimes, in good people. I don’t believe he is all-knowing and all-seeing; how could he be? You have seen the terrible loss of life; are the people that died under these tons of rubble just automatically going to heaven? What was their purpose on Earth, especially the children that have hardly begun to live, what of their lives being cut short?”

“You are correct young man, in saying that they will be in heaven, and I believe especially the children, as they are sinless,” replied the chaplain.

The rescuers that had gathered for their refreshments did not seem to take on board what had been said; shaking their heads, they walked back to where they had been working previously.

Walking away from the men and the chaplain, George looked across the rubble at the massive task that lay ahead. He glanced at the bodies in their shrouds, awaiting removal; the flies had arrived and were buzzing around the bodies. It seemed that the flies were being disrespectful. He wanted to put all this right, but of course he couldn't, it left him feeling helpless. He didn't know any of the people here, but he could not help his eyes filling up with the deep heartache for the loss of so many; the tears rolled down his cheeks and he began to cry more deeply for the loss of so many lives, his shoulders shaking from something deep within.

Looking around him, George saw that men were already back at work. He needed to do something practical. Wiping his eyes, he spoke softly to himself.

"Pull yourself together, man; you are no good to anyone like this."

The men dug, pulled and dragged materials from suspected sites, where they thought buried victims might still be alive. How, nobody knew, even in the 11th hour of the rescue there was still hope, but the blazing temperatures would make it almost impossible to survive without water. All the men from different battalions, backgrounds and ethnicity, sat together in solemn silence as they took their refreshments in dust-covered clothes, with bleeding hands and hearts. As soon as their short breaks were over, without hesitation they returned to the piles of debris that were once people's homes, schools and meeting places. The digging and searching would begin once again. After over a week of this backbreaking work, manual digging was called to a halt, the heavy equipment had arrived; hope was lost for anymore survivors. The men reluctantly returned their tools and fell into the tented city, their beds and slept.

The return journey to Jhansi was the same as the one leaving it, but George was a changed man; he had begun to view his fellow man in a different light. The effects of the traumatic events had had a deep impact on him. He promised himself that he would not take life for granted. He knew that this was a cliché but, cliché or not, he was determined to make his life count. How? At this point in time he didn't know.

George returned to his barracks and was determined to live his life to the full. He spoke very little about his experiences in the north but became a little more reflective and inward-looking, trying to find answers that the chaplain couldn't give him.

The years passed relatively quietly for him in India with the usual routine of patrols, the odd breaking up of resistance from the few named dissidents, who had decided that the British should leave India to the Indians; there wasn't too much to complain about, except of course the heat.

There were changes in the world outside India that would be of greater significance, and George was about to be thrust into a much bleaker time. The news had broken that Germany was at war with most of Europe, but what would have a profound effect, was the entry of the British in the war for Europe.

The 1st Battalion, along with their 4th Indian counterparts, would travel to form a fighting force in North Africa, to disrupt the supply lines to Rommel, entering into many bitter encounters.

*Extracts from hibbit.org.uk / queenandroyalsurrey.org.uk/ wikipedia

Chapter 9

North Africa – Egypt –Syria and Iraq

After the long sea journey from Bombay in 1939, eventually the ship docked in Egypt, Alexandria to be precise, but the men on board were both surprised and angered as they had believed their next port of call was Blighty, then perhaps on to France – even straight to France would have meant they could have sorted out Jerry but no, where were they? In another dust hole, which was…where? The men disembarked, feeling disgruntled and tired but glad to have their feet on dry land. Perhaps this was just a stopover before travelling on to be a part of a larger force. Their comrades were fighting in France in rather a hurry last time, but this was their time to show the Jerries what the Fusiliers were made of: that was the opinion of most of the men. There would not be another opportunity as far as they were concerned. The 1st Battalion, along with their fellow comrades in the Ranjipur Rifles, would knock Jerry for six: that was their feeling. They were totally unaware that this desert was to be their home for many months, if not years, to come.

Once the men were assembled on the dockside in a semblance of order, they were addressed by an officer from the station at Alexandria. He made it clear that they would not be travelling to England or France, but that they had a pretty important role here in Egypt and the surrounding territories. He went on to explain that the Italians and Germans had a stronghold in certain parts of the desert areas and were making inroads into Egypt at a rate of knots from Libya. Puffing out his chest, the officer spoke louder, with more fervour.

"We need to teach these I-ties a lesson – and Jerry too – so that we can move forward and support our comrades across the Mediterranean." The men had heard this sort of jingoism before and were unimpressed with this puffed-up officer, who probably had achieved very little in his career in the army and was quite possibly one of the many administrators. The officer continued.

"The sergeant major will move you to your transports and will designate your billeting; follow his instructions. That's all, men. Good luck." With that he moved away, taking a salute from the sergeant major, who was an old hand and soon had the men lining up and ready to either march to their billets or be loaded onto trucks for deployment further afield.

George and his comrades were feeling a little the worse for wear, especially as a few days earlier their life aboard ship had been a bit rough. They had hit some heavy seas; although you couldn't call it a real storm, it was sufficiently rough, coupled with the cramped conditions, for many of the men to feel pretty ill. Some had thrown up and it had induced a cascade effect: once one of the ranks threw up, it tipped the balance of those that were on the cusp, and then the next. Like a Mexican wave, it became a perpetual roll of sickness. George had moved from the quarters below to the upper deck: firstly, to get some fresh air so that he wouldn't succumb and, secondly, to get away from the claustrophobic and sickening stench below. The effect of these days at sea had been to deplete their reserves of energy, especially as they either didn't eat or, if they did, their meal soon returned to find fresh air once again.

The First Fusiliers were being marched to their billet by the sergeant major. For this, George was grateful, as it gave him an opportunity to get his land legs back, as well as his bearings. Being shunted around in a troop transport left him without a sense of well-being; he'd had enough of enclosed spaces. He strode out, sucking in the cooling air of the evening and feeling the blood course around his body, bringing him back to life. Not far from the port, they made a right turn out of the gates. As they were crunching along at a fair rate, one of the men further down the ranks began to whistle. The men seemed to be bolstered by the well-known tune; their steps became lighter, their mood too. By the time they had reached their encampment, their disposition had changed dramatically; they were chatting and playful, so much so that the sergeant major told them to simmer down, sort themselves out or they would miss mess and go hungry. The thought of missing their first real meal on dry land spurred them to move quickly and more quietly around the camp.

George and Bertie sat in silence for a while, eating the long-awaited and deserved food. Bertie was the first to break the silence.

"What do you think about coming up against the I-Ties, George?"

George looked as if he were pondering Bertie's question deeply; he was just enjoying the food and his mind was nowhere in particular, just savouring the moment.

"What was that, Bertie?"

"The I-Ties George, do you think they will give us a hard time?"

"Nah, they'll probably want to get home, as soon as they come up against a well organised and disciplined force like us, eh Bertie!"

The fusiliers in close proximity laughed and shouted, "Too right George." One of them added, "When they see Bertie coming at them all spick and span with his bayonet fixed, they will all probably do a runner!"

The men laughed and slapped Bertie on the back as they left to see if there was any more grub going.

Most of the men were scathing about the efficacy of the Italian army, which was 200,000 strong and banging on the front door of Egypt. Whether the men appreciated this, it did not stop them making detrimental comments about the Italians. The 1st Battalion was to be on the move again, by train on this occasion from Alexandria to Garawla, where they were rehearsing movements in the desert. The 4th Indian Rifles, who had also travelled with the men of the 1st Fusiliers, were to be deployed on the sea frontage, which needed to be occupied as an attack was imminent, according to intelligence from the War Office in London.

The men of the 1st Batallion were correct in their thinking about the Italian troops, whose hearts were not in this war, and there were several successful outcomes to their attacks on them. Nevertheless, there were also many losses that gravely affected the men. Lieutenant Colonel Johnson was one loss that was keenly felt, not only by the 1st Battalion but by the whole regiment; he had become a very popular commanding officer to all the men.

Although the men had at first thought that the battles against the Italians were to be a pushover, it soon became clear that to take matters too lightly was not the best approach; over the coming days many men were lost. The Italians had taken a real beating, so much so that the battalion had to escort 10,000 prisoners to Matruh and then return to Garawla. The fusiliers were becoming accustomed to the ravages of war; they were dishevelled, dirty, tired and rations were running low. Reduced to half a bottle of water a day, their rations were bully beef and biscuits, any spare produce being sent to the cookhouse back at base camp. They had enjoyed much success in the battles over the previous weeks and, with feelings running high, nothing else seemed to matter: your mates around you, something to eat and drink and the prospect of being relieved in time for Christmas added to their increasingly high spirits.

The men were always pleased to get back from the conflicts, to a good hot meal of beef and potatoes. The vegetables were tinned of course, but to be able to sit around a table instead of squatting in the desert sand with the accompanying flies was a great blessing. This also gave the men time to talk, to clean up and enjoy the usual ribald jokes and banter, while they gathered in groups. Food was still a precious item and was treated with great respect. After all, when would their next hot meal time be? The soldiers always stoked up when returning to base and after a desert campaign; they were totally full, as they had become used to dried rations while in the field. Their stomachs had shrunk with the short rations and without the satisfaction of feeling a good solid meal. Satisfied, replete and tired, men dozed where they could find a suitable spot to rest in the shade, some under vehicles, some in their tents, others were so exhausted they fell asleep in the NAAFI, regardless of the hard bench seats and scrubbed tables. Those completely exhausted fell face first into their food; comrades picked them up and propped them in a shady corner, where they slept the day and night through. On seeing the men in this position, kindly officers ordered the quartermaster to send blankets to cover them due to the cold night air; there they remained until reveille.

The battle in the Western Desert raged on, with successful outcomes for the Allies, although they still had a race to outmanoeuvre the desert fox and his cohorts before they reached Tobruk.

George was keeping his ear to the ground, and anything he could pick up he would relay to his mates. He had heard that the Australians had arrived – they were supporting the routing of the Italians; the 4th Indian were chasing the Italians out of

Eritrea and the 1st would soon be on the move again, lock stock and barrel.

Little did the Fusiliers know that this was just the beginning of several years of conflict in the deserts of Egypt, Syria and Iraq. The many battles they were to endure tested their strength, determination and the sheer willpower of the officers and men. With officers taking the brunt of many engagements, the life expectancy of a junior officer was now only two weeks.

Frenchman's Hill was one of many pinch points, where they were ordered to attack. They were spread across too wide a front as they approached the enemy position. There was no response, so they pressed forward, only to realize too late that the enemy had laid a minefield in the long grass at the approach to the hill. The first to realize was one poor soul, who was lifted into the air by a blast; the second and third were not so badly injured, but a fourth man was unfortunate enough to step on an anti-tank mine and there was little left to see. They were called to an immediate halt and it was decided to make the approach in single file, the irony of the situation being that, once they had arrived at the enemy position, they discovered that it had been deserted.

At Sidi Abdullah, the Germans were well entrenched and it took considerable determination and firepower to remove them; many men lost their lives at this point and the Fusiliers, not wishing to break off the encounter, persevered with one engagement after another. One brave or foolish lance corporal pushed forward, throwing grenade after grenade into the well dug-in positions, completely oblivious of the fire from the slit trench beyond, and, when he had run out of grenades, he returned to the dead bodies and took theirs until he completely ran out of supplies. Only some 30 men were left, with just one officer remaining alive. They stayed hunkered down, awaiting the inevitable counterattack.

George waited in a dugout, while they were strafed with machine gun fire; they were so hard under fire that no man was foolish enough to even contemplate raising his head to return fire. In utter frustration at the situation, a captain further down the line was out of cover and, with a Bren gun on his hip, sprayed the machine gun post, removing the opposition. He was about to signal for the men to come forward when he was cut down by another machine gun post on his right.

After the loss of their officer, the men looked to the more experienced soldiers for guidance. George had been in his dugout too long and was getting cramp.

"Fuck this," he said, "Is anyone going to move or are we going to fucking stay here until the Italians invite us for tea?"

"I'm with you George. Whatever you think, I'll go along with it," replied Bertie.

The men looked to George and he nodded to them,

"Let's take that machine gun out; it's getting on my nerves."

Without an officer in sight, George took the initiative. With gestures and whispers through the dugout, they told the rest of the men what they were about to try. There was only one dissenting voice.

"You mad bastards!" it cried back. "You'll get yourselves killed."

The men agreed that was a possibility, but their anger had turned into strategy and a will to overcome.

"We need to do this quickly and as one," George said. "You know the positions, so let's do it."

The strategy was a simple one, more to do with confusing the enemy by misdirection. There was to be as much noise, shooting from the hip, grenades being thrown and distraction techniques deployed as possible, while three of the men would come from the machine-gun post's right flank. While the Italian machine gunner was bent on taking down the 'noisy' bunch, the rest would 'hopefully' be in the clear to outmanoeuvre them.

George was anxious, his mouth was dry and his heart was beating too fast in his chest. What was he doing, taking charge like this? He questioned his motives, but he couldn't really find any, other than to get the job done.

The plan was in full swing, the men had left cover, and George had taken centre ground, where an officer would normally lead, so that he could keep tabs on the different parts of the action. All was going well, the machine gun was trying to find a target, but the men were doing as described to them and popping in and out of dugouts, throwing grenades, ducking down out of sight, only to be followed by fusiliers screaming at the top of their lungs, veins in their necks bursting with their efforts, firing from the hip in a continual stream of fire. Some of the men fell, and George felt a terrible guilt at the thought of losing them. The three men he had chosen to outflank the enemy machine gun were the smallest and fastest men, who moved like ghosts through the smoke and stench of battle. They were so fast that they were overtaking the other fusiliers. George dared not signal to them for fear of bringing the machine gunners' attention to them. He needn't have feared, as they were in sync with the plan and slowed their pace to match the others. When they felt the time was right, they moved with immense skill and accuracy. As George had hoped, the Italians were totally surprised by the three fusiliers bearing down on them. The Italians' yells of surprise were drowned by the bloodcurdling screams of the three soldiers, who gave no mercy and cleared the Italian machine-gun post of all who were there.

The fusiliers all eventually reached the post and, to George's surprise, the two he had seen fall, had literally just fallen over. He was relieved and pleased to see that, apart from a few scrapes, the men had survived the madness of the day. The men were buoyant with the thrill of their success, slapping each other on the back, laughing and recounting the last minutes of their action. Turning to George, Bertie said, "Well fucking done, you should be an officer."

Embarrassed, George replied, "No fucking way, they get shot too easily."

The men laughed at this, but reality dawned: that this was just one action in a day of devastating news; others had not been so lucky.

After many days and weeks in several fierce battles, the men heard that relief was on its way; they would withdraw and get some respite. Although their spirits were lifted by the news, they could not help but think of those friends and comrades, who would not be returning with them. Never had George seen so many acts of bravery from the officers. He did wonder whether they had become crazed with the long period in the desert, but he dismissed the thought as soon as it arose. These men were doing their best for the men under their command and should be commended for taking such initiatives. George wondered whether their families would understand what these young men had sacrificed in their fight, their beliefs and their attitude, in pressing so hard to bring the Germans to their knees.

Chapter 10

Another engagement

The wind had been relentless all night; the sand dunes had changed their shape once again. George awoke to feel the inevitable grating feeling of sand in every part, crack and orifice of his body, including his eyes that he dare not rub, for fear of causing permanent damage to his sight. Instead, he reached for his water bottle and, feeling for the cap, gave it a turn and poured some of the precious water across his still closed eyes. The relief was audible, and he gave a contented sigh as he slowly opened his eyes to the new day. He drank a little water, sloshed it around his mouth, spitting out sand and water onto the ground outside his dugout. His body ached from the cold of the night, he wanted to get up, run about to ease his limbs and get the blood coursing through his veins. He dared not, as the enemy could be watching and waiting for such an error. George was far from green so he let the moment pass, grunting and groaning to relieve the pressure off his backside, his lower back and legs.

Where was he now? He couldn't recall the name of this wadi, but he knew he was still deep in the desert somewhere in Iraq, or was it Syria? It didn't matter; their job was to intercept and interrupt the supply line to Rommel, who was still giving battle to the 8th army. Montgomery's plan was to build up his reserves to such a degree that he outnumbered Rommel. After all, the German tanks were far superior in armour and armaments, the tactic was to outmanoeuvre, overwhelm and destroy. The cutting of vital supply lines was all part of the strategy to undermine Rommel and his elite desert troops. The Rajanpur Rifles were to the east of the Fusiliers, positioned strategically to outflank the convoy, should it slip through the tightening noose of the Allies.

The sun had started its circuit of the desert for the day. It was already felt by the men lying in the shallow dugouts, and the heat of the sand around them would reach blistering temperatures as the day progressed. The reflective heat from the sand was torturous; officers scurried through the ranks, assuring the men that they would be relieved soon; exhorting them to take care of the water they had, as there were no longer further reserves until relief came. Too late, I've used a proportion of mine already, thought George as he sipped thoughtfully on a little to keep his mouth from drying out, relishing the coolness of the water still residing deep within the bottle, a coolness produced from the previous night's cold air.

The men were positioned in an arc so that the farthest on the right could see the farthest on the left. According to air reconnaissance, they were lying across a well-known route Jerry had taken over the past months. This did not mean they would follow this route again; Rommel was not known as the desert fox for nothing. His ability to outthink his opponents was legendary, and the Allies were all too aware of his ability to change plan, move on a pinpoint, and outflank with seeming ease.

The sound of heavy diesel vehicles in the far distance grew gradually louder, the sand rising in a cloud behind them. As there was no wind, it hung in the air, announcing their presence to all, like a smoking bonfire on a windless day. The men hunkered down even further into the sand; the wind from the previous night had served them well, obscuring them with a dusty, sandy covering. What had seemed a hindrance to the Fusiliers had become a blessing, giving them the best camouflage in the desert: the desert sand itself. As the men prepared their weapons, the one place they did not want sand to penetrate was the mechanisms of their rifles and machine guns, and they checked them thoroughly, while the transport convoy moved closer each minute. The Fusiliers hoped the convoy would keep on track towards them; they wanted the first crack at the enemy. They did not have heavy artillery, just machine guns, rifles, mortars and anti-tank guns. They were waiting until the Germans were in such close proximity that the weapons they had to hand, combined with the combustible materials the heavy diesel lorries carried, would be sufficient to send them all sky high.

The tension grew in the dugouts, the men were totally silent and still, their breathing measured, their hands beginning to perspire as the convoy edged slowly towards them. George was trying to gauge how far out they were from the intercept; he strained to see clearly, but the heat haze was building, giving the vehicles an ephemeral appearance, going in and out of vision, at one moment appearing solid, at another seeming to be just a haze in the heat of the day. A man coughed, the others shushed him, as if above the noise that was arising from the convoy, a man coughing almost a mile away could be heard, but such was the tension.

George bit his lip, he needed to pee; tension did this to him. He rolled a little on his side, scraped a little depression and let his water trickle rather than flow; his bladder wasn't that full, but tension dictated that he needed release. He scraped sand into the little hollow and rolled back, flat on his stomach. None of the soldiers noticed George's action; they were all too caught up in their own world of discomfort.

George was back to full concentration as the vehicles continued on their path. He thought of his home and a nice cold beer at the local, but this way lay madness. His throat was dry with anxiety as the perspiration trickled down through his hair and into his eyes. The flies liked this and were buzzing around his head. He dare not make a movement, so brushing them away was out of the question and might draw attention to their position. He felt a prickle down his spine as the enormity of the situation bore down upon him and the men around him.

Inexorably, the convoy moved closer; the sound of the vehicles was not quite deafening, but they were hardly likely to creep by any outpost. Suddenly, from the convoy, came two motorcycle outriders with sidecars armed with machine guns. Completely covered in dust, their progress was much speedier than that of the convoy. Their faces were covered and they wore dark glasses, which must have inhibited their vision. If it were possible to see their faces, they would be grimacing as they sped ahead of the convoy, desperate to reach their destination in order to be able to disrobe, clean up and rest. It was not the best job in the world, being an outrider in the desert heat in full garb. A fusilier was heard to whisper, "Shit, they've sent reconnaissance vehicles ahead of the convoy."

The men looked towards their officer, who was positioned in the centre of the arc. He gestured with his hand for the men to stay down and was obviously hoping that the natural camouflage would be sufficient to hide men and equipment. His wish miraculously came true, as both motorcycle outriders whisked past and through their lines as if they were on a Sunday afternoon bike ride, kicking up a dust storm in their wake.

The heavy vehicles began to thunder past, supported by four armoured cars on their flanks, and the convoy disappeared into the distance, the fusiliers waiting with baited breath for the signal to open fire. The officer was a cool character; he would not be rushed into action, he waited until he could see the last vehicle coming into view and the majority of the convoy was in the arc of fire. With one movement of his arm, he let loose the relentless barrage of fire. It peppered the vehicles from stem to stern, until one after the other caught fire, exploding in an ear-splitting thunder of sound, ammunition trucks making the most dramatic effect. At night this would have been an amazing firework display; in the heat of day, palls of smoke and fire could be seen for miles. The armoured vehicles were all caught napping; the continuous rumble of the vehicles over the hardened sand track had mesmerized the drivers and gunners into a hypnotic state, so much so that they were hit simultaneously, taken out by the anti-tank weapons, which cut through the shallow armour like a knife through butter.

The element of surprise had worked spectacularly; men were jumping and running out of the vehicles: some were on fire, while others rushed to put out the fire on the backs of their comrades; others halfheartedly returned fire on the fusiliers, realising that they were outgunned and completely outmanoeuvred. Some of the vehicles at the rear of the convoy had sufficient warning of the firefight and were turning in their tracks to beat a hasty retreat, to where nobody could guess, but in their moment of panic they ran straight into the Rajanpur Rifles, who, having been ordered to bring up the rear from their easterly position, were desperate to get into the fight.

The trucks and armoured vehicles burnt on; the danger from the ammunition trucks was apparent, as those too hasty in their exuberant attack had fallen foul of the exploding vehicles. The officer in charge called the men away. Viewing the onslaught with a feeling of sickness as he saw the charred remains of the German soldiers, he called forward his medical orderly to do what he could for some of the men strewn across the path of the ambush, for many it was too late. The Germans had had all the resistance knocked out of them; they were oil and smoke blackened from the burning trucks. The stench of the burning oil and bodies was horrendous, the men were ordered downwind, such as it was, to keep clear of breathing the toxic mix. After waiting in the intense heat for so long, suffering incredible discomfort, they had witnessed the battle come and dissipate extremely quickly, so much so that the fusiliers did not shout with exuberant cries of victory; instead, they looked upon their victory and the victims with some distaste. The injured and dying could only be pitied; there was no glory here, only a job that they had all been called upon to carry out.

A few of the fusiliers had gathered and were discussing the events of the day. George was a little way outside the group; they were smoking and viewing the results of their ambush; shock had turned to relief as the adrenalin subsided. Bertie signalled for George to come into the group, he was in a sombre mood and at first shook his head; Bertie's insistent gestures drew George in like a reluctant dog on a leash. One of the fusiliers said, "Come on George, brighten up, we won."

George pondered the sand-covered and grime-smeared face for a moment and then said, "Won? Those poor beggars are no different from us; their comrades are burning while you stand around like a committee, discussing matters of great importance, like flower arranging. There's work to be done, so let's get on with it."

Having delivered his comment in anger, he walked away from the group. He heard one of them say, "What's up with him, we won didn't we?"

Bertie followed George quickly; he had begun to see another side of George: as a more sensitive soul, than he had first believed.

From out of the burning wreckage, a German lieutenant came forward. He saluted the captain of the Fusiliers, who returned his salute and offered his hand. The German officer looked at his outstretched hand, took it and shook it firmly. The captain was heard to offer his sorrow to the lieutenant at the loss of his men and proceeded to offer what medical assistance he could for the wounded. The lieutenant bowed his head at the offer, looking as if he were about to cry. He was very young, as was the captain; both men were acknowledging that the loss of life was a tragedy and in other circumstances they could have been friends. The captain withdrew so that the lieutenant was able to talk to his men and see to the needs of the wounded and dying.

The captain addressed his own men, praised them for their actions on this day, particularly for keeping a cool head, following his lead to the letter and for behaving well towards a defeated enemy. He dispatched one corporal and two other men to gather from the less dangerous vehicles any material that might be of use militarily: maps, diagrams, passwords, anything that could help with the ongoing conflicts. Another group of men were ordered to report to the lieutenant to see if they could assist him and his men in any way. A further group was sent to check for any intact supplies that could be of use to them, especially any containers of water.

That evening, the captain sat alone and contemplated the actions of the day: the devastating fire they had poured on their enemy. He simply wrote in his diary, "*Today my enemy was defeated, dependent on my goodwill, we offered succor to his wounded, we shook hands like friends, has he now become my brother?*" These were the last words he ever wrote, as two days later he was killed in action by machine-gun fire as he led his men one last time.

Chapter 11

Back to Blighty 1943

The relief of the men of 1st Battalion was palpable: they were to get leave. They would be sailing back to Liverpool and staying in the British Isles for several months' respite. They were not quite sure how long they would be home, but the thought of what would happen after their leave was not in any of their minds.

For George, the last four years in the desert had seemed too long. He had now been away from home for nearly eight years and the experience had left him distraught and filled with anxiety. He had watched too many good men lose their lives in the harsh sands of the desert campaigns.

After many months of eating sand for each meal, scratching around for supplies, it would be good to be going back to familiar ground, and there was much talk about that first pint in a real English boozer. Those that were married were looking forward to being reunited with their wives after such a long stint. They had not believed that they would be away for so long when they first set out for India, but the disappointment of not going straight back to England afterwards was soon put in the past; they were all looking forward.

The jokes and banter flew around the bivouacs for some days, as they gathered their gear together, until the men were told for certain that they were the ones who would be going home on leave. Those remaining shouted to their comrades leaving for home, "Give her one from me, Chalky," and the replies were just as ribald.

"You should be so lucky, you Taffy git." There was no insult that could penetrate their good humour and good fortune; it all just rolled off their backs like water off the proverbial ducks.

The men piled into trucks and set off for the docks at Alexandria. The bumping, gruelling ride in the back of a vehicle not made for comfort didn't seem to bother them quite so much on this occasion; at least they were going somewhere they wanted to go. Some of the men began to sing the well-known verses to Colonel Bogey; this soon caught the ear of the men in the following trucks and then spread down the column: not the most tuneful bunch, but joyful? – Yes!

The voyage back to Liverpool was not an anxious one, even though the men were asked to look out for signs of U-boats: several of their number were drafted for lookout duty around the ship. George volunteered for this role; not only was he was happiest in the fresh air but he was also aware that travelling with the horizon in sight made for a better passage. The return journey was a fairly smooth run; the excitement of returning home was infectious and many of the men from the various regiments were happy to mingle with each other. Some of the Welshmen on board managed to set up a choir, which was quite a thing to hear, it was heartwarming but also made the longing for home even greater.

George hadn't received much news from home so he did not know what to expect when he eventually got back to London. He was glad to be back to enjoy a good British summer after the heat of the desert and the plains of India, but on arrival he found the weather was rather cool in England. He was quite looking forward to seeing his friends and wondered which of his family would be home, if any. He surmised that at least Harry would be, as his sight impairment kept him out of the forces, but he wasn't sure where Tom would be: he could have been posted anywhere, and the likelihood of them sharing a leave was less than slim. However, he was optimistic as he turned the corner of his street.

After many bombing raids, some houses were now derelict, and it hadn't occurred to him that his house might have been hit. George took in a deep breath; he rounded the bombsites with trepidation. The thought of his family being killed, his house devastated by the bombing, hadn't entered his thoughts. He was shaking as the full perspective of the street came into view. He was relieved to see that it was the opposite side from his home that had been wiped out and then felt immediately guilty for the thought. He knew the people that lived in the houses opposite; he was shocked to see the piles of debris where there had been homes – had the neighbours got to the shelters in time? While away, he had been so wrapped up in his own plight with the war in the desert, it hadn't occurred to him to any great extent that people back home were suffering too. Some news had got through to the troops fighting abroad, but, on seeing some of the devastation here and in Liverpool, he felt that perhaps it had been somewhat sanitized.

The door was wide open and he could hear the sound of sawing as he entered; Harry was bent over the kitchen table, working on a long plank that was balanced on one end of a kitchen chair, while he held the other end in his firm grasp. Harry hadn't heard him enter, so George stood for a while watching Harry check and double-check before making his next cut. The room became quiet when Harry checked his measurements once more. George spoke softly.

"Hello Harry." Harry didn't respond immediately so George repeated his hello louder. Harry turned slowly and George said, "Deaf as well as going blind are you?"

Harry looked stunned as he asked, "George is that you? You look so different; I would have passed you in the street. Don't hover in the doorway; come in, come in, this is your house as well you know."

They were awkward in each other's presence; they weren't an embracing family, only Mum had been like that. As they moved towards each other, George held out his hand and Harry took it and shook it vigorously until George said, "You can let go now, Harry."

Then George looked around, "Where's Dad?"

Harry looked at George before he spoke, then, with a deep sigh, in a sorrowful tone said, "You obviously haven't been informed: Dad died last year."

Pulling out one of the kitchen chairs, George sat.

"How, what and when?" he enquired.

Harry said, "It was all rather quick in the end, but I'll tell you all shortly."

"Where is Dad buried?" George asked.

"Next to Mum, of course," Harry replied. "We were lucky enough to get that spot; bombings have taken their toll – there's a shortage of graveyard spaces locally."

George probed a little more, "Was there a good turnout for the old man, Harry?"

"Yes George, everyone from around here, despite the many funerals that they've had to attend."

"That's good," said George thoughtfully, "I'll take a walk over to Mum and Dad's grave soon. I can't believe they're both gone. It's like a large part of your life has just disappeared."

Harry moved to the stove and said, "Cuppa?"

"Yes please, but tell me everything that happened, was it the bombing?"

"No, it was his chest. I think that it had been coming for some while, then he caught pneumonia and that finished him."

"Poor bugger," said George, "He didn't have a great life and after losing mum he probably lost heart too."

"You're probably right, George. He didn't seem to have the same fighting spirit, and his work didn't help him much either." The brothers sat and drank their tea, then Harry said, "Tell me about everything that's happened to you since leaving home; I've been stuck here while you've been gallivanting around the world." Harry looked at his brother expectantly.

"Gallivanting, that's not what I would call it, Harry – more like pure bloody hell. I can tell you that I have seen more men blown apart and I have lost so many friends, I have decided not to make any more for fear of losing them."

"That bad, was it Georgie?"

"No one has called me that for ages." George looked away as he felt a tear might be forming in the corner of his eye. George's mother had always called him Georgie, and it brought back memories of his loss. To change the mood, he asked where his other brothers were.

"Tom was home on leave a few weeks ago, he is a lieutenant now in the Royal Artillery. He was being sent back overseas, wasn't allowed to say where, except he said he hoped for sunnier climes. Albert was the last to join up and I believe he's based in Catterick at the moment. Jack is in the Guards, but I haven't heard from him. It's a shame that you missed Tom; he looked really fine in his officer's uniform. He sat exactly where you are sitting now and he was quite the officer with his mannerisms, putting on airs and graces. Didn't wash with me, I'm his elder brother after all, I know too much about him, and we know his roots are firmly planted in the East End. Shame you missed him though."

After the two brothers had discussed all that had happened in the past years, George took his gear upstairs and made up a bed for himself. Nothing much has changed up here, he thought, still needs a lick of paint, but I don't suppose the landlord will be carrying out maintenance in the circumstances – probably hoping that it gets bombed out so that he can claim restitution after the war.

The sounds of the street entered the bedroom and he crossed to the window to look out on the familiar sights and sounds of his childhood and early youth. Apart from the section that had been bombed, the street remained very much the same. The houseproud mothers were out bashing the living daylights out of their rugs, while others stood on their doorsteps, talking about who knew what and where. Good Lord, thought George, there's Mrs Brentwood polishing her front step. Doesn't she know there's a war on? She must still be hoping that cleanliness is next to Godliness, as she always was heard to say, while she was hanging her washing out. Well I can shatter that illusion: it didn't matter how clean and shiny your kit was, it didn't stop a bullet; although, I suppose shiny kit might be said to bring you next to God, as the Boche could spot you a mile off and send you on your way to heaven.

After George had settled himself in, he asked Harry if he would like to go to the local for a pint; it was something that he had been looking forward to. Harry said he thought it would be a good idea, but the Seven Stars – the local George referred to – was no longer there.

"How about the Anchor? Is it still standing? I can't believe the Seven Stars has gone, Harry."

"The last time I was by that way it was, but I'm not sure it will be that great now. The new landlord is a bit of a tyrant, I hear."

"They still serve beer, don't they?" said George, readying himself to go.

The two of them made their way to the Anchor, avoiding the debris in some of the side streets. Wardens were organizing the clear-up to make the streets passable and easier to navigate. The two brothers had to divert around the activities in one street, as properties that were teetering on the brink of collapse were being pulled down. Arriving at the Anchor, they saw that it was packed, and they had to worm their way through the throng. Eventually, after some effort, the crowd in the smoke-filled bar parted, as one voice cried out, "Returning soldier here. Get the man a drink!"

The crowd was very welcoming; the men in the pub were elderly, and something had changed during the war that George hadn't appreciated – there were quite a lot of women in the bar too. George ordered two pints of best and the man next to him said, "Let me get that for you, soldier boy. Where have you returned from?"

George thanked him and said that he wasn't allowed to speak of military matters, but it was hot and sandy. The man laughed, patted him on the back and said, "Well it wasn't Eastbourne then; they have sand, but it's not hot."

The crowd closest to Harry and George laughed and responded with, "Good on ya, mate." George signalled to Harry for them to move away so that they could have their drinks in relative peace.

There were a few other military uniforms in the pub and they too had moved away from the crowded area, although they were probably more interested in the young women sitting in the corner. They had drawn the attention of a couple of RAF crew; the young women were having an animated discussion. The women's laughter could be heard above the noise of the smoky bar. One girl was particularly attractive. She was looking over at George, who lifted his glass and smiled at her, and she smiled back. One of the airmen noticed this and glanced round to see what the dark-haired young lady was looking at. Seeing George smile back at her, he frowned at him but didn't react in any other way. George was relieved he hadn't; the last thing he wanted on his first day back home was a fistfight in a pub over a smile.

After they had finished their pints, George made his way back through the crowded bar, managed to order two more pints and began the hazardous journey back to Harry, sliding past elbows and arms that were gesticulating and emphasizing their stories. In the process of skirting one rather large gentleman, George bumped into the dark-haired girl with whom he had exchanged a smile; they both apologised at once and then laughed. With all the gallantry he could muster, George offered to get her a drink, as she was returning to the bar with an empty glass and he couldn't have a young lady fighting through this crowd.

"A gin and orange for me please," She smiled up at him.

"Be right back," said George, "Just got to deliver my brother his beer." As soon as he had delivered the beer to Harry, he made his way back to the young lady.

"I'm George by the way."

"Amy," she said in return.

George and Amy made their way back to Harry, and George introduced her. Smiling, Harry raised his eyebrows at George and said, "I'll see you back at the house, Georgie." He got up, leaving the couple to enjoy their drinks and the rest of their evening together.

Amy worked in a factory close by; she had been packing and stacking for a food company, which processed tinned corned beef, spam and other food stuffs. The work was repetitive but a necessary part of the process of supplying the army. Amy said she couldn't be out much longer as she had to get back home or her mum would be worried.

"Where do you live?" asked George. Amy said that it was not too far and George said he would walk her home if she didn't mind. He asked if he could see her again, perhaps go to the pictures if she would like to. They agreed on Saturday and George said he would pick her up at half past six.

He was rather pleased with himself as he made his way home. He'd not been back but a few hours and he already had a date – not bad. He began to whistle like his dad used to and, like his dad's, it was a fairly tuneless repertoire. On entering the house, he was in a pretty good mood, looking forward to his date with Amy at the weekend.

Chapter 12

Amy

George was all washed and brushed for his date with Amy. He was a little nervous, as he couldn't remember being on a real date and felt he lacked the skills. The only females he had met on his travels with the army were of a different disposition; their approach was quite alarming for a young man away from home. This girl was different; her dark hair, deeply dark brown eyes and approachable nature were amazing. He tried to recall her figure – slim yes, with sufficient up top. Apart from her looks, she was also very easy to talk to. What was his fear then? He looked pretty good in uniform, he was also slim and some said handsome, with a tan from his time in warmer climes. Although not tall, he had grown upwards a little and outwards since joining the army and was now a reasonable height at five feet ten inches. He told himself to be more positive – he might be called back to duty any day, and who knew where he might be sent.

"Just enjoy yourself, George." He hadn't realised he had spoken out loud to the mirror until Harry called up the stairs.

"What did you say, George?"

"Nothing. Just talking to myself."

"First sign," said Harry as he continued sawing.

It was a warm summer evening when George called for Amy. She came to the door looking fresh and sparkly eyed, greeted him warmly and commented on his punctuality. George had gone into shy mode, being less than adept at courting, and just mumbled something about army training.

"I suppose," said Amy quite buoyantly.

While she reached back to close the door, a large older woman came to the door and gave George a stern look. Dressed in a wraparound pinafore with a small flower motif, her hair was turning grey and she looked ready for trouble. Her arms, of quite substantial proportions – not quite wrestlers', were folded across what appeared to George a very ample bosom.

"Just you make sure you bring my Amy back safe and sound. Do you hear me, young man?"

"Yes of course," George bumbled. He made a grab for Amy's hand, making a break for it. But the woman hadn't finished; she was still standing in the doorway shouting after him.

"And don't try any funny stuff or you will have to answer to me." With this invective ringing in their ears, the couple made a quick exit down the street, away from the tirade.

When the two of them were safely round the block, George turned to Amy and said, "I assume that is your mother." Amy laughed.

"Who else would it be?"

"She's quite the one; best not to get on the wrong side of her, I would imagine," said George looking a little concerned.

"You're right there," said Amy, laughing once again at the memory of George's face at the sight of her mother. "Best you remember that, you want to see her in full sail chasing the rent man down the street with a broom in her hand. Most of the neighbours come out to see it." Amy repeated George's words, still chuckling to herself, "Just best not to get on the wrong side of Mum."

"Where is your dad?" asked George.

"He's in the house, but he isn't too well. He won't take cover in the shelter; he's been in the house when there have been several near misses; he was covered in rubble and dust and his lungs haven't been too good since then."

"I'm sorry to hear that, Amy. What does he do for a living when he is well? Does he still work?"

"Oh yes, and he should be on his rounds today as the weather is good: he's an ice cream seller. The trouble is the work is quite hard, pushing his cart uphill; in the morning we get up early and make the ice cream. Then he goes out with his handcart until he has sold out".

"You say 'we'; do you mean your dad and you?"

"Yes that's right; we have to mix the milk, sugar, get the ice from the ice delivery man, so it's quite hard and we have to be preparing by 4 a.m. – it takes a lot of churning. We also have problems with supplies because of rationing, so Dad has had real difficulty in making it. Since rationing came in, he's been labouring. He's much too old for that now, but he won't listen to reason."

George was very impressed with his young lady: not only holding down a full-time job in the factory but assisting her dad in the early hours before leaving for her job as well.

Suddenly, George said, "We'd better get a move on or we'll miss the main feature." They hurried through the streets until they reached the Gaumont. They needn't have worried about missing the main picture, as the queue was still moving slowly into the cinema. They joined the end of the queue and moved at a snail's pace towards the ticket booth.

"*The Outlaw* – is that what we're seeing?" asked Amy.

"Yes, is that alright?"

"Jane Russell stars in that, doesn't she? I hope you're not taking me along just so you can see a woman with large breasts?" George was quite taken aback and didn't know how to respond to Amy's last comment. He blustered and flustered an answer that was quite incomprehensible, until he realised by her smothered laughter that she was pulling his leg. This girl is quite unusual, thought George, as he approached the ticket booth.

They sat quietly together, holding hands and occasionally stealing a look at each other in the semi-darkness.

After the film, they walked home in the warm, quiet evening, not speaking much at all, just happy to be holding hands, breathing the warm night air. Amy spoke first. "We were fortunate there wasn't an air raid warning; recently there had been quite a few false alarms and it would have been a pity to spoil such a good picture." George turned to her, smiled and nodded in agreement; they walked on until they reached Amy's home. Now here was the dilemma for George: should he try to kiss her? He certainly didn't want to just shake the hand he had been holding all the way home. He would go for the kiss. He leant forward; as he did so, there was a tap, tap on the window from the house; Amy's mother was there as large as life in a voluminous nightdress, with her hair in rollers. A very scary sight, thought George, it gave him a nasty shock, as Amy's mum gestured for her to come in. Amy turned back to George, looked at his bemused face, put her hands either side of it and kissed him full on the lips.

"Goodnight George," she said as she turned to go in.

George was taken by surprise and felt his heart beat that much faster at the unexpected kiss from Amy. He returned the kiss a little more fervently than Amy's attempt. This made his pulse gallop and he mustered his thoughts quickly, not wanting to miss the opportunity of seeing Amy for another date.

"Can I see you again soon?" enquired George.

"Of course, meet me after work on Monday and we'll make a plan."

George waved to Amy as she entered the house. Walking back home with his hands in his pockets, he whistled a nondescript tune, but he wasn't a good whistler. Nothing seemed to matter in these magical moments; he had met a wonderful girl, with a terrific sense of humour: a hard-working girl, a terrific looker, with a beautiful figure, but most of all he liked that he could talk to her about anything; she listened and made intelligent comments. Monday eh! Well, I wonder what sort of a plan I should make for us next, thought George. Where would a girl like Amy like to go? He would give it some thought, maybe ask Harry.

George was unsure of what to do with himself on Sunday. He was looking forward to seeing Amy on Monday, but that seemed an age away. He managed to pass some of his day in the Anchor and he helped Harry clear up around the house. For the rest of the time he read a little and dreamt of seeing Amy again. Tomorrow couldn't arrive soon enough.

He met Amy from work as planned and walked her home; he said.

"I would like to take you to tea at Lyons Corner House in the West End."

She replied excitedly, "I would like that very much. I have looked into some of these places but not actually been in one as they were rather posh with their nice white linen, their wonderful crockery and cutlery. It would be such a treat to eat in one."

They both agreed that it would be quite a highlight, and afterwards, if the weather held, they would make their way to one of the parks, perhaps St James's, see the ducks and just wander. Amy thought this was wonderful after her life of drudgery in the factory and the early mornings helping her dad.

The week passed slowly for George, only seeing Amy on the walk between work and home. He couldn't wait for the weekend to arrive so that he would have more time with her. Eventually Saturday came and George picked her up from home; they had to get the bus, so they walked hand in hand to the bus stop and chatted in quite an absorbed manner as only couples finding out about each other do. Amy told him about her family. When George asked about her brothers and sister, she told him,

"Three of my brothers are away in the forces, except for my younger brother, who works in a sheet metal factory, helping with the welding. He's quite clever and draws and writes very well. He also makes plans for construction; this is what he wants to do after the war is over. My sister is still very young so I have to help mum quite a lot in looking after her. Mum suffers from arthritis so can't bend or pick up very well, but this doesn't stop her chasing men down the street with a broom," she laughed.

"So you have four brothers and a sister, not a bad size family. There are five of us, all brothers, all at war except one," said George keeping tally.

"Well, Mum had three other children so we would have been nine, but she lost the rest at birth."

"That's a bit sad," George replied.

"It happened before I was born, so I have no feeling of loss," replied Amy. "Of course, my mum and dad being good Italian Catholics, they just put it down to God's will."

George was thoughtful and made no reply for a while, and then asked, "Why haven't your mum and dad been interned as others?"

Amy replied, "Mum has been in a bit of trouble recently, as she won't stay within her area in London. Did you know that some aliens were ordered to stay within three miles of their homes?"

George shook his head.

"Well she's taken off to see my little sister in Kent, after she was evacuated. This wasn't allowed under the rules of her being free of internment. My father is too ill and old, so I suppose the authorities showed some leniency as the boys are fighting for England. They were all born here and so they are British citizens."

"I see" George replied. "Is that why your mother greets strangers in the way she does, with a broom held high?"

"Not at all," Amy laughed. "But she does greet anyone she feels might be a threat to her family in that way."

"I should consider myself almost welcome then," responded George.

The tea house was just how Amy had imagined it: the white of the tablecloths nearly blinded her with their brightness, the cutlery and crockery clinked and clanked against each other as the customers ploughed their way through the food as if it were going out of fashion. How did they manage with rationing, she wondered; they still seemed to have enough flour and sugar for cakes and sandwiches. The tea was excellent too, one large pot between two; they went for the fixed price tea selection. Although there was a war on, they both had sufficient to eat.

The ‘Nippies’, who were dressed in the traditional black and white uniforms, were buzzing around the floor to ensure that everyone had what they wanted; no one was neglected. George paid the bill; unsure about how much to tip, the amount he left was far too generous. Amy looked at him in surprise; he shrugged and said that he hadn’t spent any of his hard earned cash for quite some time. They both agreed their little foray into this new world was worth it, and were looking forward to their planned walk in the park. The weather had been kind to them; they hurried along to get out of the busy restaurant into a more serene atmosphere.

“Thank you George, that was really lovely. I hope it wasn’t too expensive.”

“It was my pleasure, Amy. I’m glad you enjoyed it. No, it wasn’t too high a price to be with such a beautiful woman.” As soon as George said it, he felt himself blush. Thinking he was trying to be too suave, he felt awkward and repeated, “I’ve nothing much to spend my pay on anyway.” No, he thought to himself that sounds terrible too. Amy just smiled at George in his struggle to impress, and gently squeezed his hand.

They enjoyed their walk around St James’s Park, as they were able to stroll and occasionally kiss without the distraction of a heavyweight mother bearing down on them. Falling into a rhythm, they walked arm in arm, with Amy’s head bent towards George’s shoulder. Too soon the day was over; it was time to retrace their steps, back to the bus, then home.

Chapter 13

Call to Barracks

Amy and George enjoyed their long summer together; it stretched through autumn and beyond until the dread day that George was called to return to barracks. His heart sank at the thought of what this might mean. His thoughts plagued him, they were tumbling about his head and he feared the worst all the way to the Tower of London.

In fact, he hadn't been called back to barracks for either of the reasons running through his head; it was to inform him that he had been made up to corporal, to be ready to take charge of the men in the next few weeks as they were preparing for an undisclosed destination. George protested: he didn't want this promotion. Every time an officer registered his performance as a regular, they wanted to promote him; he just wanted to be an ordinary soldier. This "undisclosed destination" was not what George wanted to hear either. After leaving the barracks, all that could be heard from George as he walked home was, "bugger, bugger!" and again "bugger!" Some of the people he encountered scurried past this potential madman, swearing out loud as he made his way through town. As the months went by, he had thought that he had been forgotten and he was only to return to barracks for drills and machine-gun training, which mainly consisted of dismantling and rebuilding the machine gun under the watchful eye of the sergeant major. Unbeknown to George, the reason for his prolonged leave was simply a difference of opinion as to where the 1st Battalion Fusiliers were to be deployed. The 2nd Battalion had already been dispatched to France, while the 1st were still awaiting their final orders. Should they be sent to France or did the desert campaign need the skills they had sharpened? That was the big question.

On returning home, he thumped around like a spoilt child, slamming his door, throwing his clothes in a heap on the bed. The trouble was that he did not want to be in charge of men, sending them into a situation and getting them killed or maimed. He had become too comfortable seeing Amy regularly; he had almost forgotten that he was a soldier: a soldier at war, at that.

The next morning he thought about how he was going to break the news to Amy that he could be leaving in the not-too-distant future. He would meet her after work and see if she would go for a drink with him. Weekdays meant she was usually completely shattered after an early start and a day at the factory. When they met, she could see he was not happy; they sat in their usual corner, in their usual pub, talking quietly, while others came and left.

"Well done George," Amy said. "Congratulations! I knew that you would get recognition one day."

George's response caught her by surprise.

"I never worked for this, or wanted it, I just don't want to be in charge of men; the responsibility is too much. I just don't bloody well want it, can't you understand that?"

Amy's reply angered him further. "Well, the army obviously believes in you." Being of a positive nature, she said, "It is meant to be, and you should be grateful."

This was the first time George had ever been angry with Amy, and the look in his eyes and the harshness of his voice surprised her so much that she just said, "I had better be going home; Mum will be wondering."

Before George could respond or stop her, she was gone and he was left drinking alone. Others in the pub had heard George's outburst and were staring at him as Amy left him to his own devices.

Ordering another drink, George was aware of the stares and shouted, "Who the fuck are you staring at, you bunch of wet weeks?"

"Steady on son," said the publican.

When he eventually arrived home a little the worse from drink, he stumbled into the house to find Harry sitting at the kitchen table.

"George, is that you?"

"Of course it bloody is. Who were you expecting: the King of England?"

"Are you alright George, are you drunk?"

"Bloody feels like it, I think I've just had a row with Amy and she's gone home."

"Well a policeman came by earlier, left you this; it's marked 'Urgent'."

"What the bloody hell is a policeman calling here for? Open it, will you, and read it to me".

"I'll try, but if it's small print I won't manage it."

"Oh give me it here will you." George snatched the envelope from Harry's hand then, after ripping it open and reading it, said, "That's bloody typical that is, just to round off the day, I have to report back to barracks immediately."

"You'd better sober up first George; I'll put the kettle on."

Once Harry was satisfied that George was sufficiently sober to go to the barracks, had had several cups of tea and was properly dressed and had all his kit, he looked George up and down carefully, and said, "You'll do, you stupid bugger."

George turned to his brother.

"Sorry mate, I've acted stupidly. Now I have to go the barracks with all my kit and I know what this means: they will be shipping us out again. Do me a great favour, take this letter to Amy as soon as you can, get past the monster mother and tell Amy how sorry I am for the way I behaved tonight. Tell her that if I am posted, I will write as often as I can."

"I will George, and don't feel you have to apologise. We're brothers; I know you must have gone through a lot. I wish you didn't have to go back to it." Shaking his brother's hand, Harry told George to take care of himself and to keep his head down.

The barracks was crawling with men and vehicles; some soldiers were scampering about the yard, others were looking bemused from being called back to barracks so suddenly or because they were still in civilian mode after a couple of months' respite. George entered with a heavy heart; he was desperate to speak to Amy, but he knew the likelihood of being released from duties was remote. He would just have to put his mind into another gear. Seeing someone frantically waving at him from across the yard, to his delight he found it was Bertie Bakewell; at least that was one person he was happy to see. George made his way across to his friend and saw Bertie's eyes gravitate to George's stripes.

"Should I salute you then?" asked Bertie with a twinkle in his eye and a mocking tone to his voice. "Or maybe I should bow or go down on one knee?"

"Stop taking the piss and take me to the quartermaster," George responded, and the two men soon fell into their familiar banter, happy to be in each other's company once again.

The next few days were part tedium, part preparation for their departure; George was frustrated that he couldn't wangle some leave to return home and speak with Amy. He wrote prolifically and then threw away the letter he wrote to her; everything he had written seemed inadequate, but he persevered until he thought he had written something worth sending and hoped his protestations and explanations were sufficient. He passed on his letter with some trepidation, knowing the censor would have to go through it with a fine tooth comb; he had written with this in mind.

The assembled men were all in the same situation of frustration, boredom and – to some degree – fear, while they awaited their fate. All they had been told was that they were to be shipped out to an unknown destination. One sarcastic bright spark was heard to say, "Well that clears that up."

The day came when they were climbing onto lorries, still none the wiser about their destination. At least the change of scenery would make a difference, and maybe one of the officers would let slip their ultimate destination. Some of the men were taking bets: some said France, others reckoned it was back to North Africa, but the bright ones thought the Mediterranean sector.

Chapter 14

Mediterranean Expeditionary Force 1943/44

In the last weeks of August 1943, Allied warships had sailed, guns blazing, through the Straights of Messina, and artillery batteries had been moved up to face the coast of Italy on the western shore of the straits. The bombardment of the beaches north of Reggio di Calabria started at 4.30 a.m. on 3rd September. The artillery alone fired 400 tons of ammunition. (Reprinted by kind permission of Matthew Parker)

Central Mediterranean Force 1944

There was hardly any resistance from the two German divisions in the 'toe' of Italy. Their artillery positions were quickly silenced by air attack, and they moved back into the mountainous terrain of Calabria, leaving the fighting to the Italian coastal defence divisions. These quickly surrendered, faced as they were by so many threats from the sea and the air, and even supplied eager hands to unload the landing craft. (Reprinted by kind permission of Matthew Parker)

The rain that fell on the Allied troops moving up the central backbone of Italy was relentless. It was as if the weather was on the side of the enemy; there was no possibility of moving heavy armour or trucks up the slippery sides of ravines, and men and mules became the order of the day.

The Germans made matters worse by flooding areas and dismantling bridges and dams. Their skills and precision at making the move northwards even more difficult could not be surpassed. The Allies made many tactical errors in their movements; the Germans mocked them by dropping leaflets to demoralise them, depicting the Allied troops as snails crawling up the central passes of Italy.

The men had seen nothing like the weather. Rain, sleet and snow hit them in the face like a series of piercing needles, thrown at them as if it were a punishment for past transgressions. Their misery was heightened by the slowness of the supplies to catch up with them. The Germans' harassing fire and perpetual tenacity in sniping at the slowly progressing troops added to their wretchedness. What made matters even worse was that the further north they progressed, the colder it became, the rain turning to heavy snow and the roads becoming a quagmire to hinder them further.

Eventually, after weeks of hardship, the 1st Battalion had reached the outskirts of Cassino town – or what was left of it. Cassino had been flattened by the continual bombardment from both the Germans and the Allied forces. The local people had fled the town long ago, moving south to relative safety: behind the Allied lines. The strategic importance of the town, and in particular the abbey perched high on the hill above Cassino, could not be underestimated. The Germans held the high ground and were well entrenched around the abbey. Overlooking the whole valley, the Germans around the abbey could spot any vehicle or men travelling the road to Rome: they could be easily shelled. The abbey stood on the main road from Naples in the south to Rome in the north, and the Allies were pressing hard from the south to reach Rome. The Gustav line, erected by the Germans, straddled the width of Italy and was enforced with concrete bunkers, barbed wire and heavy artillery, halting progress north of Monte Cassino, but Cassino was still the prime and first objective.

The green hills on the approach to Cassino had been decimated: not a tree stood, nor a house that had not been reduced to rubble. The pretty red-tiled and whitewashed walls of the villages were no longer. The narrow lanes were now a quagmire; the efforts of the tracked vehicles had scored mini ravines into the hillsides, so much so that roads could not be distinguished from hillside; the churning of the vehicles and heavy bombardments had been too much for this once picturesque principality.

The mud had not abated, and tracked vehicles could not make their way up the narrow passes. The constant sniping of the Germans made every move a nightmare. In frustration, the commander of the 1st called up artillery and armoured support so that they could enter the town. Three tanks were despatched from the 5th Tank Squadron; they would be some hours, if not days, the commander was told, as the terrain was particularly difficult and the German artillery had all routes covered in a pattern that allowed not even a mouse to squeeze through. However, he had three tanks that were prepared to give it a try.

In one of tanks dispatched on this suicidal mission was young Ben's tank. Called up, trained and shipped out to Morocco and then to Italy at the age of 18 years, Ben was now the driver of the last tank in the patrol. He and all the tank crew were of the opinion that being the last tank in a patrol was probably the worst position to be in. As the patrol made its way up the narrow ravines, they could hear the sniper shots pinging off the metal of their Sherman's armour; this was a comfort, on one hand, but also a realisation that they had better stay inside the relative safety of their armoured vehicle.

They hadn't been travelling for more than an hour or so when there was a great thump on the underside of Ben's tank; it lifted them on the port side and dropped them back down again with an almighty thud. Ben realised that they had lost traction, and the tank began to whirl around to the starboard side, resulting in debris, dust and a mixture of the tank's own exhaust filling the interior. The men began to shout in panic as the tank dropped back to the ground. Ears popping and hearts racing, they all thought that this was the end for them. Smoked filled the tank from the explosion, men were coughing and yelling at the same time. Despite his years, Ben shouted in a cooler voice, which belittled the dilemma they were in.

"Bloody hell."

As the tank sank into the ground on one side, he shut off the engine and shouted back to the crew.

"We've lost a track on the portside, seems we hit a mine."

He peered out of the driver's slit to see the other two lead tanks moving away, totally unaware of their plight. Ben wondered when they would realise that his tank was no longer with them: not until nightfall he assumed. There was no way of contacting them; they would have to sit tight and hope that night would cover their dilemma. No one was going to risk going out to check on the state of their vehicle; snipers could be in the rocks all around them, awaiting their opportunity.

It was a cold and long night. The men in the tank slept fitfully, keeping watch as best they could but most importantly keeping as quiet as they could. As dawn began to break over the rocky hillsides, they heard in the distance a clanking and thudding sound that would wake the dead. The men inside the tank were relieved, as they knew that a recovery vehicle was on its way, but, at the same time, it was declaring, "Here we all are, just sitting ducks," to every German within a five-mile radius. The recovery vehicle was a cobbled together, makeshift vehicle that wasn't totally fit for purpose, but it was all that was available to them.

As Ben had suspected, the leading tanks hadn't realised that the tank bringing up their rear was missing until they reached their destination late that night. They had radioed back to HQ to get the recovery vehicle to search for them. Although not sure that the men would still be alive by morning, they felt duty-bound to send in the recovery vehicle with suitable armed cover, which consisted of an armoured personnel carrier with George, three fusiliers and five Ghurkhas, bristling with machine guns and automatic weapons. On reaching the stranded tank, the rescue team encircled it: a position to cover any eventuality of enemy fire. George was first to jump on the tank, banging with a rat-a-tat-tat on the top.

"Anyone home?" he shouted, "or have you all gone out for a constitutional, on such a bright morning?"

The turret flew open and the tank commander popped out his head, saying, "Thank Christ you got to us before Jerry."

"That's quite alright sir, pleased to be of assistance," replied George. "Now if you and your men wish to rest easy, we will cover you while you stretch your legs. As you can hear, your rescue vehicle is not far away."

All the crew were glad to stretch their legs, have a smoke, but best of all was the sense of relief that they were not to become captives or corpses. The rescue vehicle arrived ten minutes later; the recovery team soon had the tank shackled to their vehicle and were just as keen to get going as the men that had spent the night in the tank. As soon as the vehicle, with tank in tow, was underway, the fusiliers and Gurkhas withdrew from their positions, still covering the hillsides from the personnel carrier.

The lead tanks had accomplished their task of clearing a way for the allies to enter Cassino and mop up what they hoped was a small contingent of Germans left behind after the days of bombing. Unfortunately for the Allies, and George and his men in particular, the clearing of the Germans from Cassino town was not as complete as they were expecting. Therefore, vast arrays of American bombers could be seen over Cassino town and eventually the abbey, with unexpected results.

Chapter 15

The Cellars

Early in the morning the forward battalion of the New Zealand 25th Battalion holding the Northern outskirts of the town withdrew up the Caruso Road and at 8.30, in bright sunshine, the first wave of heavy bombers appeared overhead.
Never before on the Italian front had a town been obliterated by carpet bombing. For three and a half hours, 575 medium and heavy bombers and 200 fighter bombers, the largest air forces ever assembled in the Mediterranean theatre, dropped nearly 1,000 tons of high explosive on roughly one square mile of land. (Reprinted by kind permission of Matthew Parker: Monte Cassino: The Hardest Fought Battle of World War 2)

In the melee of the fighting, men were separated from their units. The chaos of the jumble of bombed buildings was ideal for snipers, and groups of men were pinned down around the town by groups of German machine gunners and snipers. How the Germans had survived the bombardment was miraculous; they were now just as stranded as the groups of Allies, scattered through the ruins of Cassino.

The cellar filled with dust and debris, and men lay in precarious positions, gasping for air as the ground shook beneath them like a giant shaking the land. The fire upon their position was virtually continuous until the building seemed to breathe a sigh of relief and then collapsed upon them. George shouted across the dust-filled room, "Is everyone ok?" Gradually the dust was settling, the men in a rough circle coughed and spluttered

"Fine here, Corp."

"Me too," said another.

Further away came a "shit, shit, shit," from a less impressed voice. "What the fuck was that?"

"I think we've been hit by a tank shell," George replied. "Bang on our position."

"Well," said Bertie Bakewell, "I don't think we should hang about here, I don't think we're very welcome". The men began to splutter and then they began to laugh out loud.

"You old tart," said one, and another added, "You have to make a joke about everything."

"Made you laugh though, didn't it?" Bertie was a jovial, round-faced individual, with a shock of blonde hair and blue eyes, which contained mischief. He was slim and when walking about his home town, he would swagger down the streets of Nottingham as if he owned the place.

The four men had been holding out in the cellars under and close to the town's jailhouse. The Germans were their nearest neighbours, next door in fact. The game of cat and mouse had been played out over several days, with neither party willing to concede defeat. All that separated them from the adjoining courthouse was a brick wall; they had to repel the Germans on several occasions as they tried to dismantle it. Each of the parties had tried to push through grenades but had failed at each attempt.

They quickly realised each party had put themselves in danger from the back blast.

George was the corporal in charge of the group of men, who were in turn in charge of the machine gun. They had managed to get stranded as the main body of troops moved out; their sergeant had moved forward a little too rapidly, leaving them to become pinned down by German sniper fire and more recently tank shells. Along with Bertie and George, the other two fusiliers with them were Gerald Berman, a dark-haired, swarthy man with dark eyes and a blue haze around his face, even after a close shave. Terrence (Tel to his friends) Hurley was a skinny, brown-haired, hazel-eyed young man from Bristol, whose speech had a slight burr at the end of his words.

George didn't want this responsibility of looking out for other ranks, but as the older regular soldier, he had been promoted, at first without extra pay then, when he complained, with pay. All he really wanted was to be a fusilier without the responsibility of these men. This was the second time he had been promoted; the first time he had requested to be relieved of the responsibility. When they refused to relieve him, he behaved so badly that they had no option but to slam him in the guardhouse and demote him back to fusilier. This second attempt at being in charge was his worst fear, having to decide what to do, not just for him but for others too.

Bertie was the first to speak.

"Well what are we going to do now, Georgie boy, I mean Corp?" This was a familiar term, only used by family and now close friend Bertie. George didn't hesitate with his reply. He ignored the familiarity of Bertie's remark; they had been friends too long to worry about the niceties of rank, especially in the situation in which they found themselves.

"We're going to dig ourselves out and give those Jerries a bit of a dusting, a little bit of a surprise." Trying to raise their spirits, George stated emphatically, "Gerald and Tel, see what you can find in the way of a shovel or something. Bertie, scout around this dust hole and see where you think the best spot is to start digging. Be careful we don't dig through to Jerry."

"Rightoh Corp," they all said, one after the other, as each man set about his appointed task. George began checking the machine gun; dusting off the loose debris, he worked the mechanism, blowing, dusting each part, hoping that there was nothing to stop the gun from functioning.

"See if your rifles are still ok as soon as," he told the men. "We're going to need all the fire power possible."

"Shhh,"Bertie suddenly warned. "I think I can hear Jerry moving about too. You don't think they are trying to break through again, do you?"

"Everybody quiet," said George. They all listened intently. The dust and rubble was still settling after the blast, but above their heavy breathing they could hear a muffled digging sound. George held his hand aloft, then to his mouth, gesturing to keep still and be very quiet. They listened some more; there was definitely a digging sound now, it was growing in strength and coming from the wrong side: the German side. George gestured to them to pick up their rifles and to check them as quietly as they could.

"What's the ammo situation, Tel?" he whispered.

"We've only got what's on us. The rest of it's buried under the rubble, and we can't give ourselves away by digging," Tel whispered in reply.

"Shit," said George, not so softly. The digging sound stopped.

"Think they're listening to us now," Bertie whispered.

The next few hours continued in this manner, first digging, then stopping, then waiting. The cat and mouse game continued for what seemed forever. Each man was at his wits' end; the terrifying ordeal was taking a heavy toll on their nerves: so tense, they were at the point that they raised their rifles at every tumbling piece of concrete. George was concerned they would end up either shooting one another or their own feet, such was the nerve-wracking silence. Everything was graveyard quiet; the heavy breathing could be heard across the small cavern, so they tried holding their breath to hear more effectively. Suddenly, there was a burst of rubble, tumbling towards the men in the cellar. Each man had drawn up his rifle and held it ready to fire, when in burst a burly Scotsman, shouting at the top of his voice, "Don't shoot me, you silly beggars. I'm on your side."

With that reassuring cry, the men in the cellar breathed a sigh of relief, all beginning to speak at once in an incoherent babble. The Scotsman was followed by three others from his company and they all began to share their experiences and anecdotes, the main theme being that they all thought the others were Jerries.

Once everyone had been introduced, George was able to discuss the current situation with the sergeant of the Scots Guards. George was doubly pleased to see the sergeant because this meant that he was no longer the leading rank. The Scotsman explained that they too had been cut off in a similar way to the fusiliers. Now they needed to pool their resources and work out a plan to get out of the cellar, back to their lines, wherever they might be at this time.

Alex, the Scotsman, was a regular soldier, who had seen action in North Africa, very much like George and his fellow fusiliers. His two compatriots, Duncan and Fergus, were also regulars, and there was not a lot the three of them had not seen or done together. They were like brothers, sticking together and watching each other's backs like hawks. Their accents were broad, and George thought almost that Fergus was speaking a different language until he got his ear in.

The plan was very much as George had described to his men. They all agreed that they needed to get out of the cellar; they would probably have to take down Jerry in the process, if they were to get clear of the town and back into a safer position. George explained this would be tricky as they were not sure where the Germans were located. They had been under considerable fire prior to the collapse of the building, but the cellar walls were holding for now. Alex said that he didn't know where the Germans were for certain either, but he had an inkling that they were close to the right of the building. As they had taken cover in the cellars, they had been under heavy fire from their left, which had made their entrance collapse. Alex was hoping that this might be a way out; he suspected the Germans were just a few feet away, their nearest neighbours in fact. George explained about the to and fro with the Germans in the cellar next door, Alex nodded and rubbed the back of his neck.

"The only thing for it then, George, is to dig on the far side of the building, hoping that we're not overheard and bring a whole load of Jerries crashing down on us." George agreed.

The men formed a gang, passing the debris by hand, one piece after another, and stacking it at the far side of the cellar, which they hoped was the German side. The thinking was that Jerry would have more to break through if he tried, which would give them more time to respond. The work continued laboriously and as quietly as possible, with the men stopping every now and then to listen. It was thirsty work and the men soon ran out of water, which meant that they had to speed the whole process up or die of thirst in the creaking, unstable dust-filled hole. The temperature was rising in the confined space and sweat was pouring off the men. They were attempting to escape what could become their tomb if they were not careful.

Fingers bleeding with the effort of moving so much heavy masonry, their eyes filled with dust and sweat.

"I think I can see daylight," Gerald whispered.

"Let me see," said George. "You're right, you lovely old Berman, you."

"Steady on, Corp," said Gerald. "You don't want the others getting jealous now." George chuckled, but he couldn't say how relieved he felt, as his spirits were lifted.

"Now as quickly and quietly as possible, everyone, we've been lucky so far, so let's not bring the roof down on our heads after scraping and digging away for hours."

George signalled to Alex, who wormed his way between the men to daylight, where Gerald had made an opening.

"Where do you think this will bring us out, Sarge?" said George.

"Fuck knows," replied Alex. "But out we must get, that is for sure; we're out of supplies and water."

"We've sweated buckets moving this lot," added George.

"Exactly," Alex replied.

The men continued with their backbreaking work for a few more hours, until they could see that the hole was now wide enough for a man to crawl through; it was also quite timely, as night was beginning to fall.

Tel was the smallest and so he was volunteered to be the first out as scout. Even so, he struggled to get through, but he eventually made it with a wriggling and crawling motion. He whispered back to the men ready to follow.

"Pass me my rifle; there's enough room if you pass it up the left-hand side." Tel didn't want to be first out without anything to defend himself, as this was not friendly territory. He had made it to the outside, but he signalled back to the men to hold fast, while he had a good look around. The men sat crouched in the tunnel they had excavated. Time seemed to pass slowly; they were beginning to think that Tel had been captured. Hope was disappearing when he returned to the mouth of the exit.

"Come on slowly and quietly," he said. "I believe I can see where Jerry has set up his position; he is very close."

The men heaved themselves out one by one. It was a massive undertaking for the bigger men, and they had to be pulled out like a cork from a bottle. They decided to leave the machine gun where it was, as most of its ammunition was buried under the collapse. The men were now huddled in a tight group by the rubble close to the jailhouse. Their position was extremely vulnerable; they were in such an exposed place that, if spotted, they were done for. Alex had noted their vulnerability; he said that he would make the first move to see if he could make it across the road into the ditch, hoping that he didn't land on Jerry or a mine in the process. There was little moonlight; therefore manoeuvring through the rubble was in their favour, but the slightest noise and Jerry would spray the area with machine-gun fire. Alex drew in his breath, made a quick dash across the road and fell into the ditch as he tripped over debris strewn by the bombardment. Everyone gasped at the noise of Alex's dramatic dive and waited in alarm for the inevitable gunfire. There was none, but they heard German voices. They assumed the Jerries had thought it was one of their own moving about; at least they hadn't begun firing indiscriminately. They let a few minutes pass before Fergus made a dash to the ditch, followed shortly after by Duncan.

"Okay, lads, it's our turn to go now," George said. "Let's hope our luck holds." These words were barely out of his mouth, when the Germans opened fire. No one had moved; they couldn't believe their bad luck. Pinned against the pile of rubble, the fire seemed to sweep in front of them in an arc. Of what had given them away, George was totally unaware. They hadn't moved a muscle, yet Jerry seemed to be on their case.

"Right guys, as soon as there is a lull, we will all make a run for the ditch. Time is not on our side, we'll eventually be under their fire. It might just be a nervous gunner or it could be that something caught the gunner's eye, but we can't stay here." On the count of three, the men lifted themselves up from the rubble and ran like they had never run in their lives before. All the men made it across without getting hit. They were an unseemly bundle as they landed in the bottom of the ditch, but, apart from scraping themselves on the rubble strewn ditch, no one was injured.

Bertie was the first to speak.

"Oh Tel, have you just farted, is that your awful pong?" All the men were sombre as Bertie turned to them beaming his goofy smile. "What?" he said. "What's up?"

Tel just pointed to the far end of the bomb crater-cum-trench to a pile of decaying corpses. On closer inspection it turned out to be at least 20 very young Americans. All their gear was still strapped on them, but none of them had seen action until they were cut down in their youth. Probably they were straight up the road from Naples, believing they were heading for a Roman holiday.

"Poor buggers," they all whispered.

"Nothing we can do for them now, boys," said Alex. "Grab their tags; we'll drop them into HQ – if we make it ourselves, that is." They drew lots for the job, but in the end Bertie said he would do it, as he had made the joke. He hadn't meant to offend the dead boys from the USA; this would, he hoped, make amends for the remark. The others understood and, as no one was in a hurry to take up the gruesome task, they left Bertie to take care of it.

They all gathered around Alex, who was showing on a roughly drawn map where he thought they were in the town and where they needed to get to, if they were going to rejoin one of the main brigades.

"Whatever we do boys, it's going to be pretty sticky out there. The moment we pop our pretty little heads above the parapet, all hell will break loose. In fact, I believe we have been damn lucky to get this far. Jerry will have posted snipers, probably machine guns covering the open ground, so we'll need to manoeuvre as far as possible on our bellies through these thoughtfully prepared craters."

"We're ready when you are," said George. "You have the maps and the general idea where you believe the latest HQ is, so we will put ourselves in your hands."

"Right," said Alex. "Gather all the gear you need; take the water bottles that Bertie has brought back from our American friends, we leave in five minutes."

"Ok boys," George whispered back to his men. "We need to make sure we don't lose sight of each other; we need to be well clear of here before daylight, otherwise we're all sitting ducks."

Chapter 16

Toward Their Lines

Alex led the ragged group of sorry-looking men back along the trench, away from where he supposed the Germans were. Covered in dust and muck from the cellar, they were pretty indistinguishable from the rubble around them at present. As long as they didn't make a sound, they might just get far enough away to make it back to their lines. The men scrambled onward, seeing only the feet of the man in front, puffing and cursing the rough ground, but at least they were out of sight of snipers so far. After they had been crawling for about an hour, Alex sent the word back to halt, to rest, and drink some water before moving on again.

After another half hour, the men were perspiring profusely, the sweat stinging their eyes. They could see the glimmer of the dawn coming up above the holes they were crawling along and knew time was short, if they were to make it to the far side of town before daybreak. Coming to another halt, this time the word was that the way was blocked, that they would have to venture above ground blindly, as Alex couldn't see the next piece of cover. They were told to rest awhile, take on some more water and prepare themselves for a run across some open ground.

Each man's heart was thumping in his chest at the prospect of the dash: the dash to where? Alex dared a peek above cover; he could see the wall of what was once a shop and the remains of what was the Hotel Roses, across the other side of the street, where they had first broken out. The distance they had travelled seemed minute, but the time on their stomachs made it seem like forever: they must have completed the only stomach marathon in the world. Alex was assessing the distances, hoping that he had guessed correctly and wasn't leading his men into further danger. Asking the men to squeeze up, he whispered the best course of action.

"Look men, we have only one option as far as I can tell if we want to make it out of here, rather than make this our final resting place. We'll have to make a run to the pink building on the right of the square. I think this will give us adequate cover once we're there. The first man across will be able to give covering fire across to the hotel, should it be required. I believe Jerry is still held up in there, across the street from there in this building," he said pointing to his roughly drawn map. "Any questions?"

Gerald had taken up the rear and asked if he could see the map so that he could get his bearings; this was passed to him with due reverence, then passed back equally so.

"Right," said Alex. "My show, so I will go first, then signal for the next man. Clear?"

"Yes Sarge," the men mumbled rather unenthusiastically, but they all knew that, if there was a sniper, the first man, maybe even the second, would get across while the sniper set his sights, but thereafter: who knew?

Alex took a deep breath and hoisted himself out of the crater. For a big man, he made a very good sprinter. He crashed into the wall with so much force that from the top of the unstable pile, rocked with his weight and power, some dust with small pieces of rubble tumbled down. Not a good start, thought Fergus, who was the next to go. If he had brought more of the wall down, the Jerries would be alerted. Fergus was of slighter build, more like a greyhound; whether he could travel like one was soon to be discovered. Both men waited to see if anything stirred, reconnoitring the buildings opposite to ensure there wasn't a glimmer of a barrel protruding, lying in wait for the next unfortunate. All seemed to be clear so, with a signal from Alex, Fergus jumped like a jack-in-the-box out of the crater, only to slip ignominiously back into the crater as the edge had given way. Sliding back, he cracked his chin on the side, drawing blood. The language from all parties was strongly directed at Fergus for his folly. The men were horrified because of the noise of Fergus's fall, plus Duncan wasn't too happy because Fergus had also managed to drop his rifle on Duncan's outspread hand.

"Fucking hell, Fergus! What the bloody hell you playing at, man?"

Fergus sheepishly tried to apologise, but the men all waved him forward, to get on with it. His second attempt was more successful and he made it across to Alex without further incident. The day was now brightening and the men in the crater were getting more than a little agitated about being spotted. Picking up their mood, George said to Duncan, "We have to move this along much faster or we'll be caught in the open with our trousers down."

"Gotcha," said Duncan and, with this statement hanging in the air, he bounded across the open space without waiting for Alex to signal. When Alex saw Duncan racing across like a greyhound out of a trap, he didn't look best pleased. There was nothing he could do about it now, but Alex had spotted what seemed like a German patrol assembling; he just hoped that Duncan made it before they were fully awake. Not wanting to distract Duncan, Alex he let him come on; anything else would have caused more problems and Duncan would probably have hesitated, drawing much more attention to the hidden men. Duncan reached his destination without the Germans noticing, with a "Made it," and a big grin.

"You great lummox," Alex said. "Why didn't you wait for my signal?" Feeling aggrieved, Duncan said in his defence, "The Corp wanted me to speed things up. He was getting worried as it's getting light." With this information, Alex knew he had to act quickly; he had to change the plan. The group of fusiliers were going to have to make a dash in one move. The trick was finding the most appropriate time to do so.

George moved to the edge of the crater in the hope that he could see Alex and his signal. He hadn't meant for Duncan to dash across without the prior signal; he hoped that Alex appreciated this. The matter in hand was how to get all of them safely across without being picked off by snipers. George was trying desperately to signal Alex, he needed to communicate that they must move as one; the time was running out for them. He needn't have worried, as Alex was signalling, holding up four fingers and waving them towards himself so as to beckon the group as a whole. His mime, especially his facial expression, would have looked most amusing in other circumstances, but this wasn't the time or place. Alex was holding the palm of his hand toward the group, indicating for them to stay put, as he had a better vantage point than the group crouched in the crater. They were becoming extremely uncomfortable, as this part of the crater was disgusting, partially full of slimy oil-contaminated water, the coldness of it gradually soaking into their bones, making them shiver. Alex was busy keeping his eye on the group of Germans at the hotel. As far as he could tell, they were mounting a machine gun in one of the blown-out windows. While one German waited outside, the others ducked back to see whether they were well covered. Alex was amazed at the camouflage. If he hadn't seen them place the gun there, he would not have been able to pick it out at a later time – until it was too late, in fact. This gave him a spur; he had to get the men across now, before that machine gun was set up, or they would be cut down. There was no doubt about that.

Alex gained George's attention, not that George had been looking anywhere other than at Alex at the present time; his neck was aching from the strain of peering over the edge of the crater, just enough to see Alex but not enough to be seen by the Jerries. Raising thumbs up to Alex, George hoped he had guessed what this latest signal meant. Turning to the men, he said, "We are going as one. I need you all to move to my end of the crater and, when I say 'Go', we go as fast as we can to the cover where our Scots lads are. Got it?" They all nodded and George turned back to look at Alex and wait for his signal for their dash to safety, he hoped.

The signal was given, and the men rose as one smelly, wet, fearsome-looking bunch. The water was dripping from them, and the combination of the dust from the cellar and water from the crater made them appear to be one entity, when they rose as one grubby but tightly attuned group. Stiff from scrambling along the craters and from lying in wait for so long, their limbs were shaking with cold and their hearts were pumping to a quick march like a trombonist in a military band. They looked neither right nor left but straight at the Scots, who were beckoning for them to run to them. The Scotsmen's faces were filled with horror as they saw the Germans across the open space gathering together, fortunately in some confusion. In any other circumstance it would have been funny, as some of the Jerries were running into each other in their haste to get to some sort of weapon to fire. Alex had timed it to perfection; either the German machine gun was not completely set up or their disarray and confusion at the dishevelled group of humanity heading across the open space had completely thrown them. Whatever it was, it was playing into their luck.

Despite the unevenness of the ground, scattered with debris from the myriad of bombings and artillery shells, the men were making good progress, although to them it was playing out in in slow motion. They could hear each breath and count each heart beat pounding in their chests and ears; they knew that, by taking this mad but essential dash to apparent safety, their lives were in the balance. If you were to ask them what they were thinking at this moment in time, they wouldn't be able to tell you, but they could recall every step they made as each one lasted a lifetime and was burnt deep into their bcing, as each step was a stride closer to the bombed-out pink building and to a degree of cover.

The men were now just a matter of four or five large strides away from the building. They could see the Scots gesturing for them to hurry – as if they needed encouragement – as they became aware of the clamour of the Germans, who were preparing to open fire.

"Just look straight ahead lads," George shouted. "We're nearly there."

With that, there were several almighty cracks and dust spat into the air as the shells hit the ground. Two of the Scots swung their rifles toward the hotel, from which they believed the fire had originated.

Shouting, "I see the bastard," Duncan let off three successive rounds at the top of the building. Meanwhile, Fergus was firing at the Germans, who were struggling to get the machine gun operational.

"Tuck that in your sporran, you little shit, and that and that," they could hear him shout.

Although Fergus's shots were full of vehemence towards the enemy, they were not at all successful in hitting anything. Nevertheless, they did keep the Germans' heads down and delayed them in getting the machine gun fully operational. Glancing over his left shoulder, Alex could see that the Germans were in a much better position to start firing in a coordinated fashion; soon even this crumbling building would not hold much protection for the group.

Arriving in a dishevelled, stumbling mess behind the safety of the pink building, the fusiliers were gasping from their frantic efforts and from the adrenalin that was still coursing through their bodies. While the men tried to gain some semblance of order and gather what intelligence they could about their surroundings, Alex was already planning their next move out from behind the building. He was just about to speak to the fusiliers, when a barrage of fire struck the wall, leaving him unable to even think, let alone speak. The men were returning fire for all the good it would do them, as the Germans were well dug in, now they were prepared. They could hear orders being barked amidst the fury of the shots to the men on the machine gun. Soon their position would become untenable as, on the rooftops opposite, they could see German soldiers, who would obviously do their best to outflank the group huddled behind the pink walls.

There was a momentary lull. Alex spoke first.

"We need to get towards Castle Hill; I think we have a contingent based there and if not we'll have to think again."

"I believe that the RF 2nd Battalion were going to be moving up to Castle Hill and toward the monastery to the west," George replied. "But this may have changed since we've been separated from the main battalion position for some days."

"That settles it," said Alex. "Let's make a move sooner rather than later, as I believe the Germans might have something heavier to remove this wall and we'll be buried under it." As he spoke, the machine gun picked up its rapid beat, taking large chunks of masonry with it, the bricks and mortar cascading down on top of them.

"Prophetic," was all George said.

Alex snorted, and George wasn't sure whether he was stifling a laugh or about to swear, as he dusted himself off and added, "As I said, let's get out of here."

Alex moved to the centre of the men. As it was nearly impossible to hear, he used a myriad of hand gestures: a lot of gesticulation to get across what he was planning for them to do. Basically, he was going to lead the men and George would guard their rear. He wanted the men to be separated by at least five yards to prevent them all being taken out by a machine gun. He also he hoped it would make it more difficult for the Germans to ascertain their numbers.

The firing continued against the remains of the pink building; it would not be long before it collapsed completely. Crouched low, well-spaced, as Alex had commanded, the men moved without a word between them. This was serious stuff: they were now exposed in the remnants of the town. Many utilitarian items lay scattered across their path, as George brought up the rear. Seeing the articles from a normal household lying scattered in the rubble, he thought of the family and friends back home. His home in the East End of London had also taken a tremendous beating; he wondered how well they would be coping, whether they were any better off or even still alive.

Chapter 17

New Neighbours

Alex was relieved to find that there were more bomb craters not far from where they were crouched, so he made a beeline for one of the larger ones. He had jumped into the crater before he realised that it already had occupants, landing with a crump as he tripped over a radio and other equipment scattered about the crater.

"Hello Jock," came a cheery voice. "Been out for a bit of stroll, have we?"

"You have stirred Jerry up no end, you 'ave, that's for sure," came another voice from the other side of the crater. By this time the other men, hearing the voices and seeing Alex drop into the crater, quickly gained pace. Soon they too were sliding into their new temporary home.

"Well, well, it's nice to 'ave a bit of company, ain't it?" said the first soldier, as the others arrived en masse.

"How very rude of me," said a sergeant. "Let me introduce myself and my jolly band of warriors. I am Sergeant Reading of the 2nd Battalion Royal Fusiliers. These chaps are Lance Corporal Smethurst and Fusiliers Hibbard and Washington. We were out for a stroll, Sergeant," he continued, having noticed the insignia on Alex's arm. "Or, as some would like to call it, recon, when we heard the commotion that you and your jolly tribe have caused, we thought it best to come and investigate; good job we did too, eh lads?"

"You will have to excuse the sergeant," said Lance Corporal Smethurst. "Too much time rubbing shoulders with the management, that's what that is."

Not to be diverted, Sergeant Reading continued, "Well Hibbard, give HQ a tinkle, will you? Tell them we have seven more for tea, would you? There's a good chap."

Quite used to the affectations of Sergeant Reading, Hibbard just replied as always, "Rightoh, Sarge," and got HQ on the radio. He also fed back the coordinates of the Germans gathering in the shattered part of the town, where the positions of the machine gun and snipers were.

"That'll shake them up a bit," said Reading.

Soon after Reading's words, there was the whistling sound of heavy artillery overhead. Shells fell on the town, the hotel and the jailhouse section, where they had been harboured what now seemed a lifetime ago but was in fact only a matter of some hours. The ground shook with the reverberations; they could see dust clouds rising from the town. The men that had suffered the bombardment and entombment in the jailhouse cellars were just pleased it wasn't them. Addressing Alex, Reading said, "We'll make a move in a trice, if that suits you, Sergeant?"

Although Reading played the part of a vocally affected soldier, he was a good and responsible one, taking the task of caring for his men most seriously. Hence, once the tomfoolery had stopped, he was back in the mindset of a serious soldier and could not be faulted. With one whistle from him, his men gathered up all their kit; like a well-oiled machine, they were back on task. The whole demeanour of the sergeant changed as he led his men into dangerous situations. Reading was no fool; he was using the barrage to cover his movements back to safer lines. Having gathered sufficient intelligence for this foray, now it was his responsibility to get not only his own men but also the others that had joined him back to safety. Immediately he had taken charge, although Alex and he were of equal rank, there was no doubt who would be the leader in these circumstances.

Without hesitation, the other men picked up their kit, the little they had, and followed the fusiliers, who were now crouched low and moving fast. Like snakes, they slithered through ditches, craters and amidst scrub. Reading knew the landscape like the back of his hand; he had the innate ability to work out the best routes and the safest direction to take within seconds. The lie of the land was ingrained in his very being and he moved like he was born for just such a task. Reading held up his hand and the column dropped as one, waiting for his next command.

A German transport vehicle with paratroopers spilling out of the sides was blasting across the track in front of them, kicking up choking dust, but the men held fast. Reading realised the town was being evacuated; they were moving fast and furious back to their lines near the monastery. He was surprised to see the vehicle, as most of them had been taken out in the bombardments. Once the vehicle was clear and Reading was sure it was safe enough to cross, he made a slight movement of his hand and the column moved forward once again.

They came to a further danger point, where Reading had learned a sniper was covering the area; they had tried for days to winkle this lone shooter out from among the debris of the buildings. He was good. When he made his shot, it was usually a kill, bad news for anyone careless enough to show any part of their body to him. He would then move position so when they brought down mortars or artillery on the point where they thought he was, he had usually moved on. Otherwise, there was a nest of snipers, not just the one lone shooter. Reading thought this was the work of one man; he would like to get him in his sights, but no one had even had a glimpse or a flash from this Jerry's telescopic rifle. As he had said before, this boy was good.

Reading's breathing rate had increased; he lay on his stomach scouring the surroundings.

"Where are you, you bugger? Where are you?" he said in a rasping whisper. He could not see any movement, but that meant nothing. He had the task of getting these men across the open area; although he would never admit it, he was a little scared. Not of getting himself shot – although he would rather avoid that if he could – he was aware of his duty and he would not like to lose any of these men to this elusive sniper. After a while, he believed he had waited long enough; nothing was going to change to make this situation any easier. He rolled over onto his back and whispered back to the men following.

"There is probably still a sniper ahead. We will need to move fast and low; this chap is good. If they haven't managed to get him, he's very dangerous, so on my signal you will make it across the gap to the other wall and lie flat until I have every man across. Clear?" Although phrased like a question, there was no answer to this, just a sullen nodding of several heads.

Reading tapped the first man on the head and indicated for him to go. All the time just hoping for that shot to get the sniper, he kept a very careful eye on the remains of the buildings that could possibly house him. First man across and lying flat against the wall, now for the next. It took over 25 minutes to get them all across safely; now it was left for him to make the trip. Was that sneaky so-and-so waiting for him? He felt he had a special relationship with this man; he was just lying in wait for him. Reading let the others go so he could gain his prize, but on every other occasion the sniper had managed to thwart him. It was probably just his imagination, but no one would have been able to persuade him otherwise.

There was no time like the present. Reading readied himself for the crossing just as it began to rain. It gained power; now this could be a good thing, thought Reading. The rain was coming down like a torrent and had misted out the other side of the gap where the men were. So, if I can't see them, he won't be able to see me, he thought. With that, he rose to a crouching position and made a dash for the other side of the gap. As he did so, he was aware of a thud between his legs; realising that he was under fire, he threw himself towards the men, landing on Hibberd, who said, "Steady on, Sarge, we aren't even engaged."

"Shut up you bloody fool," retorted Reading. "The sniper is having a go at me. I knew it; the bugger was just waiting for me to cross. Well he left it too late; although he got the distance, he didn't get the height right." With that, he spun around and peered over the wall that was protecting them, in the hope he might see something, but the heavy shower of rain that had probably saved him was keeping the sniper from scrutiny too.

A Coldstream Guardsman recalled how the German snipers would always target the very rear of the patrol, so they 'scrambled like scalded rats not to be the last man'. (Reprinted by the kind permission of Matthew Parker)

The rain eased fairly quickly; over the past months they had had enough rain, snow and sleet to last them a lifetime; just when they thought it might be clearing, the rain would fall. It was getting darker now. Reading wanted the group to make haste, get back to base, report his findings, have some hot grub and, as he always jokingly said, "a rub down with an oily rag". By the time they got back to base, they were worn out by the strain of the day and the sheer exertion of the crawling and climbing they had had to do. Alex and George's men were ready to drop, as they had been awake for 36 hours; all they wanted to do was crash and sleep, but George insisted that they eat or they would feel feeble when they awoke.

Alex and George went to report to the captain in charge of the base camp. The two men eyed each other when they saw Captain Merryweather of the Guards; he was so young and fresh-looking that both were of the opinion that he ought to be at school. How did he manage to keep himself so clean? George wondered. Did he have a secret bathroom somewhere, with people lavishing creams and potions on him? The captain's voice, however, had strength in it, and both men stood to attention.

"Take it easy men," said Merryweather. "No need for all that pomp and ceremony out here." Alex and George told as briefly and concisely as they could the set of circumstances that had brought them to the base. Merryweather listened carefully then spoke.

"Ok chaps. Send in Reading, will you? And get something to eat and somewhere to catch up on a bit of sleep, but, as you can see, we don't have a lot ourselves. I will radio HQ to get fresh orders from them. Meanwhile, make yourselves as comfortable as possible; sounds like you chaps have had quite a slog."

Chapter 18

Travelling to the Mountain

The men were roused from their sleep by Reading, and he wasn't looking too pleased.

"What's up?" asked George, rubbing the sleep from his eyes, trying to recall where he was. This was the first time he had slept for some while; he was stiff from the scramble out of the jailhouse and the crawl along the ditches and bomb craters. All the men felt the same drowsiness; they were bivouacked on a slope, but this hadn't prevented them from falling into a deep, if fitful sleep; they would have slept anywhere after the events of the last few days. There was a general grunting and turning over to avert their eyes from the possibility of being plunged into reality. Above them, they could hear the rat-a-tat of the machine guns and the louder cascading and reverberating sound of mortars. How they had slept through such a continuous bombardment always astounded Reading. Exhaustion can do that, he thought.

"Well chaps," he started. "How do you fancy a little stroll up a mountain? I hear the view is terrific. Although the weather is still quite inclement, it's nothing you chaps aren't used to."

"Oh cut it out," cried Tel. "Don't tell me after everything we've got to climb that ruddy mountain?"

"Got it in one old chap," retorted Reading. "But not only that, you will have some chaps from your lot, 2nd Fusiliers, accompanying you, and oh you will be helping a great deal as the boys up the hill a way are running short on supplies." The men were heard grumbling under their breath; what they were saying was indistinct, but Reading knew men well enough to leave them to their own devices – leave their own NCOs to sort them out.

George realised it would be his job to get the men in some sort of state to make the ascent; it would not be easy, as the mountain still held many surprises. Coupled with the fact that the mountain itself was treacherous, churned up and lethal if you didn't take care, the whole platoon could end in disaster. They would be climbing the mountain in the dark to avoid snipers, carrying massive packs of food and live ammunition; it would be easy to turn an ankle in these circumstances. The mountain afforded very little cover, the scrub had been mostly macerated, and there were no large outcrops of rocks to hide behind. The perpetual cascade of mortars and unexploded ammunition meant a dangerous and difficult operation.

George explained the situation to the men; they were all seasoned soldiers now and had been together in the desert campaign in North Africa. It was the injection of younger inexperienced soldiers that brought the liability, but fortunately not many of them, apart from the Yanks, had got this far into Monte Cassino.

Breaking off to feed up and to make the best of things, the men tightened their boots, arranged their personal kit about them securely and waited for the order to move.

"Who will be leading us up the mountain, George?" asked Bertie.

"Not sure who we have with us; we'll find out soon enough, I expect."

The men from the 2nd Fusiliers joined the rest of the men. Greetings were exchanged and a little light banter, but mostly the men were gearing themselves up to make the climb. They all knew many men had lost their lives in doing just what they were about to do, and the mood became subdued while they waited for an NCO or an officer to take the lead. Eventually, a young lieutenant, wearing the insignia of the Grenadier Guards, came across to them. He looked very young, thought George, while the same thought ran through the minds of the other men.

"I'm Lieutenant Braithwaite of the Grenadier Guards and I am about to lead you men up the hill to the point here," he stated, pointing at his map, which was pristine, just like him. "I don't believe we will have too much trouble in achieving our objective; there are a few New Zealand chaps, who have got themselves stranded and, as far as we can tell, are running out of ammo and basic supplies. That is where we come in; we will make as quick an ascent as possible and give these chaps a hand. Any questions?" Braithwaite was turning to leave, when George spoke.

"Sir."

Braithwaite turned back to see who had spoken and George raised his hand.

"Yes Corporal," responded Braithwaite.

"I don't want to seem negative, Sir, but a quick ascent will not be possible carrying the amount of supplies we will be carrying. It may take us a day or two to reach the point you have indicated on your map, and we will be doing this under the cover of darkness."

"On the contrary," replied Braithwaite. "We will be leaving immediately so that we can get ahead before it becomes dark, to avoid all the dangers that you may fear." Braithwaite seemed a little ruffled; he had turned pink in the process. Fingering his collar nervously, he glared at George, who hadn't finished with the Lieutenant yet but was trying to phrase his next comment without being too confrontational.

"Sir, we should move in darkness. We will be easy targets unless we do so. Progress may be slower, but it will be safer, and we are less likely to lose our men to snipers."

"I hear you, Corporal, but I have evaluated the situation and I believe to move as far as possible in daylight is our better option. That is an order, Corporal. Now get the men ready to move. Sergeant Reading has the supplies organised, we will move as soon as practical." George wasn't having any of this. He responded without thought for himself, only for his men.

"That is sheer lunacy, Sir; you are putting my men at risk, for what?"

Now fuming, Braithwaite spun round and, like a petulant child, almost screamed at George.

"You, Corporal, are on a charge for disobeying a direct order. Any further disobedience and I will have your stripe." George was now equally angry if not more so.

"You can have my fucking stripe and stick it where the sun don't shine, but you are making a terrible error of judgement!"

Braithwaite was now beside himself and called for the sergeant, who happened to be Reading. Although he had known these men only a short while, Reading understood their loyalties and their performance under fire. Braithwaite insisted that George be put under arrest for insubordination and that he was to be demoted back to a private. Reading could see matters were getting out of hand, but he could not go against a superior, so he approached George and told him he was under arrest, asking in a whisper what on earth was going on. George as quickly and quietly as possible told Reading, who just mumbled, "Bloody idiot," back to him.

The men were now in a mutinous mood; they didn't like this new officer and they also knew George was right. However, it was too late for George; he had been charged with insubordination and would lose his stripe. George had got his way, as by the time it took to go through all the machinations – the where and whyfors – darkness was creeping down the mountain; the men would not be leaving before dark. The general opinion on George's action was that it was foolhardy but correct, in as much as his men would be safer in the process. Other officers spoke with Braithwaite and pointed out that he had taken away the stripe of a good soldier, whom his men trusted and relied on.

Braithwaite was not pleased at his dressing down and unfortunately, due to army discipline and the closing of ranks, George was to remain a private. Not that this bothered George, as he was a reluctant corporal; he had been made up before and asked to be relieved of this responsibility, but some of the officers and NCOs were disappointed at his demotion.

"Can't you intervene somehow, Sir?" Reading was heard to say to Merryweather.

"He seems like a good man and his men would follow him anywhere."

"I am as sorry as you are, Sergeant, but you know I can't go against another officer: not good for morale and all that."

Reading just finished off by saying, "Damn shame that's all, damn shame, he would have made a good NCO."

Merryweather nodded in agreement. As Reading made to leave, both men's eyes met, each understanding the other's frustration.

The men were assembled and ready to move out. They were to be led by a fusilier who had traversed the mountain on several occasions and would act as their guide. After much intercession, George was allowed to join what were formerly his men. They were all pleased to see him and appreciated he had sacrificed his rank for them; they jostled him and joked with him, calling him a jolly good chap.

"Well at least I won't have to nursemaid you lot any longer," George responded. He thought it best to bring up the rear, as far away as possible from Lieutenant Braithwaite, who, by his expression, was none too pleased to see George swelling the ranks and even less pleased at his enthusiastic reception.

Braithwaite tucked in behind Fusilier Graham, who had the unenviable job of leading the patrol up the mountainside. He knew where there were hazards, where snipers lurked, and was picking his steps very carefully among the rocky outcrops that were covered in a fine drizzle, making them extremely slippery and difficult to navigate. It wasn't long before the men fell into a mesmeric rhythm, as the mountainside grew steeper. Their breathing became more laboured as they moved with their extremely heavy loads, straps cutting into their shoulders like blunt knives at first then as a dull ache as time passed. If these mists stayed, they might make it in one go and not have to find a spot to take cover during daylight hours. It would be preferable to being found clinging to the side of a hill when daylight came, with nothing but their oilskins to cover their exposure: a pretty large target for every German with a rifle. The thought made Graham shudder; one well-placed shell in their ammunition boxes could send them all to a different place.

Stopping every hour to take rest and refreshment, they didn't bother taking off their loads, as refastening them on the mountainside would be difficult. Rather, they wedged themselves with feet outstretched, using their packs as a counterbalance and leaning back on them when possible. They munched down some biscuits, taking on board as much water as possible, although this was very precious on the mountainside; they were advised to drink because, despite the rain and the cold, they were sweating like the proverbial pigs under their loads.

The patrol was making good time when Graham held a hand aloft to signal them to stop and drop. They had reached a point of danger, where they would be highlighted in silhouette against the slightest light emanating from behind them. He glanced around carefully and looked for a long time into what could only be seen as a dark, damp emptiness. Graham had built a great awareness in his travels up and down the mountain; he wasn't going to be caught like some beginner on this occasion if he could prevent it. Passing along a message to be extremely quiet, he lay listening. The very slight sound of a chink of metal on rock came from somewhere to his right, putting him on extreme alert; he shushed everyone again, listening. He heard a voice and it wasn't English. Trying extremely hard to gather as much information through his whole body, he shook – he wasn't sure whether from the cold or the anticipation. At this moment in time he wished he had bats' ears; he had to be careful not to react too quickly, as they may be Poles, not Germans. If he were to let go with a burst of fire towards the direction the voices were coming from, he might shoot Allies or maybe draw attention by their muzzle flashes to their own positions. Always, these choices to be made in split seconds.

Braithwaite drew alongside Graham and whispered, "Who do you think they are?"

"Germans I believe, Sir, but they seem to be moving away from us. Noisy buggers, thank goodness, or we might have blundered into them in this mist." When Graham believed it was safe to move forward, he signalled for them to continue their climb. There were a few groans, as they were already beginning to cramp up with the wait in the rain. Putting his fingers to his lips, Graham whispered for them to be extremely quiet.

The men continued the gruelling climb for several hours and eventually made it to the New Zealanders, who were beyond pleased to see them. They were dug in, if you could call it that, lying in scrapes that they were confined to for most of the daylight hours or be picked off by snipers. The scrapes were just enough to hide them from snipers and they were achieved by hours of scraping with shovels and picks, grating on the rocky terrain. It was hard to make them comfortable, despite the hours of work to ensure some measure of cover. His men were gathered around in similar scrapes, and he explained that they had been cut off after an offensive against the German position. He spoke emotionally about the lack of reinforcements.

"We could have bloody kicked their arses if we had been reinforced. We have lost a lot of men on this hillside. About two thirds of the men who came up here are either dead or wounded. What is the bloody matter with the top brass?"

Braithwaite was at a loss to say anything to this captain, who, along with his men, had obviously suffered a great deal.

The men distributed food and ammunition to the New Zealanders in their scrapes; they grasped it eagerly, eating their food rations ferociously.

"Excuse my men," said the captain. "They haven't eaten for two days. Oh and by the way, I am Captain Dylan Sheerin; mustn't forget my manners, even in these conditions." Trying to be as magnanimous as possible, Braithwaite mumbled, "That's quite alright, Sir. I am Lieutenant Braithwaite, and what are your orders?" Appreciating that he was junior to the captain in both experience and rank, he would need to gain the other's approval of their next action. Braithwaite had been told to find and distribute the provisions to as many men as he could; they were not sure if the New Zealanders would even be a fighting force any longer.

"There are men further up the mountain that will need provisioning, and as to what state they are in, I can only hazard a guess. They will be a disparate and probably desperate bunch by now and quite a mixed bag of both nationalities and regiments. Rest up for now; it's becoming light and we don't want you picked off like flies."

Another reason for not climbing too high up the mountainside was the consistent heavy bombing over the slopes near and on the monastery. This bombing had been a last resort and the bone of contention between the Allied commanders; the Germans had moved the artworks from the monastery to Rome, along with the Benedictine Abbot, for fear of their destruction. The bombing was relentless, so much so that the men scattered across the mountain felt some sympathy for the Germans occupying the area. The sound of the incoming bombers sent chills down the spines of Allies and Germans alike: the whistling sound of 500 and 1000lb bombs dropping and then seconds later the explosions one after the other, the smoke piles climbing into the sky that blanketed out the weak winter sun, together with the shaking of the whole mountain under the feet of every man and beast unfortunate to witness such madness. The men did not know it yet, but it was the beginning of months of further hell.

One mountain pool just below the monastery was ringed with dead bodies of soldiers from both sides whose thirst got the better of their common sense. Under cover snipers from both sides waited for the next man to risk a drink. (Reprinted by kind permission of Matthew Parker)

Chapter 19

Machine-gunning Fritz

Climbing further up the hill was to be an eye-opener for men who thought they had seen all that was to be seen. The remains of Allies and Germans were scattered like entrails from a piñata across the escarpment. Crows picked at the parts of men like the children who burst the piñata wide open and picked up sweets, except these were body parts of varying age. The whole platoon were close to vomiting as they passed these human remains and tried to turn away in disgust, only to be faced with other bloody body parts. The realisation of the inhumanity of it all fell across the relief group as they continued their relentless climb. Nobody spoke; all that could be heard was the scuffing of their boots and heavy breathing as they bent into the hill, counterbalancing the weight of their loads to enable their climb. Dotted over the hillside were pockets of grimy-looking, cold, wet and extremely hungry men. They were joyous to see some other faces that not only brought provisions but also the hope of relief. One mud-splattered individual raised a hand in supplication.

"Oh thank the fuck, I thought I was gonna bloody die of hunger up here!"

"Brought any grog?" cried another.

"Don't be daft," called back a fusilier. "We drank that at our first stop!"

The men were incredibly buoyed by the arrival of the fusiliers. One was crying, but trying to hide it. Seeing him, Graham put a hand on his shoulder.

"I know it's bloody awful what they expect us to do, ain't it?"

The man looked up at Graham and just whispered, "Thank you for coming," as if Graham were a guest at a party, rather than a soldier in a war situation.

The fusiliers moved about the hillside as quickly and quietly as possible, delivering packages and good cheer as if they were Santa Claus or saviours, offering a few encouraging softly spoken words here and there, but mostly just distributing the goods and moving on to the next hungry man.

At last the men with Lieutenant Braithwaite were also able to take some rest and try to dig into the hillside as best they could. All those who had been in this conflict had developed ways to bring a little of home with them and some spent their time writing home in their very shallow sangars (so-called because of their sandwich of rocks, mud and anything else they could find), looking at pictures of loved ones and familiar places they had been together. Others decided the best escape was simply to sleep; how they did so on this cold, wet and exposed hillside was quite incredible: just through sheer exhaustion. Men had little brew-ups and tried to make their food rations as pleasing and satisfying as they could, holding the light from candles under their tins to shelter it from the wind and also the piercing eyes of the enemy. All had their own ways of coping with the situation and living for another day.

Braithwaite seemed a little lost in this situation and looked around to discuss their next move, but the men were too involved in their own worlds to catch the eye of an officer. The remains of an Indian contingent were deep in discussion in their native tongue and were totally in control of their part of the world. Although uncomfortable and difficult, the hillside brought only courage and forbearance to the surface. No man complained or grumbled; after all their philosophy was: Who would it help? The hillside slept, and there was little sound except for the grunting and huffing of the men as they tried to find a comfortable position. The sentries posted were not so lucky and spent the night scanning the darkness for any movement.

George and his fellow fusiliers had charge of a machine gun, as George had completed the training way back in the day. He hadn't had much cause to use his training in India and hadn't been deployed with a machine-gun unit in the desert so this was going to be his first use of the weapon since training.

There was hardly a movement that night. Even the weather had agreed to play along, the rain had stopped, and the wind had dropped. Yes, it was cold and damp; they could wrap themselves in their groundsheets against the cold, but there was little protection against the penetrating wind and rain, which seemed to have the ability to seek out every entry point, every crevice; they soon became wet through, shivering in their soaking clothes. Just as it seemed that the hillside was having its first quiet night in such a long time, there was a flash followed by a cascade of firing; who and what was going on, nobody knew. Lieutenant Braithwaite rose like an uncontrollable rag doll from the little cover he had and began shouting and barking orders to no one in particular. This was no time to stand up and be silhouetted against the arc of the burning green white light of a German flare, but that is exactly what he did. All the men on the hillside cried out to him to get down, rule number one: keep your head down. Too late, he came to his senses; a sniper soon had an easy target and took it. The lieutenant stood there for a while with a look of amazement frozen on his face forever; he fell in a slow-motion sideways action, collapsing to the ground.

The men had no time to do anything else; after all, there was nothing they could do and so they left him where he fell. They began firing in the direction of the fire flashes, all the time expecting to be rushed in a violent attack. This is how it had been for weeks and months: attack and counterattack, gain a slither of hillside, lose the slither the next day or the day after, and so it continued relentlessly, losing ground and losing men. The men questioned the logic of this procedure: repeating the same nightmare day after day and night after night wore them down; some men were losing their minds along with their comrades. Some desperate men ran into enemy fire to end their distress, others cried uncontrollably in their sangars all night long. The blank looks the next morning indicated their despair; they had, to all intents, lost their minds.

George and his group of fusiliers began acting as a well-oiled machine, they fed the machine gun with ammunition and it traced across the hillside like some monster spitting fire, like a mythical demon. Red-hot tracer could be seen hitting the hillside, and the screams of men were heard over the thundering sound from guns and now mortars. For several minutes this continuing fire storm raged – although, if you had asked any of the men on the hillside that night, they would have told you it lasted for hours. But minutes was all that it took that night and then darkness and silence once again, disturbed only by the sound of men weeping or crying out in pain from their wounds and the loss of their friends and comrades.

The machine gun was red-hot from the action of the night, and the men fell back into cover and listened to the fall of rain, which had returned once again, sizzling on the hot muzzle. Exhausted from the exertions of the action and from the climb, they all fell asleep in a sprawling mess like discarded toys that a child could not be bothered to clear away. Fitful and twitching, they drifted in and out of sleep, occasionally waking in a cold sweat and wondering where they were; once they had realised, they fell back into their restless sleep once again.

Chapter 20

The Battles Continued

I only know what we see from our worm's eye view, and our segment consists only of tired and dirty soldiers who are alive and don't want to die; of long darkened convoys in the middle of the night; of shocked, silent men wandering back down the hill from the battle; of mess queues and atabrine tablets and the smell of cordite and foxholes and burning tanks and Italian women washing and the rustle of high-flown shells; of jeeps and ammunition dumps and hard rations and olive trees and blown bridges and dead mules and hospital tents and shirt collars greasy black from weeks of wearing; and of laughter too and anger and wine and lovely flowers and constant cussing. All these it is composed of: and of graves and graves and graves. Ernie Pyle, Cassino, March 1944.

What I saw took me back across twenty-eight years, when I experienced the same loneliness crossing the battlefield of the Somme. Fridolin von Senger und Etterlin.

(All reprinted from Monte Cassino by Matthew Parker)

The mist covered the mountain like a shroud; men hunkered down as best they could against the cold night air. It seeped through their clothes and coverings like a wily thief in the night, stealing the little warmth that was stored in their innermost core.

The sangars provided little protection against the bullets of the enemy or the cold, damp, mist-filled air; the men did the best they could to pass the long nights, speaking in whispers in case they were overheard by Jerry snipers, who would take a shot if they were rattled or believed they had found a target. No one could see further than the hand in front of their face, but this did not stop a speculative shot in the deepening mists.

George turned to Bertie, who was the closest to him; both men lay stretched out in their home-built protection of the sangar.

"What are you doing, Bertie? I can hear a rustle of paper," George whispered.

"I'm just reading the good book, that's all Georgie."

"What good will that do you, Bertie, when the Hun start shooting at you?"

"George, I find comfort in the Lord's word."

"What part are you reading?" was George's enquiry.

"It's from John 14, 'In my house there are many mansions, if it were not so would I have not told you that I go to prepare a place for you'. It's Jesus talking to his disciples and those gathered around him; he is telling them of eternal life."

"And you believe all that shit do you, Bertie? I didn't realise you were so religious."

"Well, Georgie, I'm not, but my parents are. They come from Wales originally and were Chapel. They only moved to Nottingham for better working conditions than in the valleys, but my father ended up back in the mines."

"Is he still mining then?"

"He was when I left home, but mum's last letter said that he was suffering from the effects of the coal dust, so I'm not certain that he is now. How about you, Georgie? Don't you believe in anything?"

"No, not really. Mum did, but she couldn't get any of us into church, although I do remember mum reading the Bible to us on Sundays, and some of it must have stuck. I remember the bit about Samson: a bit of a boy's adventure story, where he said that he had slain thousands with the jawbone of an ass."

"Oh that's from Judges," responded Bertie, "'And Samson said, "with a jawbone of an ass, heaps upon heaps, with a jaw of an ass I have slain a thousand men".' Most appropriate that you remember that verse, Georgie."

"Too fucking right it's appropriate; I think we're fighting an Old Testament war, not a New Testament one, where everyone turns the other cheek, Bertie. How come you haven't told me any of this in the past? I've known you for years and you've never spoken of your beliefs."

"I was afraid that the others might have poked fun at me I suppose: 'you religious nutter' and all that."

The two men fell silent, just lying on their sides, tucking their legs up to their chests to reserve as much body heat as possible, with nothing else to do but to pass the night, watching their breath mingle with the mountain mist. Both men contemplated the conversation that had passed between them, wondering about their past lives and whether they would ever see their homes again. Several minutes passed before George broke the silence.

“Bertie, are you still awake?”

“Course I am; bloody brass monkeys, I can’t get to sleep with this cold.”

“I was just thinking,” said George.

“You don’t want to do too much of that; you might strain something.”

“No seriously; what you said – about the mansions – do you believe you will go to heaven then?”

“Yes I do, I just hope that I can be forgiven for killing all these Germans. Do you think God can forgive that, Georgie?”

“I’m the wrong person to ask, Bert. The way I see it is, the Germans have families too, they believe they’re fighting for a just cause, just like we have been told; apart from the fanatics, I believe they’re no different. Whether God can forgive this killing on a mass scale, only He knows, assuming that you are a believer in all that.”

“Good point, Georgie. The Old Testament God would have urged us on, but Jesus has asked us to forgive those that sin against us. When this is all over, I hope there is forgiveness, George.”

“So do I Bert, so do I.”

A harsh voice rang across the mountain, “Will you two lovebirds pipe down? There are some of us on this fucking mountain trying to sleep.”

The men slept on the mountain in whatever manner they were able, wriggling into the sangars, hoping for some respite with a morning sun that did not have the warmth of summer, but anything would do. Then of course the battle for the mountain would commence. The cold air was at least keeping down the smell of the rotting corpses about them.

Bertie spoke solemnly; he said he had an awful feeling that he wouldn't leave this mountain. George told him not to be so daft and get some sleep if he could.

Month followed month on the hillside, and the cold, wet and occasional hail and sleet did not help their situation. Some of the men passed the time as best they were able: taking what relief they could from the cold by volunteering to get supplies. This was a hazardous and highly dangerous occupation – but anything to alleviate the boredom – followed by extreme anxiety and outright fear when they were counterattacked with such ferocity that it ended in hand-to-hand fighting. There wasn't anything as nightmare-making as the feeling of sinking a bayonet into another man, another human being. They all rationalised that it had to be done: it was him or me, but the look of horror on young men's faces was not one that would easily be eradicated. These nightmares would follow them back home, no matter how they justified themselves on this obscene hillside.

Amongst the men, the main discussion over the past months had centred on what the top brass were doing.

"All they keep talking about is battle number one, two, and three. And where are we now? Number four."

"This is far from a game, this is not dealing with counters on a board, and these are men's lives that are being thrown away, almost it seems at the throw of a dice."

Chapter 21

The Mountain

As the stakes were raised, more and more men were asked to throw themselves at the virtually impregnable German defences. Monte Cassino is a story of incompetence, hubris and politics redeemed at a dreadful cost by the bravery, sacrifice and humanity of the ordinary soldiers. (Reprinted by kind permission of Matthew Parker, Monte Cassino; The Hardest Fought Battle of World War 2)

George slumped into the oozing muddy sangar he had called home for the past how many days, he couldn't recall. He looked down the rocky mountainside with its outcrops of scrub and rocks; the smallest ones were in some ways worse, as they stuck in your boots and got into clothing and became an irritant, rubbing every seam of your body. The mountainside was treacherous, steep and a killer; if the Germans didn't kill you, the hillside would. If you took a tumble you could break a leg or your neck and you might become a rolling, moving target for Jerry. The Polish troops were amazing, as they ran uphill like mountain goats in the rush to new pasture. How they managed it was extraordinary; perhaps it was a combination of hate and fear that drove them on.

There was murmuring that had rippled down the line like a seeping smoke canister, a Chinese whisper, growing in volume as it reached his mud-caked and bloody ears. Apparently the battle was over and the German 1st Parachute Division, reputedly the best division in the German Army, after holding the Allies at bay for almost five months, had surrendered at last: five months of pounding artillery, aerial bombardment and the loss of countless lives over the battle-torn mountainside. George wasn't sure he cared less; he had lost all feeling, been drained of all emotion. At the end of his tether, he wanted to cry but couldn't, not because it was unmanly, he just couldn't. Like many of his comrades, he had seen too much, he had done too much. George questioned where humanity was in this godforsaken place, what was his life for, if it just came to blood and guts spilt on the side of a mountain, living in bile and intestines? Was this to be his life until someone took it? Never mind fighting for right, God and country, the devil was real and he lived in everyone, of that he had no doubt. He saw him in the eyes of his comrades and the eyes of the enemy. There were those that talked of a just war; what utter tripe, he thought. He had had enough; that was all.

Ten armies from across the Commonwealth and the USA had been shipped into Monte Cassino over the past months with little regard for them as human beings; they were numbers on a balance sheet. How many men does it take to remove Jerry from the hill top? The officers had thrown everything they had against the securely dug-in German infantry, everything that is except the kitchen sink: maybe they should have tried that.

The Kiwis were a brave lot and had fought tenaciously for many days and weeks, while they waited for reinforcements that never came. That could have been the turning point; the Kiwis had begun to make inroads into the German defences, but some high and mighty 'plonker' at brigade had decided not to reinforce them. That's what George thought anyhow. After fighting through wind, rain, snow and icy conditions, the watery summer sun of June brought little comfort. It had taken George and his platoon over four hours' arduous climbing to reach the battle zone each time; carrying their equipment and rations made the journey more treacherous. Sliding and slipping up the unforgiving mountainside: this was no holiday hike – that was for certain.

There is a lot of to and fro now: excited voices in the somewhere beyond his thoughts; he feels light and somewhat disembodied. It is as if these past months and the previous years have never happened. George lights a cigarette, draws the warm, soothing, noxious fumes down deep into his lungs, letting the smoke drift out slowly from his mouth and nose. This process has served him well over the years and brought some small crumb of comfort each time he performed this ritual. When did he start smoking? He can't recall. His army ration of smokes soon disappears now – that's for sure. He can also use the fags for currency, and some blokes will even give up their beef ration for a pack. He sits quietly on the edge of his sangar – he

couldn't have done that a few hours ago – and draws on his cigarette until it is just a stub.
"Fag end of this war for me," he says aloud. "I've had enough of this shit," he mumbles to no one in particular and, with this statement on the air, he begins to strip, throwing his uniform in a crumpled heap, starting with his helmet, then his webbing belt, leaving the rifle that he has carried across the seas and through the mountain ranges of Italy lying in the ditch that has been his home on the side of this godforsaken hillside – and it is godforsaken, he thinks. Why else would such abominations happen? He glances at his hands; they are splattered with several-days-old blood – not his; this blood belonged to Bertie Bakewell. He was next to George in the heat of battle not many days previously and when George turned to tell Bertie to keep his head down, a German sniper, who probably believed in God and, furthermore, believed he was fighting a just war, decided to pop Bertie's head like a ripe melon.

The day had started with the usual sporadic small arms' fire, growing in force as the day proceeded. No matter how prostrate the men made themselves, pieces of rock and mud showered over them from near misses. Bertie shouted to George in his scrape hole.

"Do you think this will ever bloody well stop?"

"Only when we are all dead, Bertie!" George shouted in reply.

Bertie snorted at George's response and, with mounting anger, shouted back once more,

"That's it for me; you little fuckers are going to get some of Bakewell's bullets, right between your beady eyes." Jumping up, he fired recklessly in the direction of his now very personal enemy. George was alarmed by Bertie's strategy and shouted at him again.

"Keep your bloody head down, Bertie; they will get your measure."

"I'm indestructible, Georgie, just you watch me!"

Horrified at the demented actions of his best friend, George tried to stop Bertie popping up and down like a jack in the box. Believing that if he did the same as Bertie, he would create a diversion from his friend's activity, George popped out of his sangar, fired several bursts at the enemy and sank down, before they were able to return fire.

Bertie seemed rather manic; looking across at George, he hollered, "It's great, it's exhilarating! Do it again Georgie boy, you then me, and let's keep the Jerries guessing."

Against his better judgement, George complied. They both became extremely excited by this dangerous game; after each sortie, they fell back into their sangars, giggling as if they were just schoolboys, firing peashooters at the older boys.

The German sniper off to the left of the men was so well hidden by bodies and detritus that he was invisible from the schoolboys. He waited. He took a long slow breath, waited for the next one to pop out of his box, and crack! No one was aware of any sound, as the bullet cracked open Bertie's helmet. Not even Bertie heard the shot, his brain absorbed the shot like a sponge, and the life went out of him in an instant.

Unaware of the shot, George thought that his friend was playing a stupid game. Bertie was not moving; after a few minutes, George decided he would try to make it over to Bertie's sangar, all the time hoping it was a stupid game. He kept as low as he could, thinking to himself, I will really let him have it if he is play-acting.

The sniper was still in position, George moved on his belly, trying to stay behind every small mound of earth, sliding into every recess in the ground, as snake-like as possible. Just a few feet away from Bertie, he could see his friend was lying on his back, gazing into the air. George cried in desperation.

"Bertie, you stupid fucker, stop messing about; you will get me killed!"

On arrival at Bertie's sangar, he sidled up to him and shook him, with no response; he shook him again and again. He realised that Bertie was gone, but he didn't want to believe it. George slid under him; with Bertie on top of him, he could see over his shoulder and the hole the bullet had made in the helmet; his best friend had been cruelly taken from him. He lay in this embrace of the dead, for quite some time, as the fighting subsided and the blood ran down onto George. Making no effort to move away from Bertie, he sobbed as he repeated over and over, "You stupid sod, you bloody stupid sod, what I am going to do without you?"

Bertie was a good sort and didn't deserve to die in a scrape hole on the side of a mountain many miles from home. George can't remember where Bertie came from now; he's trying to recall: was it somewhere in the north? It doesn't matter now anyway. They called Bertie an 'old tart' for obvious reasons; George chuckles at the thought and begins to wonder why he is giggling.

"Nothing funny here!"

He turns to tell his oppos he is leaving. They cry back in jest, "Bring us back some vino and a few girls, Georgie, and be quick about it!" They turn away, not even noticing that he has shed most of his uniform and is clothed in just his trousers, shirt and boots. He is stopped by the sergeant a few hundred yards down the line.

"And where the fuck do you think you are going, my old cocker?"

"To fetch some vino and girls for the boys," he replies.

Everyone seems to be in a strange euphoria; the sergeant lets it go and watches George scramble down the mountainside, as he quizzically scratches and shakes his head.

"All sorts," he mutters, "all sorts."

George is on a mission, he wants to get away from the grime, the killing, and the blood. He can't escape the disgust that he feels inside. How many have died? He has lost count. How many has he killed? He has no idea. A loathing deep inside makes him want to throw up; he has no concept of what he is doing or where he is going. It has taken him far less time to get down than it did to get up the mountain: no need for a pack, no need to keep your head down. He crosses a track that also crosses the main road to Rome and scrambles up the rocky path and away into the warmth and protection of another world, continuing on up the path that looks as if goats use it as a thoroughfare.

As he moves further up the mountainside and deeper into untouched scrub, there are droppings from the goats and the warm embracing scent of rosemary. It is as if he has stumbled onto another planet, far from the noise and bustle of an army getting geared up for a clean-up operation, far from the scent of blood to the scent of rosemary and wild marjoram. He stumbles and falls to his knees as if in prayer, but he does not feel like praying. Letting his body slump down, he curls into a foetal position and falls into a fitful sleep, while the warmth of the June sun, gaining its heat, beats down on him. It is mellow and warm, like Chianti that has had time to breathe. That's what he needs now: time to breathe, time to think, and time to be.

As George slept, the heat of the day began its climb; a heat haze shimmered over the hillside like a mirage, as bees and other insects buzzed around the marjoram and rosemary in their summer dance. He slept on, totally unaware of the magical day, away from the horrors of war.

Footnote: General Alexander wanted to bring back the death penalty for deserters, as he was losing too many men this way. He was fortunately overruled. Not that George would have necessarily known this.

Those men who kept fighting through the terrible Italian winter of 1943-44 and into the bloodbath of

Cassino did so because enough factors outweighed the rational, essential survival instinct: they did not want to let down their comrades or their families; they were more frightened of the shame of showing cowardice in front of their group; because it was kill or be killed; because they had to. (Reprinted by kind permission of Matthew Parker)

Chapter 22

Deserting Gustav 1944

A light drizzle had moved across the mountain and surrounding hills. George awoke in the dampness of the oncoming night rain. His eyes becoming more accustomed to the darkening skies, he realised how alone he had become: not just amidst the solitude of the hills, but deep within.

The warmth had gone from the June sun so quickly, and the surrounding hills had lost their glorious iridescent reds and golds; these had been replaced by dark clouds, which were now caressing the hills with gentle rain. There was little sign of war on this side of the hill and, as he took the time to look around him and breathe in the cooling air, unexpected tears rolled down his face until they became a torrent; then a deep animal sobbing racked his body until he could take no more, and a primal scream shook the valley. A flock of birds resting in the olive trees nearby scattered in panic, as if chased by a wild bellowing monster.

What to do, what to do now, thought George. How long before they came looking for him and declared him a deserter? It didn't matter anyhow because George had vowed he wasn't going back to be put into prison or sent to another frontline; they would have to shoot him. The way he was feeling right now, the latter seemed the easiest way out.

Coldness had crept into his bones, making him shudder and shake, like a demented shaman.

His teeth chattered violently as he scurried down another outcrop, tripping and sliding where the recent rain had made the indistinct path slippery. A number of times he had fallen, unsuccessfully grabbing hold of the scrub to save him. There was a faint glow in the distance from a small building; he could make out a shape as he drew nearer. Panting, sliding and grabbing anything that would aid him in the darkness that was overtaking him, outwardly and inwardly, he made his precarious way towards the faint glow.

He entered a small yard unceremoniously, tripping over a metal bucket with a clatter. Some type of animal squawked at this blundering entry and there was a shout from within the small building that he could now see was a shepherd's cottage or what he thought a shepherd's cottage would look like.

"*Chi e la*?" and again "*chi e la*?" [Who is there?] the voice from within the cottage declared.

"*Inglese*," George shouted back, assuming that the person within was enquiring who was stumbling about their yard. "*Inglese*," he repeated reassuringly. "*Il sono un soldato Inglese*!" [I am an English soldier.] He scrambled for the little Italian he had picked up while pushing through Italy.

An old dishevelled-looking individual came from within the cottage. The door squealed as he pushed it open further, holding up a lamp. George could see the man was old and wizened and whiskered. Even in this poor light, George could see the man was terrified, and he searched for some words of comfort or reassurance.

"It's ok, old man, I mean you no harm," he said in English, not knowing how to say this in Italian. He searched for some words that might help.

"*Securo*," [safe] he ventured. It was the best he could think of at the time. George gestured with his hands that he needed some place to sleep and rest. The old man seemed relieved and gestured back for George to follow him into the cottage.

The inside of the cottage was warm and welcoming, though rather dark. The smell of recently cooked food hung in the air. George didn't know what the smell was, but his stomach began to grumble. It had been a long time since he had eaten and he was shaking with hunger and cold. The old man saw this and beckoned him to warm himself by the small fire in a fireplace, which seemed very large for the size of the cottage. He then put his hand to his mouth, making the motion to eat and drink. George nodded and said, "*Grazie*" [thank you]. The old man beamed, and his cracked and wizened face seemed to light up, showing a sparse collection of teeth. Shuffling to the large fireplace, where there was a large pot, he began spooning some of its contents into a rustic-looking bowl.

"*Conlignio e buona*," [Rabbit is good] he said, making ears like a rabbit and grinning even more.

"*Grazie*," George repeated and fell upon the food from the bowl balanced on his lap like he hadn't eaten for weeks. The old man shuffled off again to the rickety-looking table in the far corner and brought George a ceramic pot. Offering it to

George, he said, "*Vino*," then returned to the table to get himself a pot. He sat opposite George, watching him eat and drink. The old man studied George and waited for him to finish his meal. George sighed and leaned back against one of the side pillars of the fireplace.

The old man pointed to his own chest and said "Pietro," and then gestured to George for his name. "George," he said in return.

"Ah," said the old man, "*Si tratta di un buon nome.*" [It is a good name.] He spoke more to himself than to George. Pietro made the gesture for sleep and said, "*sonno,*" [sleep], pointing to the bench with some blankets on it – you couldn't call it a bed. Understanding, George shook his head and pointed to a place in front of the fire. Pietro would have none of it and pointed again to the bed in the corner saying, "*Tu sei mio ospite.*" [You are my guest.]

After much gesturing and argument, George gave in, and Pietro seemed pleased. Looking down at George as if he were his boy, his unusually blue eyes appeared to twinkle a little as George drifted into the abyss.

When the doctor John David left Cassino with the division his sense of relief was overwhelmed by sadness. 'I experienced a wave of acute sorrow,' he wrote. 'So many friends lost or broken, so many with their nerve gone.' (Reprinted by kind permission of Matthew Parker)

The sun streamed through broken shutters. The storm front of the night had passed. George couldn't remember where he was, but he was more comfortable than he had been in a long time. Peering through caked eyelids, he looked around the room and recalled the generosity of Pietro. He had put him to bed like a child. Where was Pietro now? Had he gone to give him up? He heard a thumping outside: it was the sound of chopping and splintering wood. Pietro was preparing wood for the fire. What a simple way of life, George thought: few complications, food on tap, wine – he did not know from where but assumed locally produced – and the comfort of an open fire. A hard life though, he reasoned, as he looked around the one-room cottage: not many home comforts, but then again how much do you need? As a soldier, he knew how to survive on very little. It was amazing what the body could put up with when required.

Pietro came bustling in, moving much faster than the night before, maybe something to do with the warmth of the sunlight on his ancient bones.

"*Mossa, mossa,*" [move, move] Pietro exclaimed, as he entered with arms full of kindling. With the same shepherding movement, he ushered George outside, pointing to the water pump in the yard.

"*Lavaggio,*" [wash] he said, making washing motions with his hands.

Pietro must have been up and about for a while. As George returned from his wash, the fire was alight and the pan on the hotplate in the fireplace was spitting and gurgling with eggs that he must have gathered from the outhouse or from round the yard, as the chickens seemed to be everywhere this morning.

"*Uova*?" [eggs] enquired Pietro, pointing to the pan in his hand.

"*Grazie*," said George, his mouth salivating at the thought of fresh eggs.

Pietro motioned to the table, where two of the rustic-looking plates were set and two equally rustic and unstable chairs stood. He must have brought them in from the outhouse, as George didn't remember seeing them last night. Bits of hay and cobwebs were stuck to parts of the joints in the chairs, so probably a good guess. Pietro motioned to the chair opposite him and said, "*Si prega di prendere un posto a sedere*." [Please take a seat.]

"*Grazie*," said George once again.

The two men ate in silence, tearing off chunks of bread that had been conjured up – from where George had no idea and at this moment he didn't care about anything except the task of eating and drinking the cool fresh water from the jug on the table.

As the men sat back in silence, evaluating each other and enjoying the contentment of eggs for breakfast, the early morning sun and the quiet of the countryside, George considered how he was going to explain to Pietro what he had done. It took some doing, but after half an hour of gesturing, a smattering of Italian and scribbling on pieces of scrap paper with a carpenter's pencil, George finally believed he was getting his story across.

Pietro sat for what seemed an interminable time but was just a minute or so. Then he pushed his chair back with a scraping sound, put his head in his hands and, when the old man looked up, George could see tears forming in his eyes and beginning to roll gently across his sun-leathered skin.

"*Cosa fare per gli uomini tra di loroed,*" [What men do to each other,] he muttered, making tutting sounds and shaking his head. Reaching across and patting George's knee, he looked him in the eye and said, "*Io vi aiuterò tutto quello che posso.*" [I will help you all I can.]

Pietro sat back at the table, reached for a small piece of paper and began to write a note to his younger brother, who lived further into the hills, 12 km away. He wrote as follows:

> *Mio Caro Fratello Aldo, io vi mando questo uomo (George) , che ha sofferto molto da guerra, si prega di prendersi cura di lui , e dargli un letto e cibo per tutto il tempo si è in grado . Credo che è un uomo buono e richiede il nostro aiuto . Tuo fratello amorevole Pietro.*
>
> [My Dear Brother Aldo, I am sending you this man, George, who has suffered greatly from the war. Please take care of him,

give him a bed and food for as long as you are able. I believe he is a good man and requires our help. Your loving brother Pietro.]

Pietro embraced George as he would a family member. George was taken aback at this sign of affection and felt a lump in his throat and stinging behind the eyes. He shook himself back to his situation and pulled himself together as he had been told to do so often in his past.

Pietro had explained to George that he would be safer with his brother, Aldo. Through their gesturing and despite the difficulty with each other's language, he had managed to communicate the facts of where George needed to go and why. In fact, they had become rather good at guessing each other's intentions and meanings. In addition, George had Pietro's crudely drawn map on a piece of card from a carton of some unknown origin. He also had Pietro's letter to his brother securely in his back pocket. George shook Pietro's hand as warmly as his upbringing would afford and set off up the hill away from the sanctuary, security and warmth of this little cottage on the hill. In many ways he was reluctant to leave the embrace of the home and Pietro, whose smoky body odour clung and lingered on George in a comforting and reassuring way. This was the first time in many months that he had felt the warmth, affection and compassion from a living being.

George strode up the rocky hillside purposefully, with a lump of bread and a flask of water wrapped in a cloth. He was determined to make it to Aldo's house in good time. Marching over rough ground was not alien to him and, although his boots had seen better days, they were still in fairly good order.

He walked for a good hour or more before the heat of day made itself felt. Hearing a distant rumbling, he at first thought it might be thunder but then realised that some miles away the battle for Italy and the road to Rome continued.

He sat for a while, sipping the water slowly and cautiously, so as not to spill the smallest droplet. Water was precious; he had always treated it with respect. When you were stuck in a hole half way up a mountain under endless bombardment, you couldn't pop down and get a cupful or stick your head under the tap as he did as a boy.

George's thoughts wandered back to those endless days and nights on the hill below the abbey. He tried his best to shut them out but failed miserably. They came cascading in like the endless tide of mortar and machine-gun fire, peppering his very being with a convulsive sobbing that just would not stop. His recalled, to his horror, the pieces of almost unidentifiable body parts that lay across the rocky tracks and boulders. There was a macabre practice of shaking the blackened hand of some unknown soldier as they passed on their way to the next engagement, as if in some peculiar way this would protect them from what was to come. Was this some means of saying goodbye to this unknown, unfortunate being, although some mumbled, "Lucky beggar," as they passed? The dead man had suffered his fate under an intense barrage some days previously. He was covered in rocks and mud, and no one had the time or the inclination to extract him. Neither the Allies nor the Germans were of a will to linger on the side of the hill to find out if he belonged to them, for fear of being picked off. The lack of any identifying marks laid doubt to his affiliations. When passing the gruesome sight of the remnant of corpses, the men thought that death was perhaps better than what they were suffering, but no one said it out loud, as if they might call a judgement down upon them all.

George and others had picked up snippets of information when they were relieved, and the stories of the 'green' Americans, who joined the strength, were too incredible to be believed. Some of these men, or rather boys, didn't even understand where they were. Their level of literacy and geographical understanding was zero; some even thought they were going to be fighting the Japanese, after what had happened at Pearl Harbour. This did not mean that their strength – and in particular their equipment – was not welcomed by the Allies. None of these boys had seen another country, let alone been in a conflict; this was not to be an easy initiation. Many of these young men were slaughtered without firing their weapons. Some were shell-shocked; they lay in their scrape holes and hid their faces, unable to bring themselves to fire upon the advancing German infantry. The scrapes became their graves, and the wiser and older men sucked in their breath and shook their heads, as nothing else could be done or said. Those that did survive their baptism of fire would soon learn some simple lessons. Keep your head down was the first rule and the second was keep your head down, not even a sneaky peek, as the German snipers were just waiting for the opportunity to take you out; they were extremely accurate marksmen.

George gave a deep sigh at the thought of a night-time patrol by the Gurkhas; they reported back that they could not understand the firmness and at the same time the softness of the track by the river; it wasn't mud. It was not until daylight came creeping up behind them that they understood that they were walking across the corpses of American soldiers, fallen where they had stood, cut down by machine-gun fire from across the river.

George shook himself out of this and tried to think of something else: home perhaps. With all its failings and faults, he wished he was home now, perhaps even at school: innocent days that could never be recaptured.

Chapter 23

Bella Signorina

On George's arrival, the Casa Monticelli offered quite a contrast to Pietro's small shack, which teetered on the side of a hill. To George's eyes, the *casa* was quite magnificent, built of stone, mellowed by the mountain winds and storms that were ever present at this altitude. The path leading to the *casa* was well compacted and had been well maintained. There was a large courtyard full of carts and tackle for harnessing animals to draw the carts. Two short, burly-looking men, who were dusty and sweating, appeared at the large oval-topped doorway to the barn by the side of the house. They glared at George, as he proceeded with caution towards the house. Standing with their hands on their hips and with their shirt sleeves rolled up, they exuded an air of curiosity mixed with wariness.

One of the men, the taller of the two, shouted something to George, who caught neither what he said nor what he might mean, although he guessed he was enquiring to his business there or who he was. George continued at a steady pace towards them, before he tried to answer.

"I have come from Pietro," he stated in English, in the hope that one of them spoke English or understood him. "I have a letter for his brother." He proffered the roughly scribbled note.

By now George had reached the two men. Reaching his arm's length, the taller man took the letter, still without speaking. If he understood what was being said to him, he wasn't letting on. This seemed to George more intimidating than if he had spoken or gestured or made some move to show his intentions. Turning away with just a grunt, the taller man gestured for George to stay where he was. The smaller of the two men sucked on a long extinguished cigarette that was no longer worth the effort: it was soggy and had stained his lips. They were both left standing in the heat of the day, each man sizing up the other: George with his obvious remnants of military uniform and the other man with a collarless shirt, his sleeves rolled, and his dark, hairy chest hair protruding from the 'v' shape that the unbuttoned shirt made. His strong arms were tanned and hairy, the hairs curling and moving slightly in the breeze that had sprung up; it reduced the heat of the day a little.

The taller man returned with another by his side. This man was obviously in charge, as he walked with a certainty that declared his stature: very much as the more experienced officers did, George thought. He wore baggy trousers, a similar shirt to the other men, a waistcoat that hung loosely apart, which was only prevented from being totally open by a chain that swung to and fro as he approached George. Although this man was dressed like the other men, his bearing and attitude spoke volumes; he approached with certainty, strength and assuredness. The man was at least 50, maybe more, with deep furrows around the eyes from working the land and squinting in the sunlight. His eyes were dark and clear and looked George up and down with slow deliberation. At last he spoke.

"You look strong," he stated as a matter of fact. "Are you prepared to work?" George was startled at the clarity of his English. Although he had an accent, there was no hesitation or stumbling to find the right words or sense or grammar, and he made his statement in a forthright manner, looking at George as he waited for a reply. "Well?" he prompted when there wasn't an immediate response.

The combination of the hot day and the dryness of his mouth, together with the fact that he was taken by surprise by the man's forthrightness, meant that George was the one to stumble a reply.

"Of course," he said, "whatever you need. I can dig, carry or whatever." Realising that neither man had introduced himself, George decided to take the initiative. "I am George," he stated, offering his hand. The man immediately responded.

"Apologies, my manners, we do not get many visitors up here. I am Aldo Luigi Monticelli, the owner and operator of this vineyard and farmland. My brother, Pietro, has written to me, asking me to take you in. We ask nothing of you, except that you help out around the farm and vineyard. We are a closely knit group here, and the men that already work here are loyal and discreet; you will be safe from all here."

"Thank you," said George. "I appreciate your help very much; your brother was also very kind and generous to me. I would like you to thank him for me, as I am not sure I was able to make myself understood."

"I will," said Aldo. "But you underestimate his level of understanding; he understood you much more than you realise," he said with a glint in his eyes of something more to be discovered.

Without further discussion, he gestured to the tall man, who had stood slightly behind him, and said, "Giovanni will take you to where you will sleep, and he will show you the way things are done here over the next couple of days." George thanked Aldo once again and then followed Giovanni towards the barn.

The barn was still half full of hay. Pointing to the rack at the far side of the barn, Giovanni said in broken English, "Tools are here and here." Then, indicating the back of the barn, he said, "A place to sleep out here." Again, he pointed, this time to a small side door to the barn, which he walked towards. Outside the barn was a small building made of wood, which Giovanni opened and gestured for George to enter. Inside were two rows of bunk beds. Patting one of the lower beds, Giovanni said, "Sleep here," gesturing with his hands to endorse the statement, which was totally unnecessary. Then Giovanni turned on his heels and pointed out of one of the windows, stating, "Wash here." Outside there was a water pump and a trough. George thanked Giovanni, who was about to leave when it occurred to him that he hadn't told George about the eating arrangements. Giovanni did not know the English for eating or meal times, so he gestured the eating motion and said "Six o'clock, not here, over there," pointing to the back of the house. George nodded that he understood and, for the first time, Giovanni smiled and nodded back. His smile revealed the lack of a number of teeth, and those he had were not in the best condition, unlike George, who was fastidious about dental care and keeping himself clean. It was something the army drilled into you like everything else: an unclean soldier was likely to contract more than he wished for.

"Your teeth and your feet are your prize possessions," his sergeant used to say. "Without them, you are no fucking good to anyone, so keep them clean and cared for or you miserable beggars will be even more miserable."

George decided he would have a wash down in the yard and then go for a wander around some of the property to get his bearings. The yard where the sleeping quarters were situated was tucked away and in a small garden area of its own. He wondered at how well everything was maintained, that even the working quarters had herbs growing outside and slatted benches to take in the day. He assumed, come harvest time, the lodgings were full of migrant workers and alive with the sounds of cheerful voices, maybe even singing and dancing. This was an oasis, and he was going to lap up every moment he could. Who knew what the future held or what might be awaiting him around the next bend?

Feeling refreshed from his wash down, he began his walk around the property. His stomach was protesting; he couldn't remember when he last ate, but he knew that food was available a little later, so he put the hunger pangs aside and strolled through the back of the property towards the vineyard. The sun was hot on his back, although time had passed and he could tell from its strength that it was losing some of its power, but for a fair-haired, hazel-eyed Englishman it was still quite hot. Not as hot as those summers in India, but, after the long drawn-out winter in Cassino, it was welcome warmth. He soaked it up until it reached his very core. He wondered what was happening about his disappearance, had they even noticed he was missing yet? He couldn't recall how long he had been gone; he guessed it was days, not that he cared, he was just curious, that was all.

He had reached the vines and could see the grapes forming in tiny bunches. They were quite green, and he wondered if they would change colour. They were far from ready and had several months of growth and absorption of the warm Italian sun before they were bursting to be harvested. George ran his hand over the leaves; like the grapes, they were dusty from the dry stone-filled paths between them. The wind had whipped between the vines and given them an icing-sugar coating of dust.

Sitting between the vines, George listened to the birds singing and the sound of distant voices from the farm. The sun was still warm enough among the vines to lie down, and George did just that. The ground was a little rocky, the stones pressed into his bony parts, but he wriggled them aside and settled, with his hands behind his head.

He dozed for a little while, but was woken with a start to the sound of running feet, pounding down the vineyard. Jumping to his feet, all he could see was a flash of blue-black hair tearing down the track; he guessed there was someone in hot pursuit; giggling and shouting wafted in the cooling evening air. He could not ascertain who this could be; for one thing, he couldn't see the perpetrators, nor would he know them if he did. The sounds had died to a faint babble in the distance; he took this as his cue to go back to the house, where Giovanni said there would be food. He was now ravenous.

George made his way back to the house through the vineyard; although he hadn't realised it, he had traversed a gentle slope in his wanderings and the walk back gave him a clear view to the back of the house. He could see a long table, laid up with produce. There were people he hadn't seen before gathered around the table; a woman was bringing out a large terracotta dish, which was obviously hot as she was shielding her hands with a chequered cloth. As he drew closer, the gathering turned towards him, and the woman with the dish looked up and smiled at him. She had a broad smile and a welcoming manner; she reminded him of his mother, in the way she bore herself rather than her build, as this woman's figure was ample, rather than the slim build of his mother. This woman had long, dark hair, tied back from her face, and, as George grew closer, he could see small wisps of grey, that her face was tanned and creased at the eyes from many sun-filled days and, despite the war, many happiness lines.

Aldo gestured for George to come forward and meet the rest of the gathering.

"George, this is Francis, Vincenzo, and Giovanni you have met. These are my trusted workers; I have others that help me out when we are busy, and the local men from round about come at harvest time."

Each of the men nodded their heads in turn, as their names were mentioned; they were fairly non-committal, George thought, greeting him neither with enthusiasm nor otherwise, but he expected nothing else. Men were the same the world over, and a new fusilier joining a contingent was also viewed with suspicion until he proved himself to be worthy of their trust. These men were so obviously field workers; one was Vincenzo, whom he had met on arrival. George could not tell how tall they both were, although he knew Vincenzo's height and gauged Francis to be of similar stature; they were not the tallest of men, very much like many of the men in these hillsides and mountains, except for Giovanni, who was tall and slender. They were both broad across the chest and had dark curly hair; their arms obviously belonged to men, who were used to working in the fields, as they were well-tanned and muscled. The dark hair protruded from their pristine white shirts. They were almost like twins, except that Francis had larger teeth, which stuck out slightly. They were both handsome young men, and George wondered if they had served in the Italian army; he couldn't tell if they were quite old enough to do so.

"This is my wife, Marie," said Aldo, directing his attention to the rest of the table. "And these are my sons, Antonio and Fazio, and of course my beautiful daughter, Margaretta." The two boys were very much in the image of their father.

They all nodded and lifted a glass as they were introduced. George was captivated by the daughter's dark looks; hers must have been the flash of blue-black hair in the vineyard. The boys – or young men – were both well-built and sturdy, as far as George could tell – in their teens, he surmised. The girl – or again, young woman, he had no idea – was very womanly, but that could mean any age, he appreciated. After all, George hadn't much experience with women, and none as beautiful as this one. She was quite startling; her dark hair was like her mother's, but her complexion was a colour that he could not describe, as it glistened in the lights from the house as if covered with some iridescent potion; her dark eyes twinkled with amusement, and her manner was captivating, as she passed food across the table to those who asked. At least, she was captivating George. His eyes ran across her as if he wished to remember this point in time forever; so much beauty in one person should not be allowed, he thought.

Aldo was saying something, but George was in another world. The table began to titter and he became aware that he was staring at Margaretta. How long he had been standing there, he had no idea, but he felt himself flush with embarrassment.

Realisation that Aldo was asking him to be seated dawned on him and he took his place as quickly as he could, so that he would draw no further attention to himself.

The food laid out in front of the hungry ensemble was glorious in George's book; he hadn't seen such a spread since leaving India. It was not what he was used to eating from ration packs; that was for sure. There were olives, fresh fruit and vegetables, mounds of bread and…what had Maria conjured up in her magic terracotta pot? It turned out to be the inevitable rabbit stew, obviously a family tradition, and George managed two helpings before he leaned back in his chair and begged not to be given anything more. His appetite was not what it used to be, after being on restricted rations. The gathering fell into familiar, friendly conversation, and George became an observer. Mainly of Margaretta, who he found it hard not to look at, but when she caught his eye, he felt embarrassed for staring. She smiled at him on one of the occasions he hadn't looked away quite quickly enough, and he felt the heat rise until he was sure he must be bright red. She chuckled at his discomfort and wiped her mouth in a way that was teasing and provocative. George became totally absorbed in her beauty; his spine tingled at the thought of being close to her and touching those beautifully formed lips with his.

The men were rising from their chairs and thanking Marie for the meal. George wondered if this were a regular event or something put on especially for him. Giovanni signalled to George to follow with, "Much work tomorrow." George understood, thanked Maria and Aldo for their hospitality, trying very hard not to look at anyone in particular, wished them good night, and followed Giovanni and the other men.

Although the three men had put a hard day's work into the vines, they felt it was too early to go to bed. The night was warm with the buzzing of cicadas in the shrubs and trees that surrounded the bunk house. They were also curious about their new workmate-cum-guest of Aldo's. They signalled to George to join them on the bench; they had a bottle close by and offered George a drink. He was in no need of alcohol, but, at the same time, as a guest, he did not wish to offend and so joined the three men, who sat relaxed and smoking their roll-ups. The conversation, such as it was due to the language barrier, centred on George's experience; he indicated and spoke the little Italian he had picked up along the way. Gesturing as he had done with Pietro, they were able to communicate enough to gain the sense of the horror that George had seen. They explained a little more about the workings of the vineyard, that later in the year they would have perhaps 20 workers here at harvest time. Some would be paid casual labourers that they had used in the past; the rest would be from local farms. In turn, Aldo would lend a hand with his neighbours' harvesting, although this year the Germans had either taken all they had or burnt the ground so that the Allies would have nothing to utilise.

The men nodded knowingly and sat in silence for a while, as they drew the last bit of life out of their roll-ups. The wine was having an effect on George, and he said that he should head to bed, as Aldo had prompted that there was plenty of work to do tomorrow. Giovanni commented that Aldo always said that; it was always true as well, there was more work tomorrow. The men laughed as if they had uncovered some huge joke and George smiled at the good nature of these men towards him.

Francis posed a question of George; he was indicating the shape of a woman, but George did not quite understand the significance of this until Francis play-acted by standing up and staring and then pronouncing the name "Margaretta". George realised that they were all pulling his leg and his poor attempt at hiding the effect that Margaretta had upon him. They were obviously all making ribald remarks amongst themselves; George didn't understand what they were saying, but he guessed at the type of comments they were making. This was not any different from being with men in the army, except for a much more relaxed nature of the joking and of course the surroundings. George made no reply; instead, saying that he must get some sleep, he left the men laughing and chatting among themselves.

George didn't hear the men come to bed; once his head hit the pillow on the bunk, sleep overtook him in seconds. The bunkhouse smelled of treated wood, and the warmth of the day still lingered inside, but he was too tired to care. He fell asleep with the chatter and laughter of men, the lingering smell of their smoking, the cicadas' continual buzz, and a slight perspiration forming on his upper lip. He was somewhere comforting and womb-like and he slept like he had not slept for a long time

Chapter 24

The Vineyard

George woke to the sound of the men in the yard chatting away at a rate of knots. He wondered what on earth they could be discussing with such fervour. He rose, dressed and made his way out into the yard, where he washed down and made ready for the day ahead. The men had all turned towards George as he exited the bunkhouse; they were grinning at him, seemingly unaffected by the night's drinking – they were very obviously used to it. George's head was buzzing a little, due either to the sudden awakening or the amount of wine that the men had managed to squeeze down him last night, probably the latter. Giovanni was the first to speak, wished George a good morning and added, "We eat now". George nodded in affirmation, following the men to the back of the house, where bread, cheese and salami were already laid out, together with a large pitcher of water. The men consumed their food in no time and George was taken aback by their speed; they were already moving back to the barn to get the tools for the day's work. Not to be left behind, George grabbed a lump of bread and followed while still eating. No messing about with this lot, he thought to himself, they're straight in there.

The men set off with their tools towards the vineyard; in their canvas bags were cutters and trimmers, together with twine. Giovanni explained that they were trimming and tying back the shoots that were blooming and removing what George had established were suckers. Giovanni waved impatiently at George and said that he would explain once they were in the vineyard. George hoped his demonstration would prove to be better than his explanation.

Although the buds were turning to fruits, this depended very much on where the vines were situated in the vineyard; some of the slopes proved to be little heat generators and so therefore their fruits bloomed earlier. Giovanni explained that if they had a sudden cold spell or frost the buds could be ruined so it was not always advantageous to have early-blooming vines. He went on to tell him that frosts arriving at the wrong time were detrimental to the future good harvest; at one time during a sudden cold spell, they had had to light fires between the vines to keep them from freezing. His demonstration of the trimming and the removal of suckers that followed was quite simple, and George quickly got the hang of it.

Giovanni watched George for a while until he saw that he was working at a reasonable speed but, more importantly, cutting and tying accurately. He then pointed to where he would be working and left George to his own devices. The work was repetitive, but being out in the warm June sun was perfect, although George was getting hotter as the morning sun progressed, increasing its heat, and he had no concept of the time he had been out in the vines.

Becoming aware of someone watching him work, he turned to find Margaretta smiling at him.

"You seem to have mastered the technique very quickly," she said. Her voice was gentle and joyful like a musical instrument and what she had to say sounded friendly and warm.

George was in her shade and had to squint to see her fully. He stood and smiled back and, a little more assuredly than he felt, said, "Why thank you, *Signorina*; that is most kind of you."

Not to be outdone, Margaretta chuckled and did a mocking curtsy. She then offered George a straw hat with a broad brim saying, "My father's old one; he thought that you might need this as the days get very hot here; this is also a large cloth that you should put around your neck as I can see that you are beginning to burn." George obediently tied the cloth, which to his mind was a large handkerchief, around his neck; Margaretta was right: he could feel the sensation of burning as the cloth touched his skin. The hat was welcome too as he didn't have to squint as much, which had made his eyes and face ache. George returned the compliment and did a gracious bow; then, swirling the straw hat in front of him as he returned to the upright position, he said, "Many thanks, *Signorina*; you are extremely thoughtful."

"It was not I," she re-joined, "but my father."

"Then thank Aldo for me," shouted George as Margaretta made her move to go back to her day.

"I have left you some more water under the vine, and if you come to me after you have washed this evening, I will put something on your red neck."

"Thanks again," said George, but Margaretta was too far away by now to hear, as she skipped her way back toward the house. Did she ever walk anywhere? he wondered to himself.

For the rest of the day George and the men worked on the vines with only a short break, a cigarette, some bread, cheese and salami to keep them going. George persevered with his work; it had become automatic by now. The heat of the day was getting to him, but he was not going to show it. That was the problem of being fair-skinned; these guys were like toughened old leather and they moved at a set pace that was neither slow nor fast, but just right. George's thoughts were not on the men or the work but on the thought of seeing Margaretta again this evening; this distracted him from the discomfort of working in the heat of the day. What happened to siesta? George thought as he worked on.

The evening drew near and the day began to cool a little, which was a relief to George, who was happy to work on in the coolness. Giovanni called to him and signalled for him to join him and the rest of the men as they made their way back to the barn. Each man set about the task of putting their tools away and cleaning them as they did so. George was keen to get to the water pump and wash down, as the perspiration of the day had made him feel quite grubby. Once clean, he changed into a clean shirt that Aldo had loaned him; now he felt more than ready to eat and drink.

The table was laid just as the evening before, and George wondered what was on offer for dinner that evening. Before he made it to the table, Margaretta appeared and called him to come to her. With his heart skipping a beat, he felt a quickening in his pulse as he approached her.

"Sit down here," said Margaretta, pointing to a wooden and gnarled stump. George obediently sat down. "Well, take off your shirt so that I can put this cream or your soreness," said Margaretta in a matter-of-fact tone. George again obeyed without comment. Margaretta applied the creamy lotion first to his neck and the top of his back. George found her touch gentle and soothing, although his neck was quite sore. She then got him to hold out his arms in front of him, as his lower arms had caught the sun too. This brought them into the position of facing each other; they looked at each other as Margaretta applied the lotion. This was the moment they both realised that there was something stirring between them, and Margaretta continued to apply the lotion to George's arms long after it was necessary. To break the tension George spoke.

"How is it that you and your father speak such good English?"

"Why thank you kind sir, that is very gracious of you," replied Margaretta.

"Well actually, now you sound like you are trying too hard, and there is quite a pronounced Italian accent in there somewhere," joked George.

Margaretta huffed and flicked George with the towel she had at her side to wipe her hands. "Do you want me to tell you, or are you going to joke with me all night?"

"Carry on then," said George, after the rebuff and Margaretta continued.

"My father has many cousins in America, and he spent some time working over there. He was probably there for about two years when he was young; he will still do an American accent if you ask him or when he has had too much wine. He enjoyed being in America and loved the fact that he had learnt English and, when I came along, I pestered him until he taught me. Simple eh?"

"Thank you for your simple explanation," George replied. "I can't say that I can detect any American accent, but perhaps that might be masked by a slight Italian one."

"Slight is it, I listen to the BBC and I believe I could have been a newsreader for them, so there!" retorted Margaretta, with a very upper class type voice. Laughing together, they made their way to dinner.

Both of them ate their meals, trying not to look at each other, trying not to give anything away to each other or the family. Aldo spoke to George about his day, and he replied that he felt the work was well within his capabilities and that army life had certainly ensured his stamina. Aldo pointed out the need to work through the day at this time of year. As it would become hotter as they approached July and onwards, all the vines needed tying off and cutting back in good time. George replied that he was pleased to be of help, especially in the light of their generosity and kindness to him. Expressing interest in the vines, he asked about the type of grape varieties that were growing on the slopes, compared to others that were lower down. Aldo was pleased at George's enquiry; he began by explaining that some of what he was to tell him was a family secret. There were three types of red grape variety, Cabernet Franc, Merlot and Vermentino, which, to his mind, was neither red nor white; he said that not many novices would have noticed the difference at this stage of growth. He went on to explain that he had red wines, white wines and the secret mix of wines; if mixed in the correct proportions, they brought a most unique wine that he kept mainly for family and friends. The Vermentino grape on its own was light and refreshing and could either be chilled or served at room temperature. When mixed with the reds, it became like dark berries with chocolate, liquorice and coffee in the background. Most of the local vineyards grew a grape variety called Sangiovesi and, although he had some slopes in his vineyard planted with this variety, he used it only to boost others or to make a vintage with Merlot. Nearer the time, Aldo promised to tell George more, but at the moment he needed to get to bed as another day would bring much more work.

The men seemed much more relaxed around the table tonight and pleased to have George's help. Giovanni observed that he looked a bit like a lobster, as his fair skin had turned quite red, and the others laughed and imitated the movement of a lobster walking, although George thought they looked more like apes in their impressions. Nevertheless, it was a light-hearted evening, and all drifted off early, ready for another day's work tomorrow.

The work of the vineyard continued to its normal rota and routine. Margaretta could be seen cutting, pruning and shaping the vines to give maximum light to the forming fruits. By cutting the vines in this way, more energy was also diverted to the fruit rather than to the growth of greenery. It was Margaretta's intention to work as closely as possible to George. She was intrigued by this deserting soldier; he didn't seem to be the fearful type and she wished to learn more of him and about him. At every opportunity she had to be near to him, she would manipulate the situation; she tried to be subtle, but this was not one of Margaretta's strong points. This was not going unnoticed by the other workers, and they raised their eyebrows and smiled at the obvious manoeuvrings of this young woman. This would not be the first time that Margaretta had set her sights on someone, who had become prey in her hunt. The workers talked amongst themselves and speculated on how long George would take to come under Margaretta's spell – that is if he wasn't already under it –she was able to manipulate most people, men in particular.

Maria called across the vines for Margaretta to come and help her pick up supplies from the local town. Margaretta was reluctant to leave her campaign of seeking out George, but at the same time she would have the opportunity to look around town and meet up with some of her friends. The trip into town was not a long drive, but the day was heating up and the fields and roads were dusty and extremely dry; the motion of the truck threw dust in the air and in through the open windows. It was a choice of suffocating inside the truck or eating dust for a while. One of the new workers was the driver today; he seemed quite pleasant, Margaretta thought, but of farming stock. He was a typical swarthy Italian, with short legs and strong back and, when he turned to talk, she noticed the broken tobacco-stained teeth. His name was Angelo and his family was still working on the hill farm not too far from the vineyard, but the Germans had ravaged the land, removed all his goats and taken what little corn he could grow. He was working for Aldo to supplement his income, until such time as the farm was able to produce enough food to sustain him and his ever-growing family of eight.

Margaretta and Maria talked as mother and daughter do; they discussed the decorating of the house, the finding of some fabric for bed coverings and for dresses. They also discussed the provisions that they required, although the vineyard was quite self-sufficient with its vegetable garden, cheese and winemaking. As well as working in the vines and around the house with her mother, Margaretta was in charge of the vegetable garden.

Margaretta asked her mother what she thought of the deserter George. She replied that she thought that he was a very personable young man, who seemed to work hard and get on well with the men.

"What else do you know about him?" asked Margaretta.

"Only what your father told me: that he first came to your uncle Pietro, who thought that he would be safer with us and that he had been traumatised by the fighting," replied Maria. "Are you taken with him, Margaretta?"

"Why no, I was just curious and wondered if he might bring us trouble, as he is a deserter." She said this only to divert her mother from the feelings that, to her surprise, were blossoming within her.

"Your father has thought of this too. He believes that we should help him; he may return to his unit eventually, but at the moment your father believes he needs time to gather himself in a peaceful setting." Margaretta seemed satisfied with this explanation and began wondering more about George, to the point of fantasy.

On arriving in the town, they immediately saw Angelina, one of Margaretta's old school friends. Leaning out of the truck window, waving frantically, Margaretta shouted to Angelina, "Are you alone or are the others in town too?"

Angelina approached the truck as soon as it stopped.

"Hello, Margaretta, are you going to be in town for long? I'm meeting with Paula and Francesca; apparently they have real coffee in the bar, the Americans have exchanged it for wine and Phillipe is pleased that, in his mind, he has got the better of the deal." Angelina paused. "Oh sorry, *Senora*, good morning. I did not see you there."

"Don't worry, Angelina. Why don't you girls go off together, and drink some coffee? I will meet you back at the truck, Margaretta, in about an hour."

"Thanks, Mamma," replied Margaretta. The two girls went off together arm in arm to meet up with their friends. Maria turned to the driver and said,

"It looks like it is you and me, Angelo. How are you at picking fabrics? That is, of course, if they have much choice at *Senora* Rossi's." Angelo looked horrified at the thought; his mouth dropped open, but Maria put him out of his misery, saying,

"It's alright, Angelo, I was only joking."

The bar was packed with prospective buyers of the coffee; smoke also filled the air – cigar smoke – someone had liberated cigars from the Americans too. Although smoky and loud, with everyone talking at once and clamouring to taste the real American coffee, the atmosphere was also good humoured. The laughter and joking from the men subsided, as the four young women walked into the bar; suddenly there was a hush where there had been raucous banter and laughter. Phillipe approached the young women from behind his bar and suggested that they sit outside, as it was a pleasant day under the vine that covered the *al fresco* dining area. He looked back at the men as he ushered the women to a large round table; flicking at the leaves that had fallen onto it, he enquired what they would like. The girls all said together that they would like coffee, giggling at the way they had all spoken as an ensemble. Phillipe held his head to one side, about to say it was not possible as the men had claimed the coffee for their own.

Margaretta sensed his hesitation and suggested that he might think again; she added that perhaps her father might reconsider supplying him with his best wine. Knowing that he was entering an argument that he could not win, Phillipe bowed out, saying he would see what he could do. Margaretta's friends quietly applauded her and then burst into laughter, talking over each other at the same time.

Angelina asked them all to be quiet as she had an important question for Margaretta. They all stopped and looked at Angelina in anticipation.

"I have heard that you have a new worker on the estate, and that he is English and rather handsome."

"How do you know that?" asked Margaretta, immediately realising that it was a stupid question: the workers all talked to each other and it was difficult to keep any secrets. Angelina just laughed and touched the side of her nose in a knowing fashion.

"I have my sources."

The group all laughed once more, bidding to question Margaretta further. Fortunately, Phillipe arrived with the coffee and laid it in front of them. They remained totally quiet while this was done, even though they were bursting to ask more questions of Margaretta and her mysterious Englishman. With this brief interlude, Margaretta was able to gather her thoughts; she began by explaining that he was a deserter, swearing them all to secrecy as her father would possibly get into trouble with the English army if they knew he was sheltering him.

“Never mind about that,” chimed in Paula. “What’s he like?”

“Yes, tell us more,” piped in the other two. “No holding back.” Drawing in a deep breath, Margaretta knew that she could not escape this interrogation and began.

“He is very handsome, he has fair hair and skin and he burns very easily in the sun, so much so that I had to put cream on him after working in the fields.”

“You did what?” exclaimed Francesca. “Where did you put this cream on him?” she continued, making a face at Margaretta, suggesting that more had occurred.

“Oh do be quiet, Fran. Do you want me to tell you this story or not?” Margaretta exclaimed in an annoyed tone. “I will continue. He has suffered a lot, my father said, and we need to take care of him until he has found his feet. He has the most wonderful hazel eyes that seem to look straight through you; he is slim, muscular and has a very kind way about him. I too believe that we should look after him until he has decided what it’s best to do. He may return to his unit, my mother told me this morning, so we should look at this as if he is on working leave.”

Angelina responded immediately in a teasing tone, “I believe that Margaretta has a soft spot for this Englishman, don’t you, girls?” They all whooped with laughter, and more teasing continued. When they all noticed that Margaretta was flushed with embarrassment, this caused even more teasing, knowing looks and wagging of fingers – all in good humour, of course.

The ride back to the vineyard was quiet, and Maria prompted Margaretta with questions about the girls and what they had got up to, but Margaretta was thinking about George and realising that what her friends had said in jest was probably true. She did have a soft spot for George; what she did next was the important thing – after all, he may not feel the same way. Although the way that he had looked at her that first night reassured her, she needed to talk with him. Her mind drifted to the time she touched him with the cream; his skin had been hot and the cream was there to cool the ravages of the sun. He had given little grunts of pleasure as she creamed his shoulders and arms; the feel of him under her hands had stirred something within her. This was unusual for Margaretta, as the boys and men around her did nothing for her. True, she had petted with some, but the feelings they stirred were carnal; the feeling that emanated from George was deeper; the carnal side was definitely there, but something else drew her to him.

As the weeks passed, the vineyard grew prolifically under the warm summer sun. There was hardly any rain at this time of the year, but somehow the grapes survived, not only survived but grew to bursting, their roots finding access to moisture and nutrients and their foliage, the gift of sunshine. The feelings of Margaretta and George had grown too; they had met quietly and, they hoped, privately. Margaretta was enthralled by the stories of lands he had visited during the war, the stories of the bravery of comrades and the terrible cost of life to bring freedom to those oppressed. Their closeness grew more intense. They exchanged a kiss now and then when no one was around, and they would brush past each other deliberately, making it look accidental, so that they could touch without anyone being aware. The fear of being found out was their concern, so they scurried about in secret until they could barely stand it any longer.

On a clear warm and star-filled evening, when the meal was prepared and the couple bumped into each other 'accidentally' on their way to dinner, they smiled at each other and

George went to speak, but Margaretta put her finger to her lips. She spoke in a voice pitched low and inviting in a husky tone.

"Will you meet me in the barn after dinner, when everyone has cleared away?" Margaretta enquired. George was about to speak when Margaretta held her finger to her lips again. George just nodded, somewhat taken aback. Marie saved the day as she called across to them both to come along as the meal was ready.

After dinner that night, George hung back until the men were out of sight and he was sure that he was not seen by anyone. Making his way to the barn, he sat on one of the hay bales and stuck a straw out of the corner of his mouth, trying to appear relaxed. He waited for ten minutes or more before Margaretta appeared in the open doorway, which she closed as quietly as possible behind her. Making her way over to George, she was wearing a thin cotton dress with a pattern of a cornfield in blues and yellows. Her dark hair hung loosely over her shoulders and her skin was a golden tan. Her eyes sparkled as she approached George, her lips turning into a nervous smile. It was the first time that George had seen her not totally in control. She spoke to George in a hesitant way and also seemed a little embarrassed. Again, it was the first time George had seen this in her.

"I expect you were surprised that I asked you to meet so suddenly and so soon after meeting?" George smiled at her and said that he had wanted to speak more with her but did not know how to begin; he also pointed out that he was older than her and a privileged guest here. He admitted too that he had been thinking about her ever since they had first seen each other. Margaretta blushed but replied quite assuredly.

"I may be younger, but I don't believe that matters. I am quite mature for my years and I find something about you that makes me want to be with you. I believe that the fact you came here was down to fate. Do you believe in fate, George?"

This was the first time she had used his name; he smiled and said, "Yes, I do, Margaretta, although the compatriots I have left behind me probably do not. They probably believe more in the devil and the evil of men."

With this, Margaretta put a hand on George's shoulder, reached across to him and kissed him on the cheek. They looked at each other for quite some moments; time did not seem to matter, and they gazed and smiled at each other before moving closer together. George drew Margaretta towards him, her warm body pressed against his thighs and her breasts against his chest. They kissed a few times lightly on the lips, then their passion grew and they kissed more deeply. George couldn't believe the feelings that were unleashed inside him; he drew Margaretta to him onto the straw bales, and they each pulled themselves towards each other, more firmly and with immense passion, feeling each other's body with frantic fervour. Margaretta's hands pulled at his shirt, and buttons flew somewhere across the barn. She was like a wild animal; he could feel her claws in his back as they raked his skin. In the next moment his light cotton trousers fell to the ground. With one swift movement, Margaretta removed her dress and he took in a deep breath as the beauty of her olive skin was revealed in totality down to the warm and inviting 'v' where she lightly placed her hand. The roundness and pertness of her breasts seemed to rise skywards; her nipples were dark and looked back at him; she chuckled at the obvious look of lustfulness on his face. She said in that musical and velvety Italian accent, "So you really want me?" And she added, looking down at him, "You look very erect, *Signor* Soldier." He didn't answer but moved towards her once again. Stroking and caressing her body, the electricity that was felt between them made them both shudder. He held back for a moment and looked at her once again.

"Just don't stop," she said breathlessly. With that, he entered her slowly, while holding her gaze so that he could see her expression of pleasure.

The couple had fallen asleep, but there was a need to move. Sitting up suddenly, they became aware that daylight was beckoning everyone back to work and the barn would soon be full of workmen gathering their tools for the day ahead. Margaretta brushed herself down, slipped on her dress and shoes and disappeared as if by magic through the side door and away, with barely a sound. George was less adept. While trying to pull on his trousers, he managed to fall off the bale; he scrabbled up his shirt and began putting it on, realising and remembering that there were few buttons left to fasten it. He was a little overawed by Margaretta and her passionate nature and was not sure how he should act; was this normal behaviour for her? They had not discussed how to behave with each other when around others or whether this was just a one-off, but exciting, interlude. He would just have to wait and see and follow her lead.

Chapter 25

Great Grandfather's Clock

George eventually pulled himself together and made it back to the bunk house unseen. He began his daily routine of washing and preparation for the day, but he felt jaded and elated at the same time. He hoped he could carry this off for Margaretta's sake. Gradually, the other men arrived at the water pump, chatting and laughing at the start of what looked like another fine day. They were all looking forward to their breakfast and they slapped George on the back, asking him if he was well, hungry, and ready for another day as they made their way to breakfast; they obviously hadn't missed him in the bunkhouse. Margaretta was buzzing, dancing around the table as if she were on loaded springs; she looked as fresh as dew on a newly cut lawn – how could this be, he thought. She caught his eye just once, the contact was held and lingered for a few more seconds than were necessary, but in those seconds the feeling of warmth crossed the distance between them.

After breakfast, all the men moved toward the vineyard. Was it only George that was captivated by the melody of the day, the bird song, the distant woodpecker swooping and calling amongst the vines, the sun making its daily climb from behind the hilltops? Were they all oblivious to the glorious day or were they so used to being in such beautiful surroundings that it became their daily wallpaper? To George, it was a Garden of Eden and he believed he had found his Eve.

The day was shattered by expletives exploding from behind them, coming from the house. It was Aldo, and he was furious. George's jaw dropped, and he was more than a little concerned that the rage was because of him. Had Aldo found out about their meeting in the barn? Where was Margaretta, had she confessed, or what? The men had all turned to see Aldo red-faced and stamping his feet like a spoilt child. Marie and Margaretta were trying to placate him; the ferocity of invective made the men feel they should hasten to the vineyard, keeping out of Aldo's way today. Whatever the cause of the outburst, they thought retreat was the best course of action: all except George, who peeled away from the rest of the group and headed back to see what the issue was.

Margaretta was surprised to see George back at the house, and Aldo was in no mood to talk. George enquired what the cause of Aldo's rage was; Margaretta explained that one of the cleaners had moved his prize possession, an ancient pendulum clock, which had been in his family for years, passed down from member to member, but which was now languishing on its side, as it had toppled in the move. Margaretta continued with the explanation about the clock and, on hearing what the cause of Aldo's rage was, George was immediately relieved. He whispered to her.

"I thought for a moment that he had found out about last night." Margaretta smiled at him and replied.

"So you came to my rescue, how gallant." With that, she danced back into the house without a care.

George asked if he could help, but Marie intervened and said that it was best he went with the other men to the vineyard. George persisted, saying he might be able to help. This seemed to break through Aldo's spell of rage and he asked, "Do you know anything about pendulum clocks?"

George replied that he had been fixing clockwork machinery since he was a small boy; there was very little he couldn't repair. Aldo's mood lightened a little at this; he explained that he had told the cleaners not to move this clock and to dust lightly only. Now he feared that it was broken completely. George insisted that anything could be repaired with the right skills and a little bit of patience. Aldo smiled at George saying, "Do you really think so?"

"The first thing is to lift off the pendulum and then get this back into an upright position," said George. "The strain on the mechanism is tremendous with a clock this size; the sooner we get it back upright, the sooner I can examine it." George opened the panelled door, removed the pendulum, which was beautifully engraved, having silver inserts with a coat of arms, and put this gently to one side. Then, with Aldo helping him, he gently tipped the clock back into its correct position. George then peered inside the clock and looked over the mechanism, speaking with his head inside the clock case, which gave his voice a distant sound, but with a dull booming resonance, which made his voice indistinct. Aldo was waiting for George's assessment when he reappeared.

"Well?" he said.

"The clock mechanism is twisted, which is to be expected, but I can sort that. I can see nothing else at this stage, other than it just needs a good clean. If there are any other issues, I am sure I will be able to deal with them as required."

"You are sure?" said Aldo. "It will work again?" George smiled, nodding at Aldo. Then the older man took him by both arms, patted them and said something in Italian, which he didn't explain, but George got the gist.

George said that he had better get back to work, but Aldo asked, "What about the clock?"

"Don't worry," George said. "I'll be back later and work on it for you; we'll have it better than before." Marie said it would be best to let George get back to work, otherwise the men would believe George was skiving; Aldo just huffed, while George made his escape and waved a cheery, but relieved goodbye.

He was glad that he was able to help Aldo but even more pleased that he hadn't been found out, which brought him to the thought that something would need to be said or done. He would have to discuss this with Margaretta. After all, George didn't want Aldo and Marie to find out through the gossip in the yard; they had been too good to him to allow that to happen, but he did wonder what their reaction would be.

George and Margaretta continued to meet in the barn after dinner each night, but they both realised that to continue in this way might be a road fraught with disaster. They agreed they would talk to Marie and Aldo at the earliest opportunity, but neither of them could decide when that might be.

The clock had been stripped down and was lying in, what seemed to the untrained eye, a worse state than it was before. George was busily working on the clock one evening, gradually reassembling it, when, as casually as Margaretta could make it look, she came by and feigned interest in its progress, gently stroking the back of his neck. George tried to ignore this, continuing the reassembly as if nothing had occurred, but Margaretta was, if nothing, a persistent young woman. As she stroked George, she made little clucking sounds and teasing kissing noises. Unbeknown to them both, Marie was witness to the interchange between them, noticing in particular when George blurted out, "Margaretta, not here, and not now!"

Margaretta just laughed and skipped away, saying as she did so, "Maybe there won't be a later tonight!" George shook his head, continuing with the work in hand, and the appearance of Marie a few moments later led him to believe they had barely got away with being discovered.

The barn was empty when George arrived; he thought that Margaretta was truly annoyed with him or was just teasing him. He didn't mind these moments on his own; he was thinking back to not so long ago when each day was full of fear, cold and shock, stuck up the side of a mountain, wondering if each day might be his last. Most men would have been thinking in a similar vein, although some did not show it. He was extremely sad about the town of Monte Cassino and the abbey: what an utter waste. He shook himself out of these thoughts, made himself recall his days here in the sun amongst the vines and working the earth. He was pulled violently from his daydreaming when Margaretta pounced on him from behind the bales stacked to the side of him. She must have crept in while he was in a daze. She was certainly in an excitable mood this evening; she tousled George's sandy hair, pulled at his ears and went running and skipping around the barn, while George tried desperately to catch her and bring her down. Every time he got near she would swerve to one side and then the other, avoiding her alleged captor's grasp on each occasion. She was a gazelle, full of life; he was the big cat that, although young and virile, did not have the moves of this young spirited gazelle. Eventually, Margaretta stopped as she gasped for breath. Laughing between gulping for air, she cried out to George.

"You're too old and slow, old man."

With that, George made one last effort, his sudden speed and manoeuvring outflanked her; he grabbed her and they both fell to the ground, laughing and rolling in the straw.

They lay there panting for a while on their backs then, with a slight turn of their heads, they looked at each and the mood changed. George stroked her cheek; she in turn stroked his, and they lay like this for some while, just absorbing each other. He looked at her with such tenderness and caring; she replied with a twinkling in her eyes, followed by a more solemn look of love and deep affection, which neither bothered to put into words. They were two young people in a world of turmoil and upheaval; they had found something really special by being together: happiness that neither had thought to capture in such times. She was very young in so many ways, yet very much a woman in so many others.

They kissed tenderly and slowly, letting each moment be tasted and noted so that the memory would last forever. They still hadn't spoken; the need to speak grew even less as they moved together more closely. Rolling onto their sides, they pulled each other even closer; this moment in time needed to be drunk in and savoured without spilling a drop. Their passion grew as it usually did and they began to undress each other, becoming more fervent as they got closer to being naked. She was over him, pulling at his clothes as if this was the last thing she had time to do on this earth. He writhed under her attentions, she moved closer, feeling their bodies pressed against each other in a tight embrace. They moved as one to a rhythm that was theirs alone, to a feeling that made Margaretta shed a tear of joy. Reaching for the tear, he wiped it with his fingertip and stroked her face once again. They both wanted this to last forever, but they knew that, as they became as one body, their passionate embraces moving closer to climax, they would not be able to hold on. The moment would crescendo, moving into another plain, and then die away for another time.

They were not going to let this moment slip away from them just yet. George slowed the pace of their bodies' interacting; teasing her with his manhood, after a few more moments, he brought them back to an even higher level of desire and passion. They both believed that their heads would explode; instead, George exploded inside her, making her scream and cry out. They hovered with the feeling of glorious rushing blood, pounding heart beats, and loss, as they slipped down the other side of climax into exhaustion. Their wet bodies were freefalling, their hearts slowing to a more normal rhythm, as a slight breeze began cooling their sweating skins and their ardour.

Turning to him, Margaretta said, "Again!" They laughed, pulled some clothes over their cooling bodies and fell asleep in each other's arms amongst the straw

Chapter 26

Summer days

This time was blissful for Margaretta and George: they enjoyed the days working in the fields and the love-making at night. One night, when he spoke to Margaretta, George was very serious and controlled. Every time she wanted to play their love-making games, he held her away.

"We need to talk about us and how we break it to your family," he said. Margaretta became concerned and told George that he needed to be aware that her father might not approve. George's response was that it was even more important to inform Aldo so that he wouldn't be surprised or angered by someone else telling him, rather than them. They agreed and planned to talk to Aldo after breakfast next morning.

"Now can we make love?" Margaretta pleaded with drooping lips and sad eyes. There was nothing George could do but pick her up and carry her off.

George heard it first: the sound of a large vehicle entering the yard. He rushed out of the sleeping quarters then slowed to a cautious, stealthy walk as he heard American voices calling out. Aldo came into the yard, pulling up his braces as he walked towards the American officer, who introduced himself and shook Aldo's hand. George was alarmed, ducking behind the barn and back into the sleeping quarters, advising the men that he would keep out of sight and asking them to find out what was happening. They agreed and stumbled out of their bunks, still rubbing sleep from their eyes, yawning and scratching, as they exited the quarters.

The lorry-load of American GIs jumped out of the truck, stretched their backs and legs, and began strolling around the yard. Some lit their cigarettes; others were just glad to be out of the troop transport for a break. They took in the yard and the surroundings, while admiring the view towards and beyond the vineyard.

"I wonder where they keep the vino from the vineyard," one GI said. "I can't see any fermentation set-up. Perhaps they send the grapes out."

"And what would you know about anything?" another responded.

The officer called over to the men to be respectful and not to wander all over the property. He also told them that they should fill their water bottles from the yard pump while they had the opportunity. The American explained they were looking to form a base camp near here; pointing out towards the hills beyond the vineyard, Aldo said he knew of a good position for them, not too long a drive away.

The officer and Aldo seemed to be in quite an amiable and casual conversation, as far as the men could tell. Aldo was gesturing with his hands left and then right and indicating a rise; it became clear to other men entering the yard that Aldo was giving directions. He was heard to say that they were welcome to stay and have some breakfast with them, but the officer declined; Aldo insisted they at least take some fresh cheese and eggs for later in the day. The officer thanked Aldo profusely and walked back over to his men, four of whom broke from the group and followed Aldo into the house, where Marie and Margaretta were preparing breakfast for the men before the day's work. All four GIs were taken by Margaretta's dark beauty; they first whistled and then called her a 'doll'. Aldo explained that the GIs were here at his invitation to take some cheese and eggs for the others. One of the GIs smelt the fresh bread resting on the central table in the kitchen and asked if he might sample some.

"Why don't you take some loaves too?" Margaretta said. "I am sure all your men would like some."

"Wow!" said one of the GIs "Not only a doll but she speaks great American too. Why, thank you, *Signorina*. That will be just fine."

The GIs came back into the yard with arms full of produce: not only the eggs and cheese but salami and bread too. The guys were really buoyant as they described Margaretta to the others, and another added, "And the mamma weren't bad either."

The GIs piled back into the truck and soon disappeared into the distance along the route that Aldo had prescribed. The dust settled in the yard and George appeared a little sheepishly, but Aldo and the men had no time to hang about; they set about grabbing some breakfast and getting out into the fields. They had lost a good part of the morning and they wished to get working before the sun got too hot to work under. When Aldo signalled for George to come over to him, he did so at a trot – as a private would to an officer. He was full of foreboding, wondering what Aldo's attitude would be towards him after the Americans' visit, but Aldo just said, "George, we will need to talk tonight; there a few things to discuss I believe." George nodded and Aldo continued, "Just get on with your work as normal; we will talk after dinner." George left the brief encounter with a heavy heart, fearing the worst.

The day in the vineyard was the same as usual: men chatted at break time, and some sang as they worked, while others went into their own little worlds with the rhythm of the day. No sooner had they begun the day's work than it was over, although, to George, it seemed to drag, as his mind repeatedly returned to the morning's events and the meeting with Aldo tonight.

Taking more care than usual after work, George made sure that he looked presentable to Aldo. "A few things to discuss" hung in George's mind, and no matter how he turned them round, he felt that he would be asked to move on. Not that this worried him unduly, except for Margaretta and how he felt about her and what her reaction would be if he was asked to leave.

Dinner was as good as always and Margaretta as beautiful, but George picked at his food and was very quiet. He normally enjoyed the banter between the men and Aldo, the singing and laughter, but tonight this was all too much; he wanted it behind him. Margaretta kept glancing across at George, but he would not catch her eye in case he gave his fears away. After the men had finished and had thanked Marie and Margaretta for the meal, they began walking slowly back to the bunk house, chatting and laughing; after a good day's labour in the field, good food in their bellies and a night of song and laughter, the men were contented with their lot.

Aldo asked George to follow him, and they went and sat a little way off from where Marie and Margaretta were clearing away; the clatter of plates and cutlery grew fainter as they moved further away. It was a pleasantly warm night and Aldo had a bottle of his wine and two glasses with him. Noticing this, George thought this was either welcome to the family or a goodbye drink. Which was it to be, he wondered.

Aldo took his time; he seemed to be reluctant or nervous about where to start. So he began talking about his great grandfather's clock, as if to break the ice with an item that was not in any way confrontational.

"How is my grandfather's clock coming along, George?"

Somewhat relieved at the subject and tone of the question, George replied, "It is almost completed, Aldo, and it should be as good as new, if not better. In fact, we could wind it up together, almost like a little ceremony to set it on its way, and with a little care it will be good for years to come."

"I am very pleased to hear that George," Aldo told him. "The clock is very special to me. I am also gratified by the way you have worked in the fields and vineyard, in fact on the whole of the estate."

"I still owe you more for your continued favours towards me," said George, but before he could say more, Aldo interrupted him. Holding up his hand, he looked at George in a way that indicated that he wasn't to be interrupted further.

"My Margaretta is a very beautiful and headstrong girl," Aldo continued. "She is very wilful, and anyone who would be brave enough to take her on would have to be very strong-minded. Her mother believes that she has affection for you and that you also have the same for her. It would be no use for me to even try to intervene, as she would do what she wanted anyway. What I wish to know is what you are intending to do, bearing in mind that the American soldiers were here this morning looking for German stragglers and deserters while they were on their way to Rome. They had heard of a German outfit along this road; they found a German vehicle with three dead Germans inside and wondered if we had seen anything. What is the relevance to you and Margaretta, you might ask."

George went to speak again, but it was obvious that Aldo wanted to get this outpouring of thoughts out and over with in one go, as he held his hand up once again to stop him.

"And the reason I am clumsily explaining all this to you is that we know that you deserted the British Army. You have your own reasons and justification for doing so, but what happens if you are captured and returned? What is your outlook? Will you be shot? Because, if you are, I can tell you that Margaretta will be devastated and will blame us for not protecting you. Or will it be imprisonment? If so, will they return you to England? If this is the case, will you return to us here or forget us? You see, George, these are all the questions that a father must ask if he is to protect his child and his family."

Silence hung in the air like a weighted balloon, and neither man looked at each other for some time. Aldo used this silence to pour some wine in the glasses and handed one across to George. Then he spoke.

"There is another issue that I want to raise with you, George, and that is about the relationship you have with Margaretta. The men have noticed and so has my wife that Margaretta has been disappearing to meet with you. You may ask why we have let this continue; all I can reiterate is: Margaretta is a very strong-willed daughter. Marie and I discussed your relationship and we thought that we would let it run to its inevitable conclusion. However, this is not to say that, as a father and mother in a very Catholic country, we have not both struggled with the modern ways of our children. Now, if you were to get Margaretta pregnant, what would you do, especially with a military sentence hanging over your head? I might take a more old fashioned approach to matters if this transpired."

Ordinarily, this would have been a pleasant interlude at the end of a hard-working day, but both men felt the weight of the dilemma. George was struggling with what he wanted to say. Did he just blurt out what his feelings were for Margaretta? Would that be sufficient? Was it childish to think that he could avoid capture forever and carve out a life here in the warm embrace of this young woman and her family? It was certainly tempting. Would it be glib just to reply and say that he loved her very much, as if this were the answer to everything? Would it be better for all of them, if he were to hand himself into the military and take the consequences, hoping that he would be able to return to them some day?

George braced himself, took a large glug of wine and spoke.

"Aldo, I am very grateful to you and your family; you have treated me with respect and kindness. As far as Margaretta is concerned, I love her very much. Now, whether this love is a selfish kind that only thinks of itself or whether it is the kind that can act in a way that will sacrifice that very love so that it might set others free of danger, I will have to discover. I wanted to talk to you sooner, but Margaretta felt that the timing was not right. I would have preferred that I had approached you, so that I could have explained and set your mind at rest. I will say this now: I will not put you or your family in danger because of what I feel for Margaretta. I would hope that I will be able to stay until the season is over, as I would love to see the harvesting of the grapes, but, if anything happens in the meantime that jeopardises your family, I will leave sooner or if you feel that I should leave now, I will do this and explain to Margaretta."

Aldo reached across to George, placed a hand on his knee and thanked him for his straight speaking; if he hadn't had sons, he would have been happy to have had him as one. George also felt very emotional; the two men looked at each other and drank their wine slowly. In an effort to lighten the mood, George told Aldo that he would have to finish the clock and then they could have a party to celebrate its new beginning. Aldo laughed and said that a party was a good idea; whatever George decided about other matters, he would back him completely.

"You are a good man, George. My brother was right, but then he usually is about people."

Chapter 27

Talking with Margaretta

Margaretta had a quizzical frown on her brow as George approached her by the house, and she asked him where he had been with her father. Putting his finger to his lips, he ushered her away from the house so that they could speak openly and privately. He outlined what had been discussed, and Margaretta put her hand to her mouth and gasped as George explained the ramifications. She then threw her arms around George's neck and sobbed into the corner of his collar.

"You won't go, will you? You won't go? I love you. Don't you see that? Can't you tell how much I love and care about you, like I have never cared before?" George gently unravelled himself from her arms and held her at the length of his, saying very slowly and carefully, "I am not going anywhere until I am ready and we have talked further. I love you very much. The time I have spent here has been the most precious and the happiest I have ever known. Why would I want to leave?"

With these words barely off his lips, Margaretta brushed his arms aside and threw herself around him, hugging him until he pleaded for her to stop as he couldn't breathe.

"I knew you loved me," she said with glee, skipping about him like a small child. This was the first time that they had declared their love to each other; all other words were lost on Margaretta at this point, as all she could hear was George's declaration. Her body trembled and tingled all at the same time, and then she began to weep.

"What is the matter?" asked George. Laughing and crying at the same moment, Margaretta said through a wet beautiful face, "I don't know, I suppose I am so happy."

George brought Margaretta back to earth and talked about the seriousness of his situation: one day he would have to return to the army and face the consequences. But Margaretta was not listening and asked him not to spoil this moment of happiness. He had appreciated that it would be difficult getting through to Margaretta, and he felt that she had not grasped all the implications of him staying here with the family. He shelved the matter for the time being and made a mental note to talk to her again, when she had descended from her clouds of happiness.

Chapter 28

Hauptmann im Generalstab - Reisling

There was a commotion from the large barn. Voices were raised and they weren't all Italian. Rushing into the courtyard, George found a group of workers gathered around the barn: some with pitchforks, others with shovels and stout sticks. There was such a commotion that they couldn't all enter the barn door at once. It looked like a rush to the January sales, but these were not hassled shoppers, they were muscular hardworking labourers and they were angry. George arrived at the barn door, working his way forward through the angry throng, and asking in English as he went, "What's up, what's going on?" And then he understood as he managed at last to push to the front of the men.

There, in all his jackbooted glory, was a German officer, a lieutenant, who still looked resplendent in his somewhat dishevelled uniform. George moved to the front of the angry crowd; one of the burly men had a rope and it was obvious from the shape of the knot he was fashioning what he intended to do. George gestured with his hands for them to calm down; this was not the way to deal with the officer. The assembled men began to be less agitated, listening to the calmness of George's voice as he spoke to them. They dropped to a disgruntled murmur, then to an uneasy stillness, as George explained that he would talk to the officer.

George turned and looked the officer up and down: he was flustered but not scared. He was amazed at the likeness to his elder brother, Tom, who was also a lieutenant in the army, Royal Artillery he believed; they hadn't seen each other for an age. The officer stood tall and, unlike the picture of the Aryan race with fair or blonde hair, this individual had black hair slicked down, parted to the left side, although at the moment a little ruffled. His eyes were of the deepest violet, probably dark blue in the sunlight; he stood proudly in his officer's uniform, staring with those piercing eyes at George.

"And you are?" he said in perfect English.

"Never mind that," George responded. "How did you come to be here?"

The officer pulled himself even more upright and said, "That is not your concern."

"On the contrary," George replied. "It is of concern to all of us. If you would rather deal with these men than me, I will just return to what I was doing previously and let them decide your fate."

The officer stood for a few moments, while the whispering throng discussed what George had said. Once they all understood, there were mutterings of agreement; they waited none too patiently while the lieutenant collected his thoughts.

"Very well," he said. "I was part of the evacuation party heading to Rome, picking up stragglers and deserters from other *Wehrmacht* companies, when we were ambushed by what I assume were partisans. My vehicle was overturned some way down the road; I was thrown clear and made my way here via the fields and ditches."

George paused a while and then explained to the officer that he was unlikely to reach Rome; if he did he would be greeted by Allied troops, as Rome had fallen to the Americans some time ago.

"This cannot be so," said the officer. George assured him that he was telling the truth, and the best he could hope for was to become a prisoner of war. The mood of the assembly had quieted considerably; some of the men began drifting back to work, as there was nothing more for them to do with the German officer. Now that Aldo, without a word, had joined the men to see what the fuss was about, the rest hurried back to work.

The officer stood glumly in the corner of the barn, while George and Aldo discussed his fate and how to deal with the German. They decided that the best course of action was to lead him back to the Allies, where he would be better off than if he caught up with his own troops, which was rather unlikely at the rate they were heading north. He would be fed and cared for and given safe quarters, whereas his fellow soldiers would not be so lucky; anyway, how would he get through the vast assembly of Allied soldiers all heading to Rome and beyond?

George introduced Aldo to the officer, whose name and full title was Hauptman im Generalstab Hermann Viktor Reisling. Both George and Aldo agreed that 'Hermann' was sufficient. No one was going to stand on ceremony, agreed the two allies, without the full consent of Hermann, who, although seemingly a little put out by the familiarity of the two men, had no option.

The men led Hermann to the water pump, where he could get cleaned up and have a good drink prior to dinner.

"He had better stay in his uniform," George told Aldo. "If we put him in civilian clothes and the Allies get hold of him, they may decide he is a spy. The rules of war, as ludicrous as they may seem, would apply; it could get him shot." Aldo just grunted and made his way towards the house. George stayed with Hermann and chatted to him without saying anything of any importance, just passing the time while the German brushed himself down, washed his face and hands and smoothed down his thick, dark hair.

"So, George, as we are all being very familiar, what are you doing here: deserter, partisan or what?" George was startled by Hermann's sudden engagement and stood a moment, looking at the now newly brushed-down officer, before smiling.

"Well Hermann, since, as you say, we are all being so very familiar, I will tell you. I am a deserter. I have been working with Aldo and his sons on the vineyard and farm since arriving some time back, not sure how long I have been here, I am not sure how long I will stay. I will have to return sometime soon, as I do not want to put the family in jeopardy. I was at Cassino for several months and when they declared the battle was over, that your lot in the abbey had surrendered, something in me snapped, I just got up and walked until I found myself here."

Hermann was now the one to be taken aback and looked glumly at George.

"I can appreciate you leaving Cassino, but why after we had surrendered our position to you, why not in the middle of the battle? That would have been the natural thing to do."

"Good question," replied George. "Not one that I can really answer, except perhaps to another serving soldier, who would appreciate the fact that I had just had enough and did not want to do any more killing."

Hermann nodded in appreciation, saying, "Thank you for your plain speaking, George. I too have done and seen enough for several lifetimes and just wish this all to stop. Thank you also for saving me from the men, who wanted to – how do they say it in the Western movies – string me up?" George laughed at the use of this Western idiom.

"My pleasure, Hermann. I am sure you would have done the same for me."

"I am not so sure," said Hermann, trying to be as honest as he could. "But all I want now is to get back to my family in Dusseldorf as soon as I possibly can. I have two young boys and my wife is very young too. I just hope and pray that they are safe." George looked away, saying nothing, as he knew that the Allies had been on a bombing campaign for months. He had heard, through the wireless in the house and the talk amongst the family and the men in the fields, that Germany was taking a pasting.

After dinner that evening, Hermann was given the barn as his quarters, which rather put paid to Margaretta and George's late night trysts; she was none too pleased. Hermann gave his word that he would remain in the barn until morning, and they all retired after a long and eventful day.

Margaretta insisted on a goodnight kiss; the couple slipped away into the shadow of the house, they kissed passionately until Aldo called for Margaretta to come in and go to bed, as tomorrow was going to be another busy day.

It was another sun-kissed morning and the men were eager to get to breakfast and then to work, as the day would prove to be a hot one; the sooner they got their work done, the sooner they could sit in the cool of the shade. Hermann appeared at the water pump in his shirt sleeves; the men stood still, staring at him for a while, and then lost interest as they heard Margaretta putting out the breakfast things. Hermann was true to his word and had stayed in the barn for the whole night; he was now busy making himself as clean as he possibly could with limited materials. When Margaretta took him some cleaning equipment wrapped in a towel, he was heard to thank her in Italian. She did not wait around but ducked back inside the house without a backward glance.

George joined Hermann at the pump, and they spoke amiably about the weather, the journey, and the supplies that they would furnish him with for his trip. He told Hermann that Giovanni would be his guide to the Americans, who had passed through; Aldo knew where they would be, as he had given them directions to the best routes, where there would be land owners who would be happy to help, feed and water them. Giovanni was also wily, very strong and he knew most of the partisans; he would not take any nonsense from them if they were still in the area.

Hermann questioned George further about his future and what he intended to do. George told him that the more he thought about it the more he believed the honourable thing to do was to return to the unit he had left, that is if he could find them. Hermann believed that this was the best answer and said that he would not mention George to the Allies but leave him to take his own time returning to his unit. George thanked him and told him to get himself ready for breakfast, and then he would take him across and introduce him to Giovanni to get his provisions. He nodded and went back to the barn, appearing a few minutes later in his uniform; he marched proudly across the yard towards George and the other men. My, thought George, don't you look something all dressed up? His uniform and boots were not as pristine as in the past, but he certainly carried himself with some distinction.

Giovanni glared at Hermann all through breakfast; even as they were formally introduced, he did not proffer his hand or greet Hermann in any way; he just slung his pack over his shoulder and walked off towards the vineyard. Aldo and George shook Hermann's hand, wished him well and hoped his family was safe in Dusseldorf. Hermann thanked them both for their kindness and supplies; he walked speedily to catch Giovanni, who was now some 200 yards away.

"I wonder if Giovanni will talk to Hermann on this journey at all," George said to Aldo, who grinned.

"They make a great couple, no?" Both men went back to the house, talking and laughing at the odd couple: Giovanni in his sweat-stained shirt and baggy trousers, alongside the tall and elegant German officer.

Aldo reassured George that, with all his faults and despite his association with the partisans, Giovanni would follow Aldo's orders to the letter and deliver Hermann safely to the Americans or the first Allied troops that he met.

"I hope so, Aldo," George replied. "In fact, I am sure he will; he is a good man, even if his teeth are bad." Aldo looked at George and just laughed at the mention of Giovanni's teeth; for that was another story.

Chapter 29

The General's Gift

The dust cloud could be seen for miles as the Jeep sped along the rutted track; it being normal driving for the GI over this terrain, he was totally unaware of Giovanni's discomfort. He carried on at breakneck speed, as if there were a group of *Panzers* after him. The track contorted and, likewise, the occupants dipped and bucked as on a child's pleasure ride, but this was not a pleasure for Giovanni. They entered the track to the vineyard, and the workers all looked up at the Jeep and the grimacing face of Giovanni. They were not sure whether he was smiling with pleasure at being given a lift by the GI or that his grin had become transfixed. He waved as casually as he was able but then promptly grasped the side of the vehicle for fear of being thrown out. The GI wore dark glasses; as he navigated their way, he had been chewing gum and humming an incessant tune, which had begun to annoy Giovanni from the outset, as it had no beginning, no middle: it seemed endless.

The Jeep pulled into the yard and did a handbrake turn, kicking up dust and grit. The GI leapt out in one bound and grabbed a package out of the back, looking back casually at Giovanni and asking if he was ok. Giovanni nodded that he was, proceeding to extricate himself in a more sedate and leisurely manner. As he did so, he rubbed his buttocks, which had been bounced for several miles on hard seats and rough tracks. As the GI approached the house, he shouted back at Giovanni.

"Will the old man be in, G?" That was another thing. What was it with these Americans? They had to shorten your name or give you a nickname; Giovanni couldn't understand the logic. His philosophy was: if your parents had gone to the trouble of choosing a name for you and having you christened, then it seemed disrespectful not to use it.

Aldo had heard the arrival and came to see what the noise and fuss was all about. He laughed when he saw Giovanni standing by the Jeep rubbing his backside.

"Rough trip, Giovanni?"

Giovanni mumbled something indecipherable and shuffled off to the bunk house. The GI introduced himself as Joseph Camaro, of Italian decent. He looked not dissimilar to Aldo's workers; he also had dark curly hair and an olive complexion; his nose had been flattened a little, probably fighting at home before he was called up, but Joseph told Aldo that his family had emigrated so long ago that it was a long time since their mother tongue had been used.

"What a pity," said Aldo, "and such a beautiful language."

Jo, as he was known, continued, "They told me back at base that you spoke good American, so not to worry, right. I have brought you some coffee, chocolate and cigarettes as a thank you from General Roberts, who much appreciated you sending him the Kraut. He also appreciated the way you helped his men when they called by and the provisions you sent."

"It was nothing," replied Aldo, "Nothing that is compared to what you are doing to rid us of these fascists from our beautiful land."

"Well anyway, General Roberts says thank you very much for your assistance; this package of gifts is just a token. He said that he particularly liked the salami, as it reminded him very much of home in New York and the Italian quarter there."

"In that case," replied Aldo, "it would be my pleasure to furnish you with some more for your general. Come, come, you must come inside and have some refreshments. My wife, Marie, will look after you, while I go to the cellar to see what else I might find for you and your general."

Aldo wasn't gone very long and returned with his arms full of cheeses and salami. He then went back to the cellar to fetch more gifts, and, as he came up the stairs, they could hear him talking to himself, as well as the chinking sound of bottles of wine from his estate.

"There you are," said Aldo, beaming with pride at the produce he laid before Jo on the table.

"Well ain't that just great," said Jo. "The old man will be pleased as punch at this little lot."

"Would you like to try a little of my wine?" proffered Aldo.

"Well, does a duck swim on water?" replied Jo.

"I take that as a yes." Without further fuss, Aldo poured some white wine in one glass and some red in another so that Jo could sample each to see which he preferred. Jo sat for some time, chatting with Aldo, while Marie busied herself in the kitchen; she had also packaged the returning gifts in sacking so that they could continue to breathe.

"Well," said Jo, "I had best be getting back or they will think that I've deserted. Many thanks for your hospitality, Sir and Ma'am. I will make sure that General Roberts gets these gifts."

Smiling, Aldo gave Jo a separate package, telling him that it was for him for bringing back Giovanni safely, even though a little shaken and fragile. Both men laughed and shook hands warmly. Jo was gone as quickly as he had come, jumping into his Jeep and roaring off into the vineyard tracks.

By this time the workers were coming back from the fields, including Margaretta and George. At first, they were both alarmed to see an American GI roaring up the track, but they soon realised that he was too busy navigating the discordant track to be concerned with them. Jo was also a little the worse for wear, after his wine-tasting session in the kitchen with Aldo, and was concentrating so hard on the undulations and the weaving nature of the road that he had little time to take in the returning work group. He just put up his hand, waved it vigorously, and shouted some greeting that was carried away in the wind and the dust.

Chapter 30

The Party, the Harvest and the Clock

Summer was drawing into autumn; the harvest had begun in earnest, and all the men from around the region had come to give a helping hand. Even Pietro had made the journey, although whether he was there to help harvest the grapes or to take his fill of the good food and wine, which was renowned at Aldo and Marie's parties, was much in debate, and George was not sure. Pietro was the brunt of leg pulling, to the delight of all.

The work was arduous and the days were long, but harvesting had to be completed in record time as high winds and heavy rain were forecast in the hills, which could mean disaster for the crop. Men and women alike worked their shifts, some cutting, others carrying the grapes to the carts that were pulled by mules and men. Although the work was hard, the atmosphere in the vineyard was one of joyous celebration: not only for the bringing in of a record crop but also for the news that the Allies were pushing the Germans out of Italy and that they were on the run. This would be the first opportunity for a feast in a free Italy, and all were looking forward to the food, singing and dancing at the end of the harvest.

The grapes were collected in large baskets and passed down the lines of vines to the carts, which in turn travelled to the press. Some grapes were still pressed in the traditional way in a large vat and trodden by the workers. Margaretta loved this process, and it was traditional for her to start the treading of the grapes, while other workers stood around clapping and singing. Gradually, others would join Margaretta until the melee of workers became overwhelming. To his surprise, George was picked up and thrown into the vat beside Margaretta; as he was a novice to the vineyard, this was also a tradition. He found it difficult to stand at first and slipped and slid and fell back into the ever-growing sea of grapes and juice. This brought a roar from the assembled workers, laughter and many ribald songs that were made up for his benefit. The greatest declaration at that moment was when Margaretta went to George, wrapped herself around him and kissed him passionately. Some looked towards Aldo and Marie; once the party-goers saw that her parents were smiling and clapping, the rest followed.

The grapes that were headed for the press were selected and treated with a little more respect, as they were destined for the 'special wine' that Aldo had mentioned to George. The juice from these grapes was to be taken to a separate fermentation plant that Aldo had hidden in the caves. There it would ferment very slowly under the careful eye of Aldo and his friend, Octavio, who was also a vineyard owner. Unfortunately for Octavio, his vines had been fired by the Germans and his farm was all but decimated. This was mainly due to his position further down the slopes; he was able to harvest earlier, but he was also in the path of the advancing and now retreating Germans, so much due to geography.

Once the 'special grape juice' was fermented sufficiently, it was transferred to large terracotta pots, not wooden casks, and similarly it would be fermented slowly in the cool air of the caves. This brought about a very distinctive flavour, and this wine had been sold at a premium before the war.

Once the other grapes were pressed and the juice placed in the underground vats, there was little more to do for the time being, and the party preparations began in earnest. Aldo was arranging for his great grandfather's clock to be the centrepiece of the celebrations. Now that George had completed all the work, the clock not only looked as good as new, it worked better than ever before, at least since Aldo had inherited it. The clock was adorned with white flowers and rich green leaves, and gold strands of material cascaded down its sides. The buzz in the house was electric; Margaretta was ecstatic as she always loved a party and was looking forward to dancing with George, even though he protested that he couldn't dance, as no one had taught him. That was music to Margaretta's ears; she replied that she would be the one to teach him. It also pleased her to think that George hadn't danced with anyone before her.

The day of the party was upon the Monticelli household. As expected, the food was not only beautifully prepared and presented; it stretched from inside the house to outside in the yard, where tables groaned under the weight of the amazing dishes, cheeses, hams, salamis, pasta and wine. There was also a whole roasted pig that had been hidden away. Neighbours and helpers too were not shy with their offerings of good eating. The yard was lit by fiery torches and the tables sprinkled with candlelight. The band of men that were to be the musical entertainment for the evening were already jolly from the copious amounts of wine they had drunk before arriving; no one seemed to care or mind that they swayed a little more than usual with the music. The band consisted of accordion, guitars, flutes and a piano; the sounds made by this merry band of men emanated across the hillside, replacing the sound of distant gunfire.

Aldo called for everyone to be quiet, as he was about to make a short speech. Clearing his throat, he smiled at the gathered guests.

"I would first of all like to thank you all most sincerely for your hard work and the wonderful and generous gifts of food. We have all been very fortunate in our little hideaway, in the beautiful hills that surround us, even more fortunate than we could have imagined. Due to careful planning and a little secrecy, we have managed to sustain our way of life, without undue attention. Neither the Germans nor the Allies have interfered with our working of the farm and vineyard. I have to thank the very astute way that my sons have dealt with this particular issue, which has avoided it becoming a problem. Who would have thought that my boys were so persuasive in their approach to the Allies and Germans alike, not to plunder, but to help us sustain them by working with us?" Aldo raised his glass and said, "To my sons, my thanks and good health to them and their future."

Those gathered raised their glasses in response, but the boys were nowhere to be seen. Aldo continued, "There is one other person I wish to thank and that is George, for the restoration of great grandfather's clock. It is now restored to its former glory and, more than this, I wish to say how pleased I am that I welcomed a stranger needing our love and help, who has now become like another son to me. To George."

Another toast, this time to George, again glasses were raised and a chorus of "George" rang out, although many of the labourers from afar had no idea who George was. Aldo quieted the even merrier crowd.

"Lastly, I wish to thank my brother, Pietro, for sending George to us, and I believe special thanks are due from my daughter, Margaretta, who, I believe, is particularly pleased."

He laughed at his own comment, while Margaretta flushed, hidden as she was at the back of the guests, whose searching eyes sought her out. George was also embarrassed by Aldo's comment and looked to see if his sons were offended by the comment about him being like another son. Fortunately they hadn't heard, as they were absorbed by two young ladies from a neighbouring farm and had had too much to drink to take offence at anything.

Aldo went on to thank his wife, Marie, and Margaretta for preparing such an excellent feast, wished everyone a good time and looked forward to sampling the first of the new wine: the first wine to have been produced in freedom and love for many years, adding that there could be no better vintage. Deeply flushed from the drink, Aldo began to weep, becoming a little maudlin, so Marie took charge of her husband, thanked everyone once again for coming and asked the band to strike up and for everyone to dance the night away.

Chapter 31

George's Fate

Long after the celebrations were over, George sat alone in the barn, staring at his feet and watching the small insects and bugs crawling about. They did not need to make many decisions, other than what they were going to eat next and how to avoid being eaten. It was no good looking for an answer to his dilemma in amongst the detritus of the barn floor. What was he going to do next? What would be the outcome if he should return and face the consequences? He knew that he had an obligation to Margaretta and in particular to her father; a step had to be taken. How would he deal with the inevitable outpouring and anger from Margaretta? He would just have to face up to it; she would have to understand that his life would be lost if he did not go back and deal with the actions of his past. They could not look to any future together if he was constantly looking over his shoulder to see if the military were on to him. He needed to make a bold decision and he needed to do it soon.

The weather was changing; being high in the hills meant beautiful summers with relative cooler nights, and so it was not too difficult to sleep. The opposite of the glorious summers were the quite savage winters on occasion, with howling winds, snow and sleet. The same slopes that had produced the sparkling white wines and the rich, deep flowery reds were about to take their revenge. All the workers could feel things changing and began preparing for the predicted bitter winter. Aldo gave his instructions for repairs that had slipped during the warm summer days and harvest time. As they moved closer to winter, the mood on the hilltop vineyards and farms changed to a more sombre note, overlaid with a sense of urgency.

George also felt the atmosphere change and, with the change in the air, so his mood took on a similar sombre note, for completely different reasons, but everyone around him noticed that he was not as outgoing as he had been through the summer. Margaretta tried hard to please and cheer him but without success; she also would be caught up in an avalanche of emotions that would overwhelm her.

George had made his decision to return to his unit and face the consequences; the big issue was going to be telling Margaretta of his plan. He spoke with Aldo at length; although the older man was disappointed that George would be leaving, he was very sympathetic and encouraged George to do what he felt best. He also made it very clear to George that, after the war was over or as soon as he was free to do so, he would be most welcome back to the Casa Monticelli. Aldo also tried to reassure George that he would take care of Margaretta until his return. Although she would be very upset in the beginning, with his and her mother's encouragement, she would soon settle back into the routines of the vineyard. George was not so sure about the latter but appreciated the kind thoughts and sentiment; he knew that Aldo was trying to make it as easy as possible for him.

Margaretta came to George after dinner. She was as buoyant as ever, talking about all the things they did over Christmas, how much he would enjoy the winters in the hills with the snow, the log fires, friends coming by with greetings and gifts for the New Year. George appreciated this was going to be a difficult evening and was struggling to find the words to begin, when Margaretta stopped in her tracks as they strolled around the vineyard and said with a stern expression, "What is the matter, George? You have been very cool towards me for some days now. Don't you like me anymore? Are you tired of being with me every day? Are you tired of my family and this way of life?"

George took a deep breath, looking at Margaretta with love in his eyes.

"It is neither of those things, Margaretta. I love this way of life; your family have been extremely kind and very generous to me. And Aldo hasn't put me up against a wall and shot me for stealing his lovely daughter's heart. The problem is that I have to tell you something very important and you are not going to like it."

Unable to stand it any longer, Margaretta interrupted him.

"You are married, that's it isn't it? You lied to me and all along you have a wife back home. I trusted you and you have deceived me."

Completely wrong-footed by these remarks, George begged Margaretta to calm down; it was not the case.

"Well what is it then?" she demanded.

"If you would let me speak, I will explain; but you must be silent and let me finish. Do you promise me that?" Margaretta nodded. Tears had begun to appear in the corners of her eyes; when one escaped and rolled down her cheek, she didn't move to wipe it away but let it run to her chin.

George began by telling her of his decision, listing the rules of war and what they meant to a soldier that had deserted. She made a puffing sound with her mouth as if to say she didn't care about that. George held a finger to his lips for her to be quiet as she had promised. She then listened intently when he said that he could be shot for desertion in the face of the enemy and that he could not live with this hanging over him.

"I have to go back, Margaretta. I cannot live with this terrible thing hanging over me. What sort of a future would we have together? I have to take my punishment, no matter how harsh that might be."

Margaretta began to weep silently, but she still didn't speak or make a move to wipe away the tears, now streaming down her face.

"I will have to go to the court martial, which is like an examining board of officers, who will look at the evidence of my absence and decide on what punishment they will give me. It is unlikely I will be shot, but who knows what the future holds? I will try and explain to them how my best friend being killed, and the strenuous battles that we fought together, were instrumental in making me crack under pressure. I just hope that they will listen and take account of my previous good record. I was so confused, upset and in a terrible state; I just got up and walked away, nobody stopped me. I think everyone was so pleased that the Germans had surrendered the abbey, they were distracted."

Margaretta was still not impressed and showed this through her demeanour but, as promised, never spoke a word., He had come to realise over the past months that, although his actions seemed understandable to him, to the army they amounted to desertion. George promised that when he could he would return to her and pick up their life together: he loved her. Her family and this way of life suited him completely; he had never been happier.

Margaretta could stand it no longer; she threw herself at George and sobbed into his neck, soaking his shirt. He could feel the warmth of her, and her breasts were heaving against his chest as she gasped and cried, and he held her very tightly against him. She begged him not to go, she pleaded: he might be shot and then she would have lost him forever. George did not speak but just held her until the tears subsided and they could talk quietly about his decision. The fire had gone out of Margaretta; she became a rag doll and leant against George as if the strength had gone from her legs. He spoke softly to her as they walked back to the house, trying to reassure her of his return, without knowing if he would be able to come back. He had no real option, as far as he could see, but to find out what his fate might be.

George had already discussed with Aldo what he intended doing, and when the household awoke the next morning, he was gone. He hadn't wanted long goodbyes and more tears from Margaretta. Aldo and he had discussed his departure; they both decided that a quick exit was the best way for all concerned. Having become like father and son, Aldo and George were quite emotional about their separation, but both appreciated that, as a soldier, he had a duty to return and face up to the decision he had made to leave the battlefield in the first place.

George would retrace his steps and stop off to say goodbye to Pietro, who had set him on his way to recovery. Through Aldo, he had been informed by partisans where the British forces were and the best route over the hills to take from Pietro's cottage. George was anxious about his return, but at the same time he was aware of a lightness in his being. Having made the decision to return, he now had a purpose; come what may, this was his life.

He had journeyed through the hills at the beginning of summer and now he was returning through the cooler days and nights at the beginning of winter. The difference was quite marked; he was glad that he could step out with purpose and raise his temperature through the exertion of the day. He was pleased to see Pietro's house coming into view: quite a different proposition to his brother's property. On seeing it through clearer vision, both mentally and physically, he saw a dilapidated property and wondered whether he should stay a few days and help with repairing the house. George dismissed this on two counts: for one, it might offend Pietro, who had given him shelter when he needed it most, and, secondly, it would delay his journey, and he might falter in his resolve in the pretext that he was only staying a few days to assist Pietro.

When he arrived at the house, Pietro was nowhere to be found so George set about the rudimentary kitchen and lit a fire under the stove. He had guessed that Pietro was somewhere out in the hills, gathering up his goats. Going into the yard, he began chopping wood for the fire; he soon had quite a pile and thought this would help Pietro at least and should not offend.

It was almost dark when Pietro arrived back, and he was very pleased to see that George had started a fire and it was burning well under the stove. Pietro threw the rabbits he had caught over a hook on a beam of the roof. The men greeted each other with affection; Pietro grabbed a flask of wine and the two sat by the stove, talking in a mixture of Italian and English, interspersed by the odd hand signal, about the decision that George had made. Pietro looked very carefully at George's expression and what he was telling him of his experiences before coming to him and Aldo.

"I just hadn't thought things through; my mind was in turmoil and I had just acted on impulse, a bit like a wild animal would, running from a sound that it could not distinguish. I blundered away from my mates that I had been with for years, although my best mate Bertie was dead. I think it was this that started me thinking: what was it all for? It was like a dream state, I don't remember how I came to be with you. I thought that I had made the walk in one day, but this could not be so. The days are a blank; I do recall sleeping and crying a lot. Pietro, you just cannot believe the terrible things the men on that hillside suffered: young men, with the whole of their lives before them, snuffed out or badly maimed. The lives of those that survived will be full of adversity in the future." Breaking down, George cried at the thought of it all again.

Pietro didn't say a word; rising from where he was seated, he walked across to George, held his head against his warm smoky goat-smelling chest and let him sob until there were no more tears left to shed. George was like a child in Pietro's strong wiry arms, and he let all the feelings that had been pent up inside him flood out. George was amazed at the fact that he could be so open with Pietro. He was such a kind and loving man – that was understood – but he also had an air about him that made you feel easy and comfortable in his presence.

After George's revelations, both men looked at each other and said, in unison, "I don't know about you, but I am starving." The red wine had dulled their senses but somehow sharpened their appetites; the act of food preparation would remove any feeling of embarrassment about George's disclosures. Pietro busied himself preparing the rabbits, skinning them with the adeptness of someone that had carried out this procedure many times before. He chopped the rabbits into large pieces and added them to the large pot by the fire, poured in some water, wine, herbs and wild garlic and placed the pot on the stove, while the men talked some more. George had picked up quite a lot of the Italian language, while working on Aldo's farm; he was far from fluent, but he had a much greater grasp of the language than on his last visit to Pietro's, and so their discussion was still punctuated with English, sign language and quite a lot of laughter, caused by some of the words that George had spoken in Italian. Pietro commented on his improvement in speaking Italian over the past months, but George still had a way to go. Both men were tired and so they ate Pietro's inevitable rabbit stew, consumed more wine than was probably good for them, and were soon asleep by the fire.

George awoke the next day with a watery sun peering through the window; the dust could be seen floating in its rays. Pietro was already up and outside, attending to his flock of goats that were bleating incessantly. George groaned as his aching head reminded him of the amount of wine he had consumed the night before. He also ached almost everywhere else, as he had fallen asleep in a not too comfortable chair by the fire. He began to stretch and groan some more as he brought life back into his numb limbs. As soon as he arose, he regretted it, as the world was moving around him.

The move to the water pump was incredibly hazardous, as George's unsteady gait made him grasp at furniture, door frames and anything else that he felt might make his journey less precarious.

Having doused his head under the cool water for several minutes and removed the sleep from his eyes, he began to recover from the night's excesses. He looked about him and saw that Pietro was halfway up a hill with his goats and, by the way he moved, none the worse for wear.

George returned to the house, stoked the fire and got it blazing nicely, filled the kettle and was about to scout around for something to eat other than leftover rabbit stew, when Pietro returned with a cheery, "*Buongiorno*" and told George he had a surprise for breakfast. The Americans that had begun passing through this way had left him some bacon and coffee and would he like some? George was just pleased to have something that would keep him going for the rest of the day and settle his stomach. The thought of bacon at first thrilled him, and then he wondered if it might do the opposite of settling his stomach, but the prospect of real American coffee was both novel and a treat. This was all kept in place by some of Pietro's coarse bread, which seemed to hold everything together.

After breakfast, the men said their goodbyes. George thought he saw a glint of a tear in Pietro's eye. He promised that, if all went well, he would return to see him, Aldo, Marie and Margaretta, but he was not sure how soon that might be. George left Pietro chasing some of the stray goats up the hillside. The old man had sent him on his way with a flask of water, some bread, cheese and the American bacon that they hadn't finished at breakfast.

As George walked away, he thought of the friends he had made over the past months.

Chapter 32

Entering GHQ

The sound of heavy vehicles reached George's ears and he assumed he was close to the base that had been described to him. As he summited the hilltop, he could see a very heavily armoured centre that was growling with tanks, trucks carrying heavy munitions and a large number of American and British vehicles, some of which were transporting fuel, others men. The centre was a hive of activity, with men running to and fro and others climbing into the back of the troop transports. They were all heading northward on the road to Rome and beyond. Reinforcements, George thought to himself: they must be pushing Jerry out of Italy completely by now; this was a major supply centre.

The walk back had not been arduous, as George was pretty fit from his farm work. He looked more like a peasant who had been working on the hillside, so no one turned their heads as he walked into the melee that was the GHQ of the 8th Army. He strolled rather than marched, as he had lost that upright soldier stature from months of walking the hills and tending the vines. The sentry at the entrance of the bustling encampment asked him his business, speaking to him in very careful English, somewhat slower and louder than necessary – the way most people do when they feel they have encountered a foreigner, who might not fully understand their language. George grinned at the sentry and, without further ado, politely, in a matter-of-fact manner, quoted his name, rank and army number and stated that he was a deserter returning to duty. The look on the sentry's face was one of utter amazement, and George had to pick up the dialogue while the sentry decided on what he should do next. George spoke very slowly back to the sentry.

"You had better get your NCO or commanding officer."

"Yes, yes," said the sentry, looking about him, "You stay right there."

"I won't be going anywhere."

Sergeant Hoddinott, together with the sentry and two military policemen, arrived at the entrance, where George was leaning against an army lorry as if he hadn't a care in the world. The sergeant seemed enraged by George's relaxed attitude.

"What the bloody hell do you think you're doing?" he asked.

"Waiting for you, Sergeant," George replied.

"Stand to attention when you speak to a superior rank and take that grin off your face!"

George's body still remembered how to stand to attention, but somehow it didn't seem appropriate in the clothing he was wearing. His baggy trousers and pale striped shirt and waistcoat seemed quite comical between the two hefty MPs, who were all spit and polish. They marched him to the guardhouse, where other reprobates were incarcerated. It was a makeshift shed with an armed guard, but most of the men inside were just waifs and strays that had been disobedient or slow to jump to their NCO's commands in good order, and they were fascinated by George.

"Wot you done, mate? Wot you in for?"

"I'm a deserter, that's all," George said.

"Well you look like you been on bloody 'oliday, that's all," was the mocking reply. The two men he was put with were the usual conscripts, that didn't believe it was right for their country to inflict this punishment of forcing them to join the army upon them; George had seen and heard it all before and so he quietly withdrew from their company.

George didn't remain with this company for long, and Sergeant Hoddinott and his two MPs marched George over to see the commanding officer, who was a Major Perry. He looked George up and down and asked him to state the details of his rank, regiment, army number and date of birth, in order that his identity could be verified. He wrote all this in a large leather-bound notebook that seemed to have travelled with him for quite a while, as its appearance was becoming ragged around the edges. There was also another NCO in the corner of the tent, who was filling out forms, which George assumed would go to his court martial; he was writing down every word that was spoken, without once looking up. After this brief interview, the major, who had pale blue eyes, light brown hair, a moustache and a nervous twitch in one eye, told George that he would be held in a separate quarter from the other men, until such time as he could put together a field court martial. He then looked George up and down once again.

"You do realise the gravity of the situation?"

“Yes Sir,” George simply replied. The major turned to the sergeant.

“Sergeant, you had better get him out of those clothes. Find him a military uniform of some sort.”

“Yes Sir,” was the immediate reply. George was duly marched out of the tent and into another, where he was told he would remain until the major had reported his return to his regiment. They would duly assemble a field court martial.

“You will remain in this tent until further notice, and don’t try running or it will be the worst for you. There will be an armed guard outside and if you decide to run, he has orders to shoot you. Understood?”

“Yes Sergeant. Why would I run when I have returned voluntarily?”

“Just ‘yes Sergeant’ in future. I don’t need a lesson in philosophy from a coward.”

With that, the sergeant turned and left George sitting on his bunk; soon after, a private from the stores arrived with an army uniform for him, complete with underwear, a belt, boots and socks. The orderly winked at George and spoke with a cheeky smile.

“You’re for it mate, you are. They’re a bit tough on deserters here.” With a wicked look on his face, he exited the tent, drawing a line across his neck and pushing his tongue out of one corner of his mouth; George assumed this was his attempt to replicate a hanging. He shrugged at the infantile attempt to put the wind up him.

Changing out of his clothes and putting on the not forgotten feel of the army kit, George smelt the fresh air mingled with smoke from Pietro's fire on his now abandoned clothes. His head and heart returned to the green hills and a very different life from the one he would now have to face. He sat back down on the bunk, awaiting his fate.

Chapter 33

Field Court Martial Part 2

The court martial hadn't taken long to arrive at what it deemed a suitable sentence. Looking at George, the major stated that, after due consideration of his prior good record and the factors surrounding his disappearance, they were sentencing him to 15 months' hard labour. He would serve the entirety here in Italy, he would not be returned home until at least the completion of his sentence and he might be returned to active duty, depending on his behaviour. After the announcement of his sentence, the MPs marched George from the field court martial and into his new life for the next 15 months. George knew that he could cope with this new regime; he was in fairly good spirits as he was marched to the lorry that was waiting to move him to his new home.

The truck lurched its way out of the camp, on the road towards Rome, where there was an encampment of prisoners sentenced to hard labour. The work would consist of road repairs, filling sandbags and the digging of waterways and trenches. The work lasted for a whole day; it was only broken up by a break of 30 minutes for lunch and an hour for dinner. The sentenced men worked until dark, even longer if there was a need for immediate emergency repairs to embankments and roads that had been shelled. The work was hard and tedious, and every day was very much the same as the one before.

The men on the truck did not speak to each other; they had all retreated into their own thoughts, shattered after a backbreaking day, contemplating either their luck or the lack of it. George's mind always returned to his time in the hills; it was a medicine for his brain. Occasionally he wondered why he had bothered to return, but he knew deep down this was the only way to come out with a clean sheet at the end of his term in the army.

Poor weather set in over the following months; the urgent repairs to roads were sorely needed, as they had been eroded by flooding and the movement of heavy vehicles wheels cutting into the soft terrain. At least the men were fed well; it was not like the previous winter, when George was stuck on the side of a hill with the enemy firing down on him, freezing cold without hot food, dry clothing or a bed to sleep on. This was almost luxury, and he looked upon it as time for keeping up his fitness levels by working hard, eating well and sleeping well.

A few months passed, and letters began to arrive. George was surprised that there was a bundle of letters for him. He was obviously back on the army records and, even though he was stationed in a prison camp, the post was a crucial means of keeping up morale; after all, he would not remain here forever. As a prisoner, he was still entitled to some of the benefits of being in the armed forces, the post being one of them. He wondered who would be writing to him, as his brothers were not the best at keeping in touch. When he found that the letters were from Amy, he was deeply shocked and somewhat ashamed, as he had not written or thought of Amy or home for some considerable time. He read the first one of the three letters bound together with string; it made him think of the girl that he had left behind, to whom he was unable to say goodbye and the last person he had expected to hear from. The envelopes had been scrawled on, as they had been passed on from the various positions in Italy where he had been stationed; he was lucky to get them at all, he thought, but now his conscience was troubling him. He had spent the last seven months with a young woman, promising her that he would return, and in the process had completely pushed out of his mind all thoughts of returning to England. But now he had letters from an English girl, to whom he had also become attached. He had been informed that he would not be returning to England any time soon; in fact, depending on the state of the war after he had completed his sentence, he would be returned to the front line. He began to weep silently as the shame washed over him; he felt as if he had been accused of murder, rather than desertion. That was it: he had deserted Amy along with his past life. How could he have been so caught up in himself as to forget his roots and the girl that he was falling in love with back home?

The first letter was in reply to his hurried note, as he had left all those months ago; so much had happened since then to change his outlook on life. The letter was warm and sometimes affectionate; Amy stated how she had enjoyed their time together. She quite understood that he had been whisked away at such short notice and also appreciated that, in wartime, this was quite likely to happen. She had taken the trouble to find out how she could write to him and would continue to do so, even if his circumstances did not enable him to write in return, but she would like to hear from him when he was able to write.

The next two letters were in a similar vein but contained added news about what she had been doing and what the war effort was like in England. The shortages were quite cutting, and she was very appreciative of the time they had spent together at Lyons Corner House; the abundance of food was quite amazing and in contrast to their meagre wartime rations. She had also visited Harry, and he was doing quite well, except that he seemed to be losing more of his sight, but still managing to make things out of the wood from bomb sites. In fact, she said, he had been so grateful for her visit that he gave her a small bedside table he had made. It was extremely heavy, well embellished with fancy corner work, and she had to struggle with it all the way home, after insisting she could manage.

Amy also told George about Harry's marriage to a woman called Dorothy, known as Dot. Amy attended the wedding at St Saviour's and, although there were not many people in attendance, the ceremony was very nice, and Dot and her friends had done their best to decorate the church and the aisle leading to the church doors with flowers and bunting. She was telling George this, as Harry found it difficult to write now and he said that he was not much of a letter writer anyway. She hoped that he got this letter in good time so that he could write to Harry and Dot and congratulate them.

George sat and sighed after reading about the familiar patterns of life back home. He was pleased that Amy had called in on Harry but was concerned about his failing sight. While on leave, he had tried to persuade Harry to go to the London Eye Hospital, but he wouldn't, out of sheer stubbornness, and got cross when George said that it would be his own stupid fault if he went blind. He was surprised at the news of the wedding; he hadn't an inkling of any romantic endeavours on Harry's part. Just shows how much I have lost touch, he thought to himself.

George sat wondering what to do next; well, you must write back to her, at least you owe her that, he mused. The real dilemma was what he would write to her. He could tell her about his situation, but how much of it? He couldn't tell her about Margaretta. As soon as he thought of Margaretta, he wished he hadn't. He had been pushing her to the back of his mind; the thought and scent of her still filled his senses with delight. He wondered what she might be doing at this time; had she already blanked him from her mind and found a young, local man? George pulled himself together, as madness lay in that direction.

That night, George wrote back to Amy and told of his predicament. He was sorry if she felt let down by him because of his actions overseas and his imminent court martial. He did not mention where he had been and how he had survived because he would have to think of Margaretta, even if he didn't mention her; he was now even more confused by his own emotions. Had he promised Amy anything, either by word or action? He didn't think so, as their parting had been so abrupt. That wasn't fair, he decided, as, by the very nature of their closeness, he had probably implied a continuing relationship. But, then again, this was war and things were changing so rapidly. He pulled himself up over this thought, telling himself that was a lame excuse. He did not know how he felt about Amy or Margaretta; it all seemed so very far away from his existence now.

He was reasonably pleased at the letter he eventually completed in the small hours; he would ask permission in the morning, this morning, to post it on to Amy. He thought that he would take Amy's advice and write to his brother, Harry, firstly to congratulate him on his wedding – the sly old dog – and to tell him of his situation too. This would be an easier letter to write; he would keep it brief and see if he could send both letters together.

Chapter 34

Back to England?

It was a warm summer's day when George was summoned to the commanding officer. A bulky man, he played constantly with his large moustache, while thinking. He had dark hair, which was well slicked down and parted in the middle and very bushy eyebrows, which seemed to balance his face with the large moustache. Looking up as George was escorted in, he immediately turned back to the papers he was completing on the makeshift trestle table that he was using as a desk. This was piled high with various depths of paperwork; even as he worked on signing his way through one lot of papers, an adjutant appeared to be piling up another lot. A disgruntled major roared at the adjutant.

"Damn and blast, Mallory! Can't you at least let me finish one pile before you start another?" Mallory hastily ducked out of the tent to avoid the major's wrath.

The commanding officer looked up again and asked, "Who is this then?"

"You asked to see the prisoner, Sir," the corporal guarding George replied. "Give your name, rank and number, Private." George duly obeyed.

"Oh yes," said the major, "I have some paperwork here concerning the prisoner. Where has my adjutant disappeared to? Never mind, I have it. Yes, yes, I'm right. This is it; it appears that you have had your sentence reduced, Private. You will now be serving until the end of this year. Some 112 days have been taken off your sentence; after that, you will be returning to England on the first available ship. Is that clear? Good. Now take him out of here. Can't you see I'm busy? And find that adjutant and send him to me."

The major waved them out of the tent and George was not sure if he was delighted or saddened by the news. The reduction in sentence was good news, but he wasn't sure that he wanted to go home just yet. He needed to see Margaretta once more so that he could explain and also to see how he felt about her on seeing her again. He would also like to know how she now felt about him, but he thought that the army would not be so free and easy about him disappearing off into the hills of Italy a second time.

The balance of his sentence seemed to pass more slowly now that the end was closer. He knew that the termination of his sentence did not mean the end of his military service; he would be returned to duty and held as a reserve at least in England. The days of digging trenches and repairing roads grew more and more tedious; the men around him were irritating him immensely. Their childish attitudes, lack of morals and thieving ways were enough to drive him mad. George felt himself slipping into a place he would rather not go. His only option was to start a boxing school within the camp; at least he could take his frustrations out on the men who annoyed him the most. First, he had to get permission and, secondly, persuade these reprobates to take part. The very action of putting this together made him feel much better; it also helped to calm his mind. He would have to make a decision regarding the women he was so very fond of, and this would be a difficult one.

One fight that George was to remember for some time was against an Irishman, who was slippery and quick like himself. The fight took place one evening in a large marquee that was used for storing foodstuff: enormous stocks of bully beef and hard rations. They had been given permission to use the marquee, as long as the boxes and crates were stacked back in their respective aisles after the fight.

The fight was scheduled for eight o'clock that evening; both men and officers were keen to see George fight, as he had become known for his unorthodox style. His opponent, who was less well-known, was Michael Kelly, also known as 'Killer Kelly', a semi-professional back in Ireland, and no one really knew what to expect.

The fight started somewhat slowly, as each man measured the other's strengths and weaknesses. The crowd became restless and there were shouts of, "Get a move on, someone hit someone" and "I have a bed to get to tonight; thump him, Kelly".

This seemed enough to spur the fighters on, and the clash was spectacular, with George receiving a cut above his eye; this enraged him and he seemed to go ballistic. He felt the anger stored from all the months past, the loss of his best friend and everything that had daunted him from his childhood rush to the surface. He struck out at Kelly, with rapid quick-fire blows that would normally have floored his opponent, but this one was still bouncing about the ring. George went for him again, but the Irishman had worked out his tactics; he ducked he weaved, and George felt the energy draining from him as the useless air punches took their toll. The Irishman moved in for the kill. Sensing George's weakening state, he delivered six or seven body blows and George felt himself buckling under the onslaught. The bell rang none too soon and saved George from a potential knockout.

On returning to his corner, he sat and spat blood, and cold water was poured over his face by his corner man, who was concerned about his eye. Growling under his breath, George sounded like a wounded animal, and he was; growling was a thing he was prone to do to raise his adrenalin and anger. George pushed away his corner man and shouted at Kelly.

"Come on you fucker, I'm going to kill you."

Kelly rose to the occasion, with a skip and a jump, ran around the ring, shouting back at George and to the spectators.

"Oh no, oh no, he is going kill me, like fuck!"

The mockery was not lost on the crowd; they were delighted and laughed, calling out, "Come on Kelly, Come on Killer, Killer Kelly, Killer Kelly."

This did nothing for George's demeanour; he stormed out of his corner like a raging bull. His eyes were red with rage, blood dripped from the cut over his eye down his cheek to his chin, and droplets fell onto the canvas floor. Kelly turned to meet him with horrified shock on his face. George exploded, delivering a triple blow to Kelly's head that was unstoppable. He didn't even have his guard up as he lay into his opponent. George was so angry that nothing would have stopped him. Kelly buckled under the combination of blows to his head, his body and then back to the head again. He was pinned against the ropes and George did not stop until the referee intervened. The bell rang out as Kelly was helped to his corner. Asked if he wished to continue, he nodded to indicate that he did.

The rest of the fight was more evenly matched, with both men drained from the earlier rounds. George felt some disgust at his own behaviour and cooled off a little for the rest of the match. When it was over, both men were called to the centre of the ring by the referee, who grasped a wrist of each opponent; the crowd simmered down and awaited the result. The ref then lifted both of their hands, while the master of ceremonies announced a draw. The spectators rose as one and applauded the fighters. Leaning across to Kelly, George said, "Sorry mate I lost it a bit there."

Kelly smiled at George, and then winced from a split in the side of his mouth.

"I'm just glad we were both fighting on the same side on the frontline."

Both men shook gloves, gave each other a hug and the crowded marquee erupted with applause, a standing ovation no less. George reflected on the events of the match and promised himself: no more fighting of any sort.

He had barely begun his boxing-promoter lifestyle when it was over. There had been 30 to 40 matches, and the prisoners enjoyed the release as much as George. It wasn't necessary for him to beat someone to a pulp to make himself feel better any longer; being the manager, rather than the participant, had given him much to do on the organisational side and, to his surprise, he had quite enjoyed this role.

George had been told that he would be returning by ship to England within the next few days. He was discharged from the prison camp and returned to join the Gordon Highlanders, who were shipping back.

Chapter 35

Not so easy an escape

George, who was buffing up his kit, had his head down working on his boots and didn't hear a tall and very spindly corporal approach.

"Private, the CO wants to have a chat with you."

"OK, Corp, just let me get my boots on and I'll be right with you." The corporal seemed to be in no hurry and perched on an empty ammunition box, casually picking the dirt out of his fingernails. George was about to say something about him flicking the remnants into the tent but thought better of it. He was always speaking out and getting himself into hot water so decided to button it.

"Ok Corp, lead on." The corporal sauntered alongside George, as if he had all the time in the world. George noticed the parachute regiment insignia then the limp that obviously plagued him.

"Where were you in action?" he enquired.

"Here and there," the corporal replied and sauntered on with the occasional limp then recovery. He was obviously not in the mood for a discussion.

They arrived at the CO's tent, saluted and the corporal announced their presence.

"What? Not you again, Private? What's he been up to this time?"

"Nothing as far as I know, Sir," replied the corporal. "Just bringing him to you as requested, Sir."

"Oh yes, let me find the communiqué. Ah here it is. Yes, yes, a note from our American friends. Apparently they have a young lady with them who wishes to see you."

George's mind was racing. Who could possibly be here? His heart thumped with expectation and fear all at the same moment. He did not dare wish for the person he wanted it to be; it was probably something mundane and he was just getting his hopes up for nothing.

"Are you sure you haven't been causing trouble again, Private?"

"No Sir," replied George, standing at attention.

"Damn nuisance if you have been roughing up the locals. Have you been putting your dick in places it shouldn't have been, Private?"

"No Sir," he replied once again.

"This is rather strange; the Yanks have sent a Jeep for you to take you to this young lady, odd that. Well you had better take him to them, Corporal. They are waiting at the main entrance. Away with you, Private, and I hope that you are telling me the whole truth or there will be consequences. Do you understand?"

"Yes Sir." With the last comments hanging in the air, they did an about-turn and marched out of the tent.

"Well Private, what have you been doing that a Yank general would send an escort for you? Have you been diddling the general's daughter?" enquired the corporal, laughing, without waiting for George to reply and leading him promptly to the main gate, where two American MPs were leaning on a Jeep, smoking while they waited for what they assumed was their prisoner. Their orders were simply to bring him back to the American base directly and report to General Roberts, not five miles further north from the British encampment.

Few words were exchanged; George was ushered into the back of the Jeep by the two MPs, who resembled a couple of gorillas or at least two American footballers, and the Jeep dipped under their weight as they threw themselves into the front of the vehicle. George asked them if they knew what this was all about as he had never met an American general.

"Search me," they said in unison and laughed at their synchronicity. The larger of the two gorillas said, "We are just messenger and delivery boys for the general. He says, 'Go there, do that' and we go and we do; that is all there is to it."

"Too right," said the other unnecessarily.

They arrived at the American base camp in about ten minutes, even though they had to weave in and out of heavy vehicles, moving men and equipment up the road northward. He had heard from Giovanni about his nightmare ride with GI Jo and now he could understand why it had been so hair-raising. These GIs had no consideration for the welfare of others on the road or for themselves; they saw their goal and headed straight for it as if they had a death wish. George was feeling rather sick from the hair-raising ride, or was it anxiety about this future encounter? He was puzzled, expectant and confused, all at the same time.

Leading him into the general's presence in a large tent on the far side of the base, they saluted sloppily and left George with the general. George was at attention and had saluted with the respect expected when in front of a superior officer. General Roberts was relaxed and much younger than George expected; his uniform looked as if it had just been cleaned and pressed recently. He had brown, mousy hair and a boyish face. He looked not long out of school, with freckles across the bridge of his nose and onto his cheeks, and he was totally clean-shaven; unlike some of the British generals, he found it unnecessary to cover himself in facial hair.

"That's OK, you can stand easy. George, right?" he enquired.

"Yes, Sir."

"Cool it, buddy, this is not official stuff so relax. I understand that you were working in a vineyard with some friends of mine. Is that right?"

"Yes Sir, but I didn't know they were friends of yours."

"Let's say they became friends over the passing months; I have been asked by a certain young lady, who lives and works on the vineyard, to find you and see that you are OK, which, by the look of things, you are."

George's emotions were about to boil over at the mention of the vineyard: it had to be who he had hoped it was. How had she arranged this? It seemed an impossible set of circumstances.

"Yes Sir, thank you Sir."

"Look George, I have said that this is informal. Talk to me as if you have met me in a bar and we're having a chat about life. OK?"

"Whatever you say, General."

"I assume that you are still fond of this young lady?"

"Yes I am." George was still struggling with the informality that the general wanted to bring to this conversation. This was due to the heightened tension and expectation; he still couldn't believe what was happening to him, and the formality brought about a routine, in what was far from a routine situation.

"In that case, I am pleased to tell you that she is here."

"What! Margaretta is here? How did she manage that?" As soon as George spoke, he knew the answer: General Roberts had organised it for her, that's why he was here.

"Can I see her?" George enquired.

"Of course, that is the purpose of your visit. I will get one of my guys to fetch her for you. Remember I am very fond of this family too, so don't go upsetting her unduly. I know that you are being shipped back to England and I have explained this to her. She believes that you conspired with her father to leave in the way you did. For a time, she did not forgive either of you. Anyhow, it's up to you to placate her and not make promises you can't keep."

The general left the tent, and George stood and waited for his reunion with Margaretta. He thought of what he might say to her. Had she changed? Did she just want to see him to tell him how angry and disappointed she was? What was the purpose of this visit? How many strings had she pulled to get to the American base?

Hearing the rustle of the tent flap open, he turned to find Margaretta standing alone in the entrance, looking at him with longing and sadness in her eyes. He looked back with the love he had been forced to bury deep, so that he could carry on with his life and the path he had chosen. She was of course as beautiful as ever; she took one tentative step towards him, and he could see that she was still slim, but her figure was slightly fuller and her face a little wiser.

"Hello, George. How are you?"

"I am well, as you can see."

"They decided not to shoot you then?"

"No, they thought they might get a little more out of me, so they gave me 15 months' hard labour, repairing roads and the like, reduced eventually by three and half months." They paused and looked at one another, each longing for the other but both afraid to make the first move or to offer any sign of doing so; the awkwardness of their meeting was painful.

Margaretta was the first to break and asked, "Will you kiss me, George?"

He made no reply but moved forward slowly as if he were in a dream. Touching one arm and then the other, he moved in closer until they could each feel the other's breath on their face. He gently brushed his lips across hers and she replied in the same way. They kissed more firmly, moving into each other until their bodies met; they both gasped, caressed each other and, as in the past, their passion grew. Her thin cotton dress was no barrier, as he could feel her ample breasts and nipples pressing against his chest and the hardness that came from him pressed against her thigh; she wanted more of him, she had missed him more than she could say.

Margaretta's voice was shaking as she asked, "Why didn't you write to me, George? I didn't know if you were injured or dead or what."

"I thought that if we broke cleanly it would be for the best. I just didn't know what would happen to me, and I didn't want to promise anything that I couldn't or wouldn't be in a position to fulfil," replied George.

"How could you leave me, when you knew how much I loved you?" She sobbed at the thought of those days when she was devastated by the longing for him, not knowing whether he was dead or alive.

"I did not want to go, Margaretta. I explained that to you, but I did not want to prolong the agony. I spoke with your father and he agreed."

She became angry then and shouted, "It was not up to him. I am my own woman, I can decide by myself. He will not interfere in my life ever again. I am 21 now and a fully grown woman, who will make up her own mind."

George had seen her cross before, but the anger toward her father was something else. He tried to plead with her not to blame her father; after all, it was her father's way of being supportive and George had come to the decision himself.

"Don't think that because I love you, that you are forgiven either."

This took George by surprise, although why he was shocked at her strength of character, he didn't know: he had seen it displayed often enough. When Margaretta wanted something, she went all out to get it. The very fact that she was here now was an absolute miracle; how she had managed to cajole the hierarchy into submission was unbelievable, and persuading a general to send a Jeep with two MPs to bring him to her was something out of the book of Egyptian queens. That's it, thought George. She is the reincarnation of Cleopatra. Why hadn't he seen this before? George began to laugh at the thought. This brought Margaretta to an abrupt halt; she then became angrier.

"Are you laughing at me?" The angrier she became, the more the thought tickled him and he laughed all the more. The situation was becoming explosive, as Margaretta did not like being laughed at. She stormed across the tent and began hitting him – not slaps, but real punches that hurt – but George laughed all the more.

"Why are you still laughing at me?"

"I'm not. It's just a thought I had." She stood over him when he collapsed onto the general's camp bed; he laughed and kept apologising. Margaretta watched him then began to laugh herself, she didn't know at what or whom, but George's laughter became infectious, and she sat on the edge of the bed while he pulled himself together.

"I am sorry," he said. "I just got this stupid thought in my head and couldn't stop laughing at it." She reached across and stroked his face; the mood had changed again and they moved towards each other once more.

"Wait, we can't do this," said George. "The general will be back at any time."

She smiled and said, "No he won't, you are not going to escape so easily."

Definitely the wicked queen's captive, thought George, suppressing the laughter.

The moments the lovers were to spend together were of the most intimate they had ever shared. For him, it may have been the reality that he would have to return to England, for her, the unsure future with his parting, but the moments were both deeply shared and of a carnal yet loving nature.

They sat in the general's tent afterwards, discussing the future and what they might possibly share. She was desperate for reassurances; he equally was reluctant to talk in positives. They came to no firm conclusions, other than that they loved each other deeply and would do whatever they could to be together once again, in the not too distant future.

There was a "huh hum" from outside the tent and George said, "I think the general wants his tent back."

Margaretta was distraught at the inevitability of their parting and clung to him, as if, by holding him tightly to her, she would prevent him from leaving her. George released himself from Margaretta's iron-like grip and opened the flap to the tent. The general was standing outside, smoking and shuffling his feet like a naughty child waiting to see the headmaster.

"I am sorry to disturb you young lovers, but the transport is here to take you both back to your different locations, and I can't keep them waiting any longer."

"Thank you very much, Sir," George said. "This has made the parting more difficult and yet at the same much better than before."

"That's ok. I just hope you two have sorted things out now and wish you both the very best for the future."

Margaretta hung back in the tent; George excused himself for one last goodbye, promised to write and was quickly gone and back along the path to the waiting MPs and his return transport to the British camp.

She appeared shortly after George's departure, once she had composed herself. Approaching General Roberts, she told him that she would never forget the kindness he had shown her and her family and wished him well for the future. Reaching up to the general, she kissed him fondly on the cheek. A little embarrassed in front of his men, he said it was his pleasure and quickly entered his tent to carry on with a mound of army paperwork.

Margaretta watched the disappearing lights of the Jeep carrying George away. He didn't turn to look back, which she thought was just as well, as she felt certain she would not be able to hold back the tears, and crying was the last thing she wanted to do in front of these American soldiers. She was politely escorted to her transport and was soon disappearing into the darkening skies of the night. A storm was brewing over the hillside; her transport was a large lorry, which was travelling to deliver supplies. She stepped up into the cab alongside a GI smoking a cigar.

"Do you mind ma'am? I'll put it out if you do."

"No it is fine, thank you for asking," she replied. Her mind was elsewhere, wondering what this England was like that her George was returning to. Would she travel there one day or would he return to her and the vineyard?

She snuggled into the back of the seat, making herself as comfortable as possible. She could see herself in the glass as she turned to keep her face from the GI, who was talking to her, although she wasn't listening. He soon gave up the one-sided diatribe and she watched herself in the truck window, as tears trickled down her face.

Chapter 36

The Leaving 1946

The ship back to England was like all the other troop transports, except spirits were high on this particular ship, because the men on board were returning home after several years away. The war had ended a year previously; George had not returned on the first available ship as he had been promised but had remained to aid the repatriation of troops. This had meant the stacking and shipping of equipment and the storage of materials that would be sent later. He was also involved in the billeting of soldiers awaiting their ship home. He didn't mind this work: it was less tedious and not as arduous as the work on the road gangs, and mostly it was undercover, avoiding either the winter rains or, later, the summer sun.

He watched as the coast of Italy was getting further away from him. In a reflective mood, his mind returned to the great loss of men in the hills of Italy, which in the summer sun looked deceptively peaceful. He knew them in a different mood. He remembered the treacherous slippery slopes of the mountains to the abbey, the men and materials cast upon the hillside that became a waste tip for humanity, the discarded cartridges, the smell of cordite and, worst of all, the smell of decaying bodies. He was haunted by the lack of warm food and supplies, the endless cold nights in a wet sangar with nothing to cover themselves, nothing to protect them from countless machine guns firing, which made it impossible to take even a moment to be able to sit upright and light a fag, for fear of being shot.

George also felt the guilt of leaving his friends behind after that last decisive battle at Monte Cassino; he believed that Bertie would have been shocked and ashamed of his actions. He felt heaviness in his throat, heart and mind, when he thought of the waste of Bertie; he was such a good soul and a good friend. Would he have left? George thought not.

He watched the wake disappearing behind them; Italy was a narrow smudge on the horizon and a deep smudge in his soul. Would he ever be forgiven for his actions? While men from his battalion were fighting their way northward through the centre of Italy, he was in the lap of luxury, being fed and cared for by strangers that came to love him. Would friends and family back home understand his actions? Was he brave enough to tell them and face their disdain? Would they understand?

Night was closing in and the wake persisted like a continuous ribbon, threading back over the sea, pulling him back to Italy, its warmth, its welcoming spirit and Margaretta. At the same time, the ship steamed homeward to England, its familiarity, its pubs and shops and the local smells of his neighbourhood, his friends, family, and Amy.

It was becoming colder as the sun went down and a cool breeze picked up over the stern of the ship. George shivered, from either the cooling air or the thoughts he had to shuffle in his mind. Turning, he went below; he would just have to wait until he reached home to see what the future might bring.

There were no cheering crowds or bunting as the ship carrying George entered Southampton waters. The war had been over for nearly a year, and the enthusiasm for returning soldiers had waned. There had been many hospital ships over the past months, bringing back the wounded that were filling local hospitals across the country. There was only so much a city and a country could endure. After the initial euphoria, there were much more subdued greetings on the dockside. The whole of Southampton and the surrounding suburbs had been devastated by the impact of the *Luftwaffe*'s bombing campaign. The attitude was to rebuild the city and its surroundings; life was continuing, there were shortages and the inevitable rationing, but on the whole people seemed relatively cheerful. That is what George thought and saw, as he made his way through the busy docks, brandishing his railway warrant to return him home to London.

The journey to London was uneventful; in fact, he dozed most of the way and was only partially aware of people getting on and off the train as it made its way through the Hampshire countryside. He gloried at the splendour and the green lush pastures surrounded by oak and ash trees, hedgerows brimming with life, birdsong and the fields where labourers were bent over their tasks; then he fell into the arms of Morpheus.

George was pleased to be back in London and to walk the familiar streets, although not as familiar as they had been. Many buildings were being either shored up or pulled down, due to their unsafe condition. There were many gaps in the streets where he had worked as a young man: houses where school friends had lived and where some of the time he had run and played. There were children now raking through bombsites and making the most of running through the debris, hiding behind half-standing chimney breasts, and, to George's surprise, firing imaginary guns with either fingers or sticks that doubled as armaments. George shook his head in disbelief. Have we not had enough of guns and war? he thought to himself, but realised kids and most adults would never know or comprehend the true horror of war and its consequences.

The door was wide open as he approached home; he could hear the radio in the background, the big band sound emanating into the street, underpinning the hustle of the area that made up the East End of London. Market callers could be heard from streets away: louder than he remembered, probably due to the missing properties and the stillness of the day. Harry was in the kitchen as usual, preparing scraps of wood. Sanding them down and touching the pieces almost lovingly, he stroked, caressed and rubbed with the glass paper to achieve the finish he was looking for.

"Hello Harry," George said to his back. "Why are you working in the dark, you daft beggar?"

Harry turned to George, but all he could see was his silhouette as the sun streamed in through the grubby windows.

"Georgie boy, you're back! Oh it does my heart good to know that you're back safe. You don't have any injuries, you're all intact, eh?"

The floor was covered in debris, not just from the wood working but from all sorts of detritus. George was a little shaken by Harry's appearance, his lack of clean clothes and his unevenly shaven face.

"Yes I'm fine, but what the fuck is going on?" George exclaimed.

"I've gone almost blind since you last saw me, Georgie," replied Harry.

"When? Who? How? What? Are you seeing the doctor?" George replied, panic rising in his tone.

"Of course I have. They say I have left it too late, I will be completely blind within a month or two, so they reckon." George dropped his kitbag on the floor with a feeling of dismay. He slumped into one of the kitchen chairs, although it was covered in shavings from Harry's woodworking.

"I don't know what to say, Harry, this is bloody awful."

"Don't fret, Georgie. I'm fine, really I am. I can still work the wood and I get an even better finish just with touch. Everyone seems to like the bedside tables I make; they just have to finish them off with varnish or paint, if they prefer."

"I don't mean that, you fool. What about the rest of your life? Who is going to be around to look out for you?"

"Georgie, Georgie, after what you have been through, stop worrying about me. I have Dot and she is very good at looking after me. I get fed and watered regularly, I have company most nights. Don't you concern yourself about me. You worry about yourself, young chap, get yourself cleaned up, get some grub inside you and we'll have a few beers together tonight. This should be a celebration – you're back, Georgie, safe and sound! That's all that matters. Right?"

"What do you mean by 'most nights' Harry? Where the bloody hell is Dot, is she looking after you?"

"Georgie, don't worry yourself about me. I've told you I am fine. Dot just likes a little drink, that's all, and she becomes forgetful."

"You mean she fucking well neglects you more like! She's a bloody drunk, that's what you're telling me, isn't it? She should be looking after you and the house. What would mum think? What a bloody state."

"Calm down, Georgie, it's not your problem, and I'm happy enough as things are."

"Harry, I don't know how you can be so happy about your situation, but you're right. We'll celebrate tonight, forget all our troubles, or pack them, as the song goes," replied George.

"That's more like it, Georgie boy, bit of the fighting spirit, eh! Oh, I nearly forgot: there's a letter from Italy, so Dot tells me; it's up on your bed. Very nice handwriting, I'm told too," said Harry, winking his partly sighted eye. "A young lady no doubt? I want to hear all about it, so hurry upstairs, get sorted; we'll make some grub and chat the night away."

On entering the bedroom, the first thing George became aware of was the smell: the familiar dusty, must-filled smell of home. Not that the room was dirty, but it had been lying vacant for his return. In fact, the room had been cleaned by Dot and she hadn't made a bad job of it either: not as good as George's mum, but not bad, it would do. He placed the rucksack gently on the bed next to the letter from Italy. George stood over the letter, tilting his head from side to side, as if a better view of the object would give him some insight into the contents. After a few minutes he decided that to pick it up and open it would be the best way forward. The handwriting was Margaretta's. Why he hesitated, he did not know, maybe it was the surprise of finding a letter that had beaten him home, having travelled from a totally different world in the Italian countryside. He sat on the bed, looking at the letter; carefully slipping his finger through the gap that had no gum to fix it, he tore a rough opening.

The paper was light in weight and almost see-through; the handwriting sloped to the right, not like his left-handed writing style, which sloped in the opposite direction. The flourishes in the style of writing were quite ornate, something left over from Margaretta's school instruction. All the letters below the line ended with a swirling action, and the crossed ts were finished with an embellishment, as found in ancient manuscripts. George slowly read the letter. There were the usual greetings and the hope for a safe journey home to England. She expressed her love for him and then there it was in bold black script: Margaretta was pregnant with his child. His hand shaking, George smiled a little, puzzled by the surge of emotions that flooded his body, mind and being. He wasn't sure if he was pleased, concerned or disappointed or all three.

He had thought of Amy a great deal on the trip home: how he was going to break the news to her – of Margaretta, after her declarations of love in her letters to him, of the actions he had taken in Italy, of the court martial. Now he had another matter to disclose to her. He would have to return immediately, but how? It was all very well being shipped across the world by the army, but if he were to return to Italy under his own steam, he would need to organise and fund it. Returning to Margaretta was the right course of action, he was sure. He realised that he had been pacing up and down the bedroom, but for how long he was not sure, when Harry shouted from below.

"George, what are you doing up there? You've been marching up and down as if you were on parade."

"Sorry Harry," George replied. "I'll be right down; I need to discuss something with you about me going back to Italy."

"What the devil for, Georgie? You've only just got back. There isn't bad news, is there?"

"I'll tell you when I come down," said George.

Harry waited expectantly as George made his way downstairs. He stood facing the stairway with mouth slightly ajar.

"Come on tell me then," said Harry, even before George had placed his foot on the last stair. "What's happened? Is there something wrong or what?"

George took his time; he walked across to Harry, grasped his arms and, with tears in his eyes, said, "I'm going to be a father."

"Who says?" replied Harry.

"Margaretta, in her letter to me. She says that we are to have a baby in six months' time. I've got to get back to her, Harry. I've just got to get back. Oh hell, what am I going to tell Amy? I wrote back to her, telling her I was on my way home. What do I do now? How do I break it to her that I am no longer available, after all she has said to me and me to her?"

"Calm down," said Harry. "I'll put the kettle on and we'll talk about it all calmly, over a cup of tea. Isn't that always the answer? Mum used to say there is nothing that can't be sorted by sitting with a cup of tea and discussing the problem."

"She did," agreed George, as he slumped down into Harry's chair that had seen better days. George was oblivious to everything but his thoughts and sat with his head in his hands, not sure whether he should be celebrating his imminent fatherhood or downright miserable about the prospect of speaking to Amy.

The tea and conversation helped George come to terms with the prospect of fatherhood. Harry was a quiet, gentle giant: exactly what George needed. He told Harry of the passionate affair that he had had with Margaretta, the fact that she sought him out and even persuaded an American officer to find him and bring him to her. She was an amazing young woman, but George had thought that Margaretta would forget him and take up with one of the many eligible and willing young men from around the villages. Maybe she would have done so in time, but the prospect of a new life had changed the pattern of events – of that he was certain. He believed that their love, shared in those moments of war-torn Italy, would have become just a sweet memory to both of them. He had assumed that distance and time would have carved their young lives in a different material, the shape of which had now changed completely. He must write back immediately and worry about the conversation with Amy later.

Now that George was set on a course of action, he felt calm and assured in his resolve to return to Italy to work with Margaretta's father and brothers in the vineyard, if they'd have him. He would be a model father; he would learn Italian and take up a totally new life in the beautiful countryside of Italy. In George's mind it was all settled; all he had to do now was implement the plan.

Chapter 37

Telling Amy

As the day drew on, George realised that telling Amy wasn't going to be that easy. At first thought, saying the four simple words, "I have met someone," didn't seem that difficult, but the closer he drew to the time and place where he was to meet Amy, the more the words stuck in his throat. He consoled himself that he was going to be a father; Amy would understand that, maybe even be pleased for him. Who are you kidding, he thought to himself. What woman, after waiting for years and receiving letters of affection, would be reasonable?

He waited for Amy at 'their pub'; he was early, nervous and wrung his hands while he sat with his pint of beer. He thought that he would enjoy his drink, but somehow it tasted strange in his mouth. Perhaps he had spent too long away from home; vino was his choice of drink now. If he had asked for a glass of red wine in the pub, he would have received some strange looks, so he had plumped for his usual bitter and that is exactly what it was: bitter in his mouth, so much so he couldn't drink anymore. Becoming aware of someone standing close by, he looked up from his dark thoughts and there, looking radiant, fresh and quite delectable, was Amy. Her cotton dress was one he had seen before but, nevertheless, the way it swished as she moved and her dark looks made him gasp. If anything, she had become more gorgeous than he had remembered. He hadn't realised that he had been staring at her for some moments and she became a little uncomfortable under his glance.

"Well George, aren't you going to buy me a drink, or are you completely mesmerised by the beauty before you?" she joked, not feeling half as confident as she sounded. George rose, knocking against the table, the action sloshing some of his unwanted beer across it.

"Of course, Amy. What would you like? I'm very sorry for staring at you like that; you look so, so, well so beautiful."

"Why thank you George," she replied. "In that case you are forgiven and I will have a small lemonade shandy please."

With this excuse to move, he made quickly for the bar and ordered Amy's drink. By the time he returned, they both had had time to pull themselves together, and they began to chat about nothing much at all. Suddenly Amy stopped, placing her hand on top of George's, which was lying by the side of his ever-warming pint.

"What's wrong, George?" she asked. "Is there something you need to say to me?" This was like a bolt of lightning to George, who wasn't expecting Amy to make the running. He appreciated women's intuition and all that, but, to him, this was mind reading. Pausing for a few moments, he looked at Amy, who now appeared agitated. Realising she was about to speak again, George held up his hand to stop her.

"There is something very important I have to say to you, Amy. It's not easy and I've been worrying about it all night." He took a deep breath, looked at Amy once again and said the words. They seemed to flood out of his very soul, "I'm going to be a father, Amy, and there is no other way of putting it. I didn't mean to lead you on at all, I was coming home and looking forward to seeing you, but there it is. What more can I say?"

Amy was knocked back in her chair, as the words were spoken. They were like a physical blow; she looked stunned rather than upset, and at first George thought she hadn't heard him correctly. He repeated, "I am going to be a father, Amy!" almost exclaiming it to the whole pub.

"I heard you the first time, George. It's just been a bit of a shock, that's all. You must tell me who, when and where."

George was at a loss at this turn of events; he wasn't expecting to go into such detail. Amy seemed to have gathered herself and was looking a little like a schoolteacher waiting for the late homework. She sat very upright, glaring at George as if he had a bad report, and, in many ways, as far as Amy was concerned, he had given just that: a bad report. As George began to explain the circumstances, he spoke of Margaretta with affection and of the family equally so. He continued with the events leading to his desertion, the family's response to him, especially his first encounter with Pietro with the sparkling blue eyes and his kindness in taking a stranger in. He spoke of his education in the care of the vines, his return to his unit and his inevitable court martial. Throughout his story, Amy had sat perfectly still, listening intently, prodding him only if he faltered over a detail that she thought to be relevant. George finished by adding, but almost to himself, “She must have become pregnant the day she came to the American camp, a short time before I embarked for England.”

“That is of no consequence,” replied Amy. “You must write to her and reassure her of your intentions and of course to her family; that is most important.”

George was a little taken aback by the straightforward manner that Amy had adopted; he was both pleased and a little surprised. He appreciated she was imagining the situation from a woman’s perspective: what she would expect of any man that had been with her and had got her pregnant.

“Come on then George. I will walk you home; you must get that letter written immediately.”

George stumbled from his seated position; they must have sitting there for quite some time, his left leg had gone to sleep and it gave way slightly as he stood. He glanced at his beer still sitting in its glass: hardly two or three mouthfuls had been taken. Amy had managed to finish her drink, but he didn’t remember her doing so.

“I should be walking you home Amy, not the other way around.”

“I don’t believe that would be the right thing to do under the circumstances, George. You have things to get organised and that letter to write.” George mumbled something about bossy women and being drawn to them, but Amy either didn’t hear or pretended not to.

When they reached George's home, Amy didn't wait for an invitation.

She said over her shoulder to George, "I'll just pop in and say hello to Harry, then I'll be away home." The door always being open or on the latch, Amy did just that. As always, Harry was happy to see her; he thought she was one of those people that brought brightness to people's lives. He gave her a hug, exchanged a few pleasantries and, before George could say a word, she was out of the front door and halfway up the street.

Harry was bursting to know how things went.

"Well Amy didn't seem too upset. As I expected, she didn't really like you anyway," joked Harry.

George was distraught by the whole encounter. He hated seeing Amy putting on a brave face; it was better than histrionics but, nevertheless, painful for them both. He hadn't taken in what Harry had said to him: his attempt at being humorous at such a time being completely wasted.

"What do you want to do Georgie, go and get blind drunk or go up 'West' and see some dancing girls? You'll have to describe them for me for obvious reasons."

George came out of his stupor.

"What was that Harry? What are you blathering on about?"

"Nothing George, just trying to get your attention; you seem a little lost."

"Sorry Harry, I am. Things haven't turned out as expected. I must go and write to Margaretta.

As Amy pointed out, I need to straighten things out with her and her family. The poor girl will be in a tizzy if I don't reassure her. I'm going upstairs to write now, so I'd appreciate it if you don't bother me with anything until I'm done."

George sat on his bed, wondering how he might begin this letter. Reassurance, he had said, and what about love? Was it possible to love both women? Well, he believed he did. They were different in many ways, but he hated the thought of either of them being hurt because of his actions. Love, though, what did that mean exactly? He couldn't bear to think of Margaretta having to explain things to her family. No matter how much they had shown their affection for him, the fact that he wasn't on the scene to marry their daughter would radically change their view of him. But he couldn't waste time thinking about that. The priority was Margaretta and their child. There, he had said it: their child.

George still had some writing paper in his kitbag; he fished deep into the side pocket and was pleased to find that it was still in surprisingly good shape after its travels. He also had a pen, but that took a little more searching out. In the end he lost patience with his kit and just tipped it onto the floor in a heap, not that it was going to aid his search, but it gave him a strange satisfaction, even though he knew there was no one else but him to clear it all up. Eventually he got himself settled on his bed. Glaring at the blank page staring back at him accusingly, he began:

Dear Margaretta,
I hope that this letter finds
you well and that your
family is also well.

I received your news with
great joy and I plan to make
the journey back to you as
soon as I can organise it.

George stopped, looked at what he had written and said out loud, "What the fuck is that? This isn't your cousin, you great heaving pillock. What the hell do you think you are doing?" Screwing up the letter, he threw it at the wall then breathed deeply and began again with a fresh sheet. At this rate, I'll end up running out of paper, he thought.

George pulled out his feelings of the past months from deep within him: the smell of the earth, the rosemary, the food, the wine, but mostly the essence of Margaretta. He sucked in his breath at the thought of her, her bronzed skin, with dark hair cascading across her shoulders, her impish sense of humour, her lack of humour when she was cross, her wild sexual nature, her strength and most of all her belief in them as lovers and more. He found that he was smiling to himself in that dark, musty room and his heart began to pick up a beat as he thought of returning to Margaretta in those glorious hills of Italy – the gorgeous dew-covered hills that had brought him nothing but joy – who knew that they would pull him back to begin his life over. What he needed to write was a letter of love. He began with renewed vigour, his heart full of great love for his new wife to be and unborn child. How could a man be so fortunate?

The next morning George was out of the front door as soon as the post office was open; he had stayed up most of the night until he felt that everything he wanted to say had been said. He was quite pleased with his efforts; he had used all the paper he had, so much so that the envelope was bulging with his protestations of love and intent. The post office was still closed when he arrived and he marched up and down outside as if he was guarding the place. Every minute or so he would check the door, to no avail. Finally, he heard the postmaster rattle the lock from inside. In his efforts to get in, George knocked the door into the face of the postmaster.

"Steady on, the war's over you know, young man." The elderly gentleman would not be hurried. "I always open 30 seconds before time, so steady up I say, steady up." Squeezing through the flap in between the wall and the counter, he said to George, "Young man in a hurry, what's your hurry for? Whatever you give me will not leave until noon today. Come on, what is it, what is it?"

George ignored his reprimand and just stated the facts, "I need this to go to Italy the quickest way possible please."

"Uhm, Italy is it? A bit exotic. Do you know anyone there then?" George was fast losing patience.

"Of course I do, just get on with it, will you please?" The postmaster raised his eyebrows and got on with his job, he beginning to see that this young man was not to be toyed with. The deed done, George made his way back home to Harry, some breakfast and possibly an apology; he realised that he hadn't been in the best of spirits last night. Then he would see what sailings there were and whether he could either afford a ship or work his passage to get back to Italy.

Chapter 38

Letter to Italy

The day was sultry with an overhanging cloud base reaching down to the vineyard's closely trimmed vines, which would normally allow maximum sunlight to reach the fruit when sun was out. The weather was akin to Margaretta's mood as she lay on her bed, beads of perspiration on her brow, a deep feeling of morning sickness that at times overwhelmed her; she was feeling very sorry for herself. She had informed her parents of her pregnancy and, surprisingly, they had not seemed alarmed by the fact that an itinerant soldier had impregnated their daughter. In fact, they were rather pleased, as they knew George well enough to believe he would return and marry their daughter, and they looked forward to welcoming him into their family. This did nothing for Margaretta's mood, as she hated being laid low by anything or anyone; for her condition, she blamed George, which, in truth, was his fault. She was still mulling over her situation, propping herself up, lying down, moving to her side, cursing occasionally, when, suddenly, her mother called to her that there was a letter from England.

With this news, Margaretta's mood changed completely. Forgetting her sickness and ill temper, she jumped off her bed, racing down the stairs, whispering to herself, "at last, at last." She ran into the kitchen, saying, "It's from George, isn't it? Tell me it's from him." Marie laughed at her daughter and her change in demeanour.

"It most probably is, my daughter. But how would I know for sure? After all, you have thousands of letters from England, now don't you?"

Margaretta snatched the letter from her mother, stating, "It is from him, I knew he would write. When is he coming?"

"Open the letter and find out; that is what I would recommend."

Margaretta tore into the letter like a demon, ripping paper, throwing it on the floor without thought. Her mother yelled at her, but she was gone, she was walking back to her room to read the long-awaited letter in private. She heard her mother yell.

"When is he coming? Margaretta, Margaretta!"

She heard, but didn't; she was totally wrapped in George's words. As she read, she wept at his declarations of love, his outpouring of love for their unborn child and then his return to how much he had missed her and loved her. Margaretta sat on her bed, reading the letter over and over. Tears ran down her face, as she continued reading and her mother entered her bedroom.

"What's the matter, my darling child?" she asked, as she looked down on Margaretta.
"Is he not coming?"

"Yes, mother, he is coming; that is why I'm crying. He loves me and wants to marry me."

Marie clapped her hands together with delight, did a jig around Margaretta's bedroom, clasped her daughter by the hands and pulled her off the bed. Together, they danced with joy, tears and laughter.

When daylight broke across the vineyard on this auspicious morning, Margaretta was up, fussing around downstairs, getting breakfast for the house and the workers as usual, except, on this occasion, there was a spring in her step. She was humming to herself, unable to overcome the feeling of happiness that welled up inside her. The morning sickness had disappeared along with her depressive demeanour, and she was about to go to town to start preparations for the wedding.

In a hurry to get into town, Margaretta was impatient with her mother, telling her to hurry along. Marie smiled at Margaretta's impatience but appreciated her need to choose her wedding dress; this was an important day in her daughter's life. Aldo made himself scarce. Although pleased with his daughter's change since receiving the letter from George, he was equally pleased that he was not being asked to drag around stores with women intent in their need to fill the 'wedding basket' with all sorts of what he considered unnecessary wedding paraphernalia. Aldo was happy to pay the bill and stay with his vines, his men and his wine. Once Margaretta's entourage, including Angelina, Paula and Francesca, had disappeared from the yard, Aldo breathed a sigh of relief, looking forward to a normal working day in the vineyard.

Margaretta's progress to town was slow, as there were pick-ups to make; they stopped at a few villages to collect more friends that were to assist with the events of the day. For this, Margaretta had borrowed the vineyard's open-back vehicle. The young women piled into the back, carrying garlands of flowers that they placed over everyone and everything, happy to be part of the ever-growing group. As they made their way into the main town, they sang, laughed and joked all the way. Margaretta, much to the disdain of her mother, leant from the truck, shouting back to the ever-growing party in the back of the vehicle. It promised to be a full and exciting day for this young lady, with food and wine in the back enough to feed an army. The more they sang, the more wine was required; soon the young women were singing ribald songs about the marriage night for young couples; these would have shocked the most strong-minded. Although they knew of Margaretta's condition, this did not inhibit them in their renditions. Marie sat in the front of the truck with Margaretta, along with Daniel, one of the farm workers, to whom she apologised constantly about the behaviour in the back of the truck. He shrugged, smiled and said it was to be expected; his sister had been even worse prior to her wedding. Marie nodded knowingly, placed her hand on his arm, and whispered, "I remember."

"She didn't," he replied, "as she was too drunk at the time." At this, they both laughed.

As the truck of singing women approached the town, they spotted a waterfall, cascading down the side of a hill. The heat rising by the minute gave the women good cause for a diversion. Margaretta's thoughts were of George, and a slight satisfied smile was spreading across her face. She was absorbing the scent of the day; the smell of propolis from some nearby hives had mixed with the scent of flowers. Was there ever a better day?

"Let's cool off in the waterfall," one of the women cried. They all agreed and hammered loudly on the truck roof for Daniel to pull over. He was puzzled and thought that something was wrong. As soon as the truck stopped, the women were out of the truck across a small field, continuing to sing and dance in and out of the glorious waterfall that had made its way through the mountains, the hills and into the valley. The water was cool and sparkling and, as it hit rocks, it splashed, leaving rainbow effects in the sun of the day. The waterfall was still full of the ice-cold water from the higher lands, and the women gasped at first at the shock of the cold water, then laughed all the more. Not to be left out, Margaretta jumped from the truck and ran across the field to join the women in their exuberant fun. As she ran towards the giggling group, petals could be seen flowing behind her from her garland of flowers; they fluttered in the slipstream like a marriage train and then fell to the ground, leaving a trail to follow. Marie called to her to be careful in her condition; Margaretta was laughing and waving as she ran to join her friends.

Chapter 39

George's plan.

George was busy organising his exit from England. He had already been in touch with a number of ships leaving imminently: none wanted extra crew, and the cost of sailing as a passenger was a little beyond his means at present. He would have to get some work to pay for his trip. He had told Margaretta in his letter that he would leave as soon as he was able to purchase a ticket, but this was proving to be much more difficult than he had expected. There was still the matter of a passport; he did not believe his army papers would see him back overseas so he decided he would make his way to the passport office, fill in the necessary forms and, if he could, he would wait for the passport to be processed. He believed he had sufficient funds for this at least.

The next day George set about looking for work, thinking that anything would do; he just needed enough to pay for his passage and he'd be away. He made his way through the markets that he knew from his childhood, but many of the stallholders had plenty of ex-servicemen clamouring for work and he realised this was going to be much harder than he first thought. Turning a corner towards the fish market, he bumped into some old acquaintances from school days; they had finished their shift and were looking for the first opportunity to get a drink. George was pleased to see them, passing a few pleasantries on the street corner, but he was anxious to get away and continue his quest to seek work. He told them of his dilemma and they thumped him on the back, saying that this was his lucky day: he could join their gang tomorrow down at the fish market. George was pleased and surprised at his luck; they in turn said that he now had no excuse not to come and have a drink with them: they could catch up on all his news.

They made their way to a drinking club, where one of them, Tim Hardy, was a member. It was in a very discreet place; most passers-by would not give it a second glance. Tim knocked the secret knock, rat-a-tat-tat, and the door opened slightly to reveal a very scruffy individual, who turned out to be the pot boy.

"Move aside Charlie," said Tim. "Let the men get to their drinking." Charlie bustled aside and George and his other two compatriots sidled in.

"Mine's the first shout," said Tim. "What ya havin?" The men all called out their requirements in unison. Somehow Tom was able to decipher what they wanted or else knew from previous occasions what they were likely to order. The three men sat together, anxious to hear George's tale. Geoffrey, the eldest, asked George to tell them about his war experiences, while Alan was of the opinion that the women George had been with would be a more interesting topic. He guffawed and prodded George in the ribs, saying, "I bet you had more than your share, eh Georgie boy?" Tim returned with their drinks, helped by Charlie, who was none too steady. He slopped Geoffrey's drink down his leg: not much, but enough to get a "Steady on!" from Tim. For the next hour, drinks were bought, tales exchanged and horror stories of war tutted over.

"Tell me about the job, how much does it pay?" asked George. "I have to get enough money to travel and keep body and soul together while aboard ship."

"Don't you worry about that, Georgie boy; if it comes to it, we'll put some in the pot for you. Anyhow, there are enough fiddles going on down at the market – you'll make your money in no time at all."

"Look here, Tim, I don't want any trouble. The last thing I need is to get banged up when I'm trying to leave the country. I just need some legit cash to get me away, that's all." George was more than a little disturbed by Tim's comments; he really could not afford any trouble. He contemplated turning the job down, so that he could disassociate himself from this gang of reprobates, but he appreciated that he did not have that luxury. Making his excuses, George agreed a time to meet the next morning and beat a hasty retreat back home.

The fish market was an early start, hard work and smelly, but the rewards were good. George never lacked fish to take home for Harry, himself and Dot, if she deigned to put in an appearance. Harry insisted that George kept his money so that he could get to Margaretta as soon as possible. There was no mention of the possible 'fiddles' again, and George breathed a sigh of relief that there was no follow-up. He even suspected that Tim had mentioned to others not to bother him with such deals. Tim was also as good as his word and, at the end of each week, he and the two other reprobates dropped by after receiving their wages.

"Wet the baby's head for me mate," they said, dropping some of their coins into George's hand. No matter how much he protested that they needn't do this, they replied, "Wot, our dosh not good enough for your babe?"

With these comments bearing down on him, he knew he had no option but to accept their gifts with gratitude. He also marvelled at the good nature of East End working men. Once you were their friend, you were their friend for life. The men were also great believers in those that stood up for themselves – even if it were against their own gang. So, all in all, the 'exit fund' was doing extremely well, with the addition of a baby fund. George was more than happy and, at the end of his shift, made his way back home, smelly, tired and whistling all the way.

Arriving home, he sensed that something was different about the house; he approached with a little apprehension only to find that his other brothers, Tom, Jack and Albert, were sitting at the kitchen table with Harry. George was completely at a loss for words; he went round, shaking hands with his brothers, with questions on his lips. Of course, they all began speaking at once so that nobody got their questions answered. George stepped in and silenced the brothers, asking after their families, wives and girlfriends. Tom was the first to pull himself together and said that Mary, his wife, was well and that she was pregnant again. This brought a cheer and further ribbing from the brothers, with comments like, "Haven't you found out what is causing it yet, Major?"

George asked about Richard, his firstborn, and Tom said that he was fine and growing up strong but was into everything now that he was able to stumble around. George then turned his attention to Jack.

"All is well, thanks Georgie. Annabelle is fine, and little Johnny isn't so little anymore."

Albert said that he was going steady with Rachel and they were discussing marriage. There was a joint sucking in of breath at this, and the brothers said in unison, "I wouldn't do that if I were you, Albert!"

They all sat back, laughed and drank together; then Tom said, "What's that smell? Oh it's you, George! For goodness sake, go and get cleaned up under the tap; you're putting us off our beer."

"Well before I do get cleaned up, I have some news similar to Albert's," said George.

"Oh my God," said Tom. "I'm losing both my brothers to women we don't know. Or do we Georgie?"

"No you don't know her. I met her while in Italy and there is more to it than that."

"Don't keep us hanging, Georgie; tell us all," piped up Jack.

"Margaretta, that's the name of my wife to be, she is pregnant with our child and I am working like a demon to get enough cash to get back to her."

"Looks like we have a double celebration coming our way, lads; let us all drink to George,

Margaretta and the baby, not forgetting our baby brother, Albert, and of course Rachel," proposed Tom, and they all joined in the toast. "Now remove yourself from our presence, Georgie and don't come back until you smell a lot sweeter."

George left the ensemble laughing in the background, while he went to wash away the smell of the fish market as best he could. As he left the others to their conversation, he heard Tom telling the others that he would be in uniform for a few months more. He had been made up to major from his wartime commission but was looking forward to retiring from the army and buying a house he had his eye on near Bury St Edmunds. The brothers were not finished with Tom and chimed in with, "Oh very posh, Major!"

They were all in good spirits, and the joking, banter and ribald comments continued; clearly, they were set for the night.

As George was crossing the courtyard to the tap, a telegram boy on a motorcycle came into the terraced houses. Looking across to George, he shouted, "Do you know where number 89 is?"

"That's me!" George shouted back. Approaching him, the boy showed him the telegram, and George said, "That's right, that's me." He signed for the telegram and handed back the pencil and form, while the boy got back onto his bicycle and rode away. His heart sank, thinking that he had been recalled already; what else could it be? His anxiety at opening the letter and it spoiling all his future plans showed in the shaking of his hands.

George stood staring at the envelope containing the telegram, loath to open it. Telegrams, to his knowledge, never bore good tidings. His hands shook even more as he slid his finger down the side, revealing the telegram. Unfurling it, he saw its contents, fell to his knees and sobbed.

By this time his brothers were wondering where George had got to and sent Albert out to find him with shouts of, "He doesn't have to make himself that pretty for us – and he never could be anyway!"

Albert found George, crouched over almost in a foetal position, his body racked with sobs, his hand clutching the telegram, as the envelope scuttled away down the street like a naughty child.

"George, what the…? George, what's going on?" said Albert. His voice shook at the sight of his brother in such distress. "George, tell me what's happened, what's the matter?"

George held aloft the cause of his affliction, while still kneeling and sobbing. There were expletives and more sobbing, as George remained in this crouched position. Taking the telegram from George's hand, Albert read it and then read it again, not believing the staccato form of words printed there.

SORRY TO INFORM YOU – OUR BELOVED DAUGHTER MARGARETTA – KILLED TODAY BY LANDMINE – ALDO AND MARIE - END

The telegram dropped from Albert's hand, and he felt tears welling in his own eyes as he stooped to comfort George, who clambered into his brother's arms, like a small, frightened child. All the brothers were standing at the door when Albert assisted George back to the house, their mouths agape. They tried to form words on silent lips, but no words came – just small sounds but nothing of any import.

George tried to straighten himself and to walk unaided, but his legs wouldn't do what his brain was telling him. Having eventually got George to his bedroom, after a short while, Albert came down. By this time the other three brothers, sitting around the table as in the past, had read the telegram. They looked at each other, and after each glance, they looked away and shook their heads. Eventually, Tom spoke.

"After all the mess he's been through, I thought this was his turn at happiness."

The others grunted in agreement. Albert took the lead and spoke to the others, who were at a loss to know what to do. They didn't want to offer condolences, as they knew George would spit them back at them. He suggested that he stayed on with Harry to help him with George for a few days; that would relieve them, so that they could return to their families. They all thanked Albert for offering; they knew they should say more, but as he was the only one that wasn't married, everyone agreed this was the best solution. After all, they were too far away to help, and what kind of help could be offered in the circumstances? The brothers all drifted upstairs, one by one, to say goodbye to George and told him to get in touch if they were needed. They all knew it was the sort of thing people said, but they had agreed there was nothing to be done. George sat on his bed, his head in hands and just nodded as they came and left.

Chapter 40

End or New Beginning?

The days passed; George hadn't left his room except to fulfil the need to go to the toilet. He didn't do this much, as he wasn't eating and it was all Harry could do to get him to drink some tea, which was often left on the side until Harry made him drink it, hot or cold.

Harry tried desperately to break this cycle of depression that George was spiralling into. Eventually, at his wits' end, he contacted Amy, who came straight away when she heard the news.

The day Amy arrived was a particularly warm, sunny, August day; she brought a cake and a cheerful demeanour. She saw that Harry was extremely worried about his brother, but she would have no nonsense

"Where is he?" she exclaimed like a school mistress looking for a naughty child.

"Where he's been since he got the news: in his room."

"Well, I will just go up and sort him out."

"Be careful," Harry ventured.

"Tut," was the only reply he received.

Amy did not knock; she went straight into George's room, determined to get straight down to business. George looked up at this dark-haired vision of loveliness and at first thought that Margaretta had come to him. Then he spoke hesitantly, almost afraid to hear the answer.

"Amy?"

"Yes, of course it's me," she replied.

"Wha…?" George was about to ask what she was doing there, but she stopped him in his tracks.

"It's of no use to man or beast you sitting in a darkened room feeling sorry for yourself. What about that poor family? Have you thought of them? Have you written or sent them a telegram or just sat here in your own self-pity?"

Not waiting for a reply, she burst across the room, almost tore the curtains from their poles in an effort to let in some light and opened the windows. Pools of dust danced about in the sunlight that had rushed into the room. George guarded his eyes against the glare and muttered something, which Amy ignored, while she continued with her tirade.

"First things first: wash shave and change of clothes, NOW!" George almost smiled and said as he made his way downstairs to wash and shave.

"You sound like my bloody sergeant major."

After George was washed and shaved, he found Amy in the kitchen. The table was laid and something was bubbling away on the stove. This woman is like a whirlwind, George thought, I hope she passes by fairly soon. Amy had made a thick homemade vegetable soup, with some bread from the local bakery; this would get George started on the road to recovery, she had surmised. There was no escape from Amy and her approach to the problem of depression or, as she called it, feeling sorry for yourself. Once the food was eaten and the crockery cleared, Harry, George and Albert sat around the kitchen table, talking only monosyllabically to begin with. The discussion picked up and centred on Margaretta's family; Amy was insistent that George wrote to them immediately. She took off the tablecloth, gave it a good shake outside the front of the house, returned with it, replaced it, gave George pen and paper and demanded he write to them now.

George did not disobey and began to write slowly and carefully; this letter was probably one of the most important letters he would ever write in his life. He remembered that the last letter he wrote was to Margaretta: full of joy for their future, love for Margaretta, their new baby and their new life as a complete family. His life was to be a dream that did not come true. The dreadfulness of the moment that he had lost Margaretta and the baby was not lost on George; he had seen the carnage left after a mine exploded. He sobbed at the thought of all that could have been but also realised the pain that Aldo and Marie must be feeling.

Amy stayed well into the evening, insisting on making them all an evening meal. Albert excused himself, saying that he felt happy that George was in good hands and would therefore return home. The meal was eggs and ham, which Amy had slipped out to buy, while George was writing the letter. George still had a hangdog look to his appearance but, as Amy had expected, with food inside him, a clean-up and a no-nonsense approach to his condition, things were nearer to normal, much more than they had been for days.

Harry excused himself and left to go to bed, while George and Amy chatted about the loss of

Margaretta. He raised the issue that Amy had appeared like some god of war against depression. The big question on George's mind was, "Why?"

Turning to George, and with a look and words that cut through to his very soul, she replied quite simply, "Because I love you George; nothing has changed." Tears began rolling down George's cheeks.

"But I have let you down. How can you?"

"I do, George, and nothing in the world can change that." Amy walked round to George's side of the table, took his head in her hands and stroked him gently, while the tears continued to fall from both of them. "It's going to be alright George; I'm going to be here for you."

Taking one of her hands that held him, George kissed it gently.

Epilogue:

George and Amy's wedding day in 1947

In August 1944, Walter Robson received a letter from a young wife of a friend in his unit who had been killed. 'I am being brave,' she wrote. 'No one ever broke their hearts with less fuss before. You wouldn't guess my world was in ruins when I discuss the good war news with people. You would never think that as far as I am concerned it can go on for ever and ever now.'

Perhaps, though, the greatest sympathy should be for the dead fathers, the 'Poor devils, well out of it', those whose worst fear was leaving behind their loved ones, the people who needed them. (Reprinted by kind permission of Matthew Parker)

<u>Excerpt from Britishmilitaryhistory.co.uk</u>

The Italian campaign opened with the invasion of the mainland across the Straits of Messina on 3 September 1943. The long slog up Italy ended with the cessation of hostilities with the German forces on 2 May 1945. The nature of the Italian campaign was determined by the geography of the country, the harsh weather conditions during the winter months, the dogged resistance by the German forces (supported by the pro-Axis Italian forces), and the international composition of the Allied forces. Whilst the majority of the Allied troops were American or British, there were contingents from Brazil, Canada, France, Greece, India, New Zealand, Poland, South Africa, plus the Jewish Brigade.

In terms of the overall strategic direction of the war, the campaign in Italy was secondary to that in North West Europe. As such it suffered from limited press coverage, and apart from the capture of Rome, rarely hit the headlines. The Allied commanders saw their resources taken away, firstly for the invasion of Normandy and then for the invasion of Southern France. In addition, troops were diverted to Greece to contain the civil war there and also sent to Palestine.

The Italian campaign can be broken down into phase [sic]. The first phase were the three landings, 'Baytown' across the Straits of Messina, 'Slapstick' at Taranto, and 'Avalanche' at Salerno. The latter was a close run thing, with the Germans nearly forcing the Allies to evacuate the beachhead. The second phase was the battle of the 'Gustav Line', including the first, second, third and fourth battles of Cassino and the landings at Anzio. The third phase was the advance up through central Italy; followed by the fourth phase which was the near breaching of the Gothic Line in late 1944. The fifth and last phase was the final offensive in April 1945, which broke through the Argenta Gap and into the valley of the River Po.

Despite the challenges, the Allies eventually defeated the German Army, but the cost was high. Casualties were severe and most formations suffered from a shortage of experienced infantry soldiers. The nature of the terrain was not favourable to the deployment of armoured formations; this was an infantryman's battle. Often fought at close quarters, in atrocious weather, their determination and suffering deserves recognition, whatever their nationality.

"The Ballad of the D-Day Dodgers" was the ironic song sung by the soldiers in Italy who felt aggrieved by the alleged remarks of Lady Astor, who began naming them as D-Day Dodgers; they were also greatly disappointed that they were forgotten and overshadowed by the D-Day action. There are several versions of this song, some more lewd than others, but it is to be applauded that the British soldiers, fighting in the Italian battles and in particular in and around Monte Cassino, could find it in themselves to turn this into a sort of poetic riposte that could be sung as they were marched from one battle zone to another.

The Ballad of the D-Day Dodgers Wikipedia

Several versions of a song called "D-Day Dodgers", set to the tune Lili Marlene (a favourite song of all troops in the desert — the British Eighth Army was a veteran formation from that theatre before landing in Italy), were sung with gusto in the last months of the war, and at post-war reunions.

The song was written in November 1944 by Lance-Sergeant Harry Pynn of the Tank Rescue Section, 19 Army Fire Brigade, who was with the

78th Infantry Division just south of Bologna, Italy.[1] There were many variations on verses and even the chorus, but the song generally and sarcastically referred to how easy their life in Italy was. There was no mention of Lady Astor in the original lyrics.[1] Actually, many Allied personnel in Italy had reason to be bitter, as the bulk of material support for the Allied armies went to Northwest Europe after the invasion of Normandy. They also noted sardonically that they had participated in several "D-days" of their own before the landings in Normandy became popularly known as "D-Day". The expression was used to refer to any military operation, but the popular press turned it into an expression synonymous with the Normandy landings only. Italian campaign veterans noted that they had been in action for eleven months before the Normandy D-Day, and some of those had served in North Africa even before that.

The numerous Commonwealth War Graves Commission cemeteries across Italy are compelling evidence of the fighting which took place during campaigns such as Operation Avalanche and the subsequent Battle of Monte Cassino.

Although we never said it to each other until the end, I love you Dad.

George Lemmon

1916 - 1970

46733806R10190

Printed in Poland
by Amazon Fulfillment
Poland Sp. z o.o., Wrocław